Letters of FATE

The premise of this historical western romance series, Letters of Fate, started out with the idea of writing a Mail Order Groom series.

As I pondered the idea, I decided rather than an agency or newspaper announcement bringing a woman and a man together, I'd have a man receive a letter that changes his life and brings him to the woman he can't live without.

This element also makes the books in the series standalone. One book doesn't have to be read before the other as they are only connected by the hero receiving a letter.

Davis
Letters of Fate

Paty Jager

Windtree Press
Hillsboro, OR

DAVIS: LETTERS OF FATE
Copyright © 2016 Patricia Jager

Contact Information: info@windtreepress.com

Windtree Press
4660 NE Belknap Court
Suite 101-O
Hillsboro, OR 97124
Visit us at http://windtreepress.com

Cover Art by Christina Keerins
photo by Paty Jager
© Can Stock Photo Inc. / rafairusta

Published in the United States of America
ISBN 9781943601943

Author's Note

This book is set in Harney County, Oregon when the Harney area was still in Grant County. The split didn't happen until 1889.

The character Peter French is a real person. He had the backing and cattle that belonged to Hugh Glenn a businessman in California and moved into the Harney and Blitzen basins in 1872. Many of the things I depict him doing in my book follow his character traits that have been noted in books about him. There were many legal battles between French and the homesteaders. In 1897, when he was unarmed, he was killed by a shot to the head by an angry homesteader.

Chapter One

Grant County, Oregon
May 1880

Davis Weston pulled the letter out of his pocket. His fingers rasped against the worn paper. How many times had he opened and read this letter since receiving it? Five, six times a day?

Dearest Davis,

Brother, I worry about you. Your melancholy words of your recent letter insisted I write to you immediately.

I understand your grief, but not the martyr. Forget what the citizens of Maplewood think. Come west and start a new life.

My friend, Mariella Swanson, has had yet another setback in keeping her late husband's homestead. With a husband, she could keep his legacy alive for their children and you would have direction in your life again.

Please think about this. You and Mariella would get along fine. She is nothing like your Sarah. You won't have to worry about past memories bringing you sorrow.

If you are agreeable to this arrangement, respond before the end of the month. Mariella is running out of time.

Your loving sister,
Ernestine

Davis wasn't sure how well a marriage of convenience would work, but he had to make a change. If another person questioned how Sarah died, he would go mad from repeating the horrifying scene over again.

For that reason alone, he'd bought a train ticket to Winnemucca, Nevada, and was now riding in the back of a military supply wagon headed for Roaring Springs Ranch in Grant County, Oregon. At Roaring Springs Ranch, his brother-in-law, J.P. Mulligan, would collect him and they would travel to the Mulligan ranch. By the end of today, Davis would have a new wife. The thought didn't set well considering how he'd lost his last wife, but he had needed a change and his sister's letter had made him want to be near family and start fresh.

"Sorry the ride's so rough!" the driver called back to him. "Had a lot of snow, it left the roads muddy and rutted."

Davis raised a hand, letting the corporal know he'd heard. The high desert area of the Harney Valley was one of the reasons he'd agreed to come here, marry a stranger, and help save her ranch. After watching his wife and son drown in Lake Michigan, he didn't want to be around water. Too many nights his dreams were filled with that day and how he couldn't get to them fast enough. Their friends and his customers stared at him as if he'd murdered his own family.

He fisted his hand, crumpling the letter. This had to work. He had concerns about knowing how to run a cattle and horse ranch, but Ernestine had insisted Mariella would deal with that. He would need to deal with the rancher Peter French who was trying to take over all of Blitzen Valley and Blitzen Canyon where Mariella and her family homesteaded.

"How long until we're at Roaring Springs Ranch?" Davis called up to the driver.

"Takes about two and a half days to get there." The corporal peered over his shoulder. "You going to work for Mr. French?"

"No."

"Didn't think so. You ain't dressed like a cowhand."

Davis stared at the corporal's back. He seemed to know quite a bit about the country Davis would soon call home. He crawled over the tarped supplies and sat behind the driver.

"What can you tell me about the Roaring Springs Ranch and Mr. French?" He pulled out his pipe and filled it with tobacco. Ernestine had told him very little about the troubles and the woman he was marrying. This man would be unbiased.

"Well, Mr. French owns Roaring Springs, the P Ranch, and Diamond Ranch. He employs vaqueros and locals to work his cattle. He's put up more wire fence than I thought could be made."

"Is he a well-liked man?" If the rancher was only having problems with the Swanson family, his new family, then it would mean they were people who were hard to get along with. Ernestine hadn't said whether or not he could back out once he arrived.

"His workers like him. Can't says he's made many friends with the homesteaders and squatters."

Davis leaned back to hear the man better. "I heard he's pushing people off their homesteads."

The corporal spun in his seat and stared at Davis. "You a gun for hire?"

"No. I'm marrying a woman who is having trouble with Mr. French." Davis smiled round the pipe in his mouth. Me, a gunslinger. I haven't held a rifle since leaving the farm.

"Several widows in Harney Valley since the Bannocks went on a killing in seventy-eight."

"Mrs. Swanson doesn't live in Harney Valley." Ernestine had mentioned the homestead was up Blitzen Canyon in the Steens Mountains.

"Oh sure, Bull's daughter."

"Bull?"

"Bull Simon. He was the tallest, broadest man I'd ever set my eyes on." The corporal nodded his head.

"What about Mrs. Swanson's husband? What happened to him?"

The corporal glanced over his shoulder at Davis. "You don't know much about your new wife."

"I don't. My sister set this up. Mrs. J.P. Mulligan."

"Mrs. Mulligan is a favorite at the fort. She sells knitted socks to the soldiers. They're better than the ones sold at the store." The corporal turned, extending his hand. "Pleased to meet you. I'm Hiram Oakley."

Davis grasped his hand. "Davis Weston."

"Mrs. Mulligan and Mrs. Swanson attended the Christmas Ball at the fort with Mr. Mulligan."

His soon-to-be wife liked to socialize. That was good. He didn't know if after being a merchant for so many years and having daily conversations with various people, if he'd do well isolated in a canyon.

"Does the fort have balls often?" Davis asked.

"The captain throws three a year. Christmas, New Years, and on the anniversary of the war."

Davis didn't need to ask which war. The war between the North and the South was the only war people couldn't forget. It pit families against one another and killed too many.

"You ever been to the Swanson ranch?" Davis asked, trying to gather as much information as he could.

"No, sir. I just drive this road from Winnemucca to the fort and back. I only know people from my layover at the fort between runs." He let out a long loud sigh. "I didn't even get to help round up the Bannocks and Paiutes when they caused trouble."

"That's when Mrs. Swanson became a widow?" Davis wanted to keep the conversation on his interests.

"Yes, sir. Her husband had gone to Winnemucca for supplies and on his way back run into a group of Bannocks. Heard they scalped him."

Davis shuddered. He didn't know the man, but he wouldn't want some renegade to take his scalp after killing him. Mariella had lost her husband as tragically as he'd lost his family. Perhaps this would be a good bonding point for them.

He leaned against the seat back and stared at the desert covered with sagebrush. *I hope the country I'm going to isn't so bleak.*

Chapter Two

Mariella Swanson stood in the small house of her friend, Ernestine Mulligan. Ernestine and her husband, J.P., were ten years older than Mariella, but they had been good friends since Mariella and her husband, Hugh, homesteaded the Blitzen Canyon.

"You look beautiful!" Ernestine exclaimed, stepping through the door of the bedroom she shared with J.P.

"I can't believe I let you talk me into this." Mariella narrowed her eyes at her friend.

"You need a husband. My brother needs a wife. He has no bad traits that I know of, but I haven't been around him for ten years." Ernestine's eyes dulled with sadness. "He's been through so much the last year. He needed this change."

Mariella took hold of her friend's hand. "I'll keep

him so busy he won't have time for memories."

"Go easy on him. He's become a dandy since leaving the family farm."

"You know we can't have a person on the ranch who doesn't pull their weight." Mariella was having doubts—for the hundredth time. How was a merchant going to fit into the hard life she and Hugh carved out in the canyon?

The rattle of harnesses, wheels rumbling, and thud of hooves meant J.P. had arrived with her groom. Mariella's stomach had been tied in knots all morning wondering if she was doing the right thing. *I have no choice. I need a husband to stand up to Mr. French and the cattle buyers. If not, all our work will go to P Ranch.* She'd promised Hugh when Zach was born that if something ever happened to him she would keep the ranch for their son to take over when he was old enough.

"That must be Davis and J.P." Ernestine's face glowed. She'd been telling Mariella all about her brother ever since his reply he'd give the marriage a try.

"You stay here. Mr. Cline, the justice of the peace, from Sagehen should be here any minute. We'll get the formalities of the wedding over, and then we'll have a nice dinner before you head back to the ranch."

"I think I should get a chance to talk with Davis before we get married." She didn't want to find herself staring at a man she couldn't tolerate.

Ernestine patted her arm. "Would you rather have dinner then the ceremony?"

Mariella thought about this. Her stomach was in such knots she wouldn't be able to enjoy her friend's good cooking.

"No, let's get the wedding over with. But I want to meet him before." She slipped her arm through her friends. Ernestine's head came to Mariella's shoulder. She was used to most people being shorter than her. Hugh had been her height and her father had been several inches taller than her.

"I promise you, Davis isn't an ogre. He's quite dashing." Ernestine pushed the bedroom door open as the front door of the stone house opened.

J.P. entered, holding his hat in his hand.

Mariella's gaze went to the man following him through the door. Ernestine had been right. Her brother was dapper and dashing. He had brown short-clipped hair and a trimmed matching brown beard. His dusty clothes were nicer than any she'd seen on a man. His brocade vest fit snug to his wide chest and narrow waist. Fancy shoes peeked out from under his trousers legs. A fancy suit coat draped over his arm.

"Davis!" Ernestine flew across the room and wrapped her arms around the man's neck. He held her tight, his eyes closed, and his face pinched in pain.

The brother and sister held one another for several minutes. J.P. shuffled his feet, and Mariella didn't know whether to watch or look away. The long embrace showed the man believed in family.

The two parted, Ernestine wiped at tears. Davis cleared his throat and turned his head, swiping a sleeve across his eyes.

Once he was composed, Ernestine grasped his hand and led him over to Mariella.

"Mariella Swanson, I'd like you to meet my

brother, Davis Weston." Ernestine stepped back, "Davis, this is Mariella."

Mariella held out her hand. "Davis."

He grasped her hand. It was smooth, but his shake was firm.

"Mariella." His gaze slid across her face and even though he stood a couple inches shorter than her, his gaze didn't drop to her chest like most men she dealt with. Her ample bosoms were her downfall when dealing with men. They couldn't see past them to her business sense. Hugh had, but the cattle buyers, and even that half-pint French whose eyes were level with her chest, couldn't drag his gaze up to her face when he talked to her.

He held her hand after the shake, peering into her face.

"Tell me about your family," he said, drawing her over to the table and chairs. He released her hand to pull out a chair for her.

Mariella sat and wondered at how he so skillfully maneuvered her to the table.

Davis pulled a chair over in front of her and sat, his knees only inches from touching hers.

"Ernestine wrote to me saying you have children. Tell me about them and everyone on the Bar S ranch," Davis said.

Mariella accepted the cup of coffee Ernestine handed her. She waited until her friend handed Davis a cup too.

"My son, Zach, is six. He wants to help with the ranch but isn't quite big enough to take on many tasks. I have my hands full making him understand he needs schooling. Lizzie, my daughter, is two. She's getting into everything right now and barely talking." She noticed Davis's eyes dull with sadness. Ernestine had told her he'd lost a wife and son in a boating accident.

"That must be hard taking care of two small children and keeping a ranch running," Davis said.

"My mother takes care of Zach and Lizzie and the house work." She missed cooking and being with the children, but there was only her and Jedidiah to handle the cattle and horses.

Davis studied her for the longest time. Her skin started tingling and her fingers tightened around the coffee mug.

"You ride and take care of the cattle with the men?" he asked.

She could tell by his tone, he didn't like the idea.

"There is only myself and Jedidiah left to run the ranch."

Davis leaned back and peered at his sister. "Ernestine said you had a large ranch."

"We do. Two hundred head of cattle and fifty horses." She and Jedidiah were getting worn out from handling all the work. From the looks of Davis, this wedding might be a mistake.

"Why are there only two of you dealing with that many animals?" Davis returned his gaze to her.

"Because Peter French offered my hands double what I could pay them."

"You didn't have any men loyal to the Bar S?" Davis asked.

"Not after Hugh was killed. There are few men who like to take orders from a woman." She'd

17

discovered that the hard way. All the years she'd delivered orders while her husband was alive the men had listened. Once the "man" of the ranch was gone, they stopped listening and several had even made untoward comments and actions. There had been many nights that she'd cried herself to sleep. For the loss of the man she loved, the loss of respect with the men, and the sinking feeling she wouldn't be able to keep her promise to Hugh and save the ranch for Zach.

Davis nodded. "Some men find it hard to believe a woman knows more than them."

Mariella's cheeks heated with anger. She didn't need a husband who believed a woman couldn't handle business dealings. "Why you—!"

Davis raised his hands. "I said some men. I don't have a problem with a woman giving me orders as long as I know she knows more about the matter."

A knock at the door stopped their conversation. All heads turned toward the sound as J.P. walked over and opened the door.

Mr. Cline, the Justice of the Peace, walked through the door. Her gut clenched. Why had she allowed Ernestine to talk her into marrying a complete stranger?

Mariella glanced at Davis. This was her last chance to change her mind.

Chapter Three

Davis knew the man who walked through the door must be the Justice of the Peace. On the ride from Roaring Springs Ranch to J.P.'s ranch, his brother-in-law had told Davis the man was meeting them here.

Mariella wasn't unpleasant to look at. She had light brown, curly hair. He knew it was curly because of the wisps curling around her face, otherwise it was pulled up in a bun. The smattering of freckles across her nose and cheeks gave her a youthful appearance. Talking with Mariella, her hazel eyes changed with her mood. His first sight of her had pleased him. She was nothing like his dainty Sarah. There was no comparison to his late wife. The dress Mariella wore showed off her wide child-baring hips, ample breasts, small waist, and broad shoulders. And her height. She stood a good two inches taller than his five-ten.

What did concern him was her riding and working cattle like a man. Granted she was as big as many men and no doubt strong, but a mother should care for the children.

"Davis, this is Mr. Cline, the Justice of the Peace, I was telling you about," J.P. said, leading the man over to Davis.

Davis stood, shook hands with the man, and wondered if he should go through with this.

After they shook hands, Mr. Cline turned to Mariella. "Mrs. Swanson, are you sure you're ready to remarry?"

Mariella shook her head. "I'm not sure. But Peter French has given me no choice."

The venom as she said the other rancher's name, caught Davis's attention. He felt there was more to the feud than she was telling. Her indecision about marrying after meeting him was a bit of a blow to his ego. He hadn't expected her eyes to light up with interest when they met, but her having second thoughts after talking with him didn't give him hope of an easy marriage.

Ernestine moved to put an arm around Mariella's waist. "Mr. Cline, I'm sure you've heard how Mr. French is pushing squatters and homesteaders out of Blitzen Valley. He's now trying to take Blitzen Canyon. That is Mariella and her children's home. She needs a husband to keep her land. My brother needed a change in his life. This is a good thing."

Davis stared at his sister. She didn't need to tell a stranger his problems. This matter was between him and Mariella. He held out a hand to Mariella. "We need to talk alone."

Mariella ignored his outstretched hand, but headed for the door of the house. He followed, tossing over his shoulder. "We'll be back in a few minutes."

Outside, standing in the warm May sunshine, Davis walked over to where Mariella stood stroking a harnessed horse's neck.

"Mariella, I understand this marriage is being forced on you. That you'd rather deal with it on your own but can't. I didn't want to remarry. Ever. It's too painful to lose someone you love. You know this, having lost your husband brutally."

She nodded and wiped at her tears with her fingers.

"What we have to decide isn't if we will ever love one another, but can we get along. Do you think we can work together to keep your ranch?" Davis leaned against the wagon wheel behind the horse she pet.

Mariella cleared her throat. "I don't know about getting along. You seem a bit citified to help on the ranch, but if you can help me keep this ranch, I'm willing to give it a try. I'm running out of choices."

"All I can tell you is I will do my best to help you keep the ranch. My goal in coming here was to change my life and leave memories behind. Helping you may just be my only salvation." Davis didn't know why, but since seeing the woman, he wanted to help her keep a ranch he'd never seen.

"You seem to be a reasonable man and with some intelligence. I'd be a fool to turn down someone willing to help." Mariella held out her hand.

Davis felt stung a bit by the 'man of some intelligence' comment but he understood her desperation. He clasped her hand and they shook.

"Come on. Let's make this legal so you can explain all the problems on the way to the ranch."

Mariella smiled. The first one he'd witnessed since meeting her. Her eyes turned a golden brown and her face glowed with youthfulness. That smile took his breath away.

He motioned for her to precede him into the house so they could get the legalities of this out of the way.

Mr. Cline read the official wedding narrative, had them sign a paper, and they all sat down to a delicious dinner prepared by Ernestine.

Davis was pleased to see that his new bride didn't eat huge helpings like a man, but she also didn't pick and push her food around.

After the meal, they hugged Ernestine, and Davis shook hands with J.P. and Mr. Cline.

"Come see me soon!" Ernestine called as Mariella drove the horses and wagon out of the Mulligan's yard and out to the road he and J.P. had taken to get to the homestead from Roaring Springs.

"How far is the ranch from here?" Davis asked as the horses settled into a lengthened walk.

"About an hour. Depending on how many times we get stopped."

The venom he'd heard in her voice earlier when mentioning Mr. French stung her words.

"What do you mean by stopped?" He wasn't understanding a lot of things this woman said.

"We have to cross land Mr. French uses for his cattle. He has riders who stop anyone crossing his land." Mariella glanced at him. "He's fenced in land he doesn't own. His cattle graze it, and he keeps everyone else off."

"How can he fence land he doesn't own?"

"I don't know, but he has, and he's keeping people from their land because of it."

Davis had never heard of this. "Have you talked to a law official about the legality of his fencing?"

"The closest one is Canyon City. That's four days from here. I can't spare the time to ride up there." Mariella sighed. "I couldn't really spare the time to meet and marry you." She glanced over. "I'm sorry. That didn't sound like I appreciate a complete stranger marrying me to help me save the ranch. I do appreciate you coming all this way to help me. Ernestine and I have been good friends since they arrived in the Blitzen Valley. When she said she'd asked you to come out here and marry me…I was mad at her. She'd aired my troubles to a complete stranger." Mariella turned her gaze on him. The golden brown of her eyes had turned to a sobering brown. "I couldn't believe when you'd accepted her offer." Her cheeks reddened. "To be honest, I didn't expect—" she waved her hand up and down, "—this."

Davis smiled. Probably the first genuine smile in over a year. "You aren't what I expected either."

Mariella laughed. It was a hearty robust laugh that was deep and sent his insides quivering.

"No one expects a six-foot, stout woman when they hear my name. Ma is the size of Ernestine, but my pa was a large man and I took after him in size." She clicked at the horses and stared forward. "When Ma named me, she was hoping I'd be petite and like needlework and fancy dresses."

Davis let his gaze roam over his new bride. "That dress is pretty and fits you nice." He hadn't expected his wife to be a large package but from what he'd seen so far she carried herself well, was articulate, and had a sense of humor.

She glanced over at him. "Your sister made this dress. Insisted I had to wear a dress when I met you." Her pink lips tipped up on one side. "I mostly wear mens clothing at the ranch. It's easier to do the ranching chores."

"When do you take care of your children?" Davis had a hunch earlier when she seemed a bit uncomfortable in the dress that she didn't always wear dresses. Wearing trousers made sense given how much time she spent outside working. But he was most concerned with the children having a mother, especially since they had lost a father.

This time she didn't glance over, she peered into his eyes. "Do you believe I put the ranch before my children?"

"From everything you've said, there is little time for them or being a mother." Davis had a strong belief in a mothers nurturing.

"I have breakfast with them every morning before heading out to take care of the ranch. If the chores are close to the house, I have the noon meal with them. And we all sit down at dinner and afterwards I see what school work Zach has done, I read them a story, and I put them to bed. It's all I have time for since Peter French stole my ranch hands."

Davis thought on this. "You need more ranch

hands. Aren't there any local men Mr. French is pushing out that would be willing to work for you to help you keep your ranch?"

Mariella stared forward, but he could see she was thinking by her scrunched forehead.

"Dan Michaels and John Tippen might hire on. They are barely hanging onto the land they squatted on in the marsh."

"Do they have families and how far from the Bar S do they live?" Davis was hoping for men who could live at the ranch, if they had to ride miles to get there every day they wouldn't be much help.

"They're at least ten miles from the ranch."

The defeat in her voice set his need to help her higher. "Have you tried a notice in the Winnemucca paper or...what is the next closest town with a newspaper?"

"Canyon City, Prineville, or Baker City are the only larger towns with newspapers."

"I'll write up an advertisement asking for ranch hands and send it to all those newspapers." He had a knack for writing advertisements. It had been one of the tasks at the store he'd enjoyed.

"It costs money to post in newspapers. I don't know how much it would be," Mariella said.

"I've posted advertisements in papers for the store. I know about how much they charge. I'm sure we can send them an amount that will be sufficient."

The wagon slowed. Davis spotted the wire stretched across the road. "This is the fence you were talking about?" he asked.

"Yes. Do you know how to open the gate?"

Mariella pulled the horses to a stop several feet from the wire.

"I'll figure it out." Davis climbed down from the wagon and inspected the wooden post on the gate and the sticks making a basket up to his chest filled with rocks that held the five strands of wire that stretched the length of the fence. The stick or limbs every ten to fifteen feet along the fence appeared to stand on their own as the wire became harder to see farther along the line.

He noticed the smaller stick through the gate and unwrapped it, loosening the gate. He slipped the wire over the top of the last stick on the gate and pulled the four strand gate open.

Mariella drove the horses and wagon through and stopped, waiting for him to close the gate.

Davis climbed back on the wagon. "Is this land owned by Mr. French?"

"No. He owns land at the Roaring Springs Ranch and P Ranch but he ran a fence from Roaring Springs to the P Ranch, closing in all the land in between."

Davis stared at the tall grass waving in the breeze. "He's locked other people out of land he doesn't own?"

"Yes. And if people try to homestead or squat, his ranch hands kick them out or make their life so miserable they sell their land to French for half of what it's worth." The disgust in her voice echoed Davis's feelings toward a man he'd yet to meet.

"And there's no law around here to make him stop?" He couldn't believe there was no legal way to make the man take his fences down.

"No. The law is spread thin in these parts. The

sheriff is in Canyon City and doesn't like to come down here when Fort Harney is so close. But the military don't like to get mixed up in the land disputes. They're here to deal with the Indians." Mariella sighed. "It's been up to the homesteaders to deal with French and it's not easy because he has so many people working for him."

Two horseback riders came into view from the south.

"Dang." Mariella said under her breath.

Davis stared at the men as their horses gathered speed and kicked up dust. "Who are they?" he asked.

"Men who work for French." Mariella kept the horses moving along the road as the two ranch hands grew nearer.

"What are they doing?" Davis asked.

"They're going to tell me I'm trespassing and harass me."

"But this isn't owned by Mr. French." Davis was having a hard time believing a person could keep people out of land he didn't own.

The two riders came abreast of them and one grabbed the head stall of Mariella's wagon horse, stopping them.

"Well, Mrs. Swanson. I see you're passin' through P Ranch's land again," said the smaller of the two men.

Davis also noticed the man's gaze wasn't on Mariella's face but was leering at her curves.

"She is no longer Mrs. Swanson, she is Mrs. Weston. I'd advise you to look her in her eyes when you talk to her," Davis said, drawing the man's attention and gaze.

The man's leering smile turned to a frown. "And who are you?"

"I'm Davis Weston, Mrs. Weston's husband. Release our horse and move on. I understand this is a public road and there is no reason for you to detain us." Davis reached over, taking the reins from Mariella. She stared at him, but didn't refuse to hand them over.

Davis slapped the horses on the rumps with the reins, causing them to lurch forward, making the other man release the headstall or be pulled off his horse. The horses and wagon headed down the road at a trot. Davis didn't look back. But Mariella did.

"They aren't following." She twisted back, facing forward. "Thank you."

Davis glanced at her. "For what?"

She glanced down at her ample bosom. "For telling him to look me in the eyes."

Mariella was pleased her new husband noticed the man staring at her bosoms. She always hated running into Peter French's ranch hands because they made her feel uncomfortable with their ogling and lewd comments.

"No man should stare at your body. Their eyes should be on your face. It shows respect and courtesy." Davis's words held conviction and a trace of anger.

The anger sent a shimmer of happiness through her. He cared how others viewed her. They'd only known each other for a few hours and he cared. It was a good sign.

"That has been my problem since Hugh died. The men only look one place and don't hear a word I say. Even some of our own ranch hands treated me differently once I was a widow."

Davis glanced over at her. "You're no longer a widow, and I'll not allow any man to be disrespectful to you."

Mariella looked down at her idle hands. It had been two years since she didn't have to drive a wagon. She wasn't sure what to do with her hands if they weren't holding reins. She clasped her hands together and stared ahead. She had no doubt her mother would be happy with Davis. But Jedidiah would be perplexed. He was hoping for a man who could step in and take over ranching chores. She had a feeling Davis would be more trouble than help while dealing with the cattle.

"When was the last time you worked cattle?" Mariella asked.

"I was fifteen. We had a few head on my family's farm."

She frowned. "The last time you rode a horse?"

"A few years back, I rode out hunting with a friend." Davis glanced over at her. "I've always been a quick learner. I understand you need me out working cattle." He stared ahead. "I also think I need to familiarize myself with Oregon land laws. One man cannot keep the public off of land he doesn't own."

Chapter Four

Davis was still thinking on the fact they had to open and close two fences that shouldn't be on a public road when the horses and smaller dirt road started following a stream.

"This is Little Blitzen. The water starts up in the Steens Mountains and flows through the canyon. It waters our cattle, horses, and crops."

The pride in Mariella's voice told Davis she would do whatever it took to keep the ranch. That included marrying a greenhorn.

A log archway crossed the road. A board hung down with a long line over a large S.

"This is where our land begins. We have this one hundred and sixty acres of grassland and the canyon." Mariella waved her arm encompassing the wide flat land covered in new green grass. "Hugh had the foresight to cut and dry this meadow for hay to feed in the winter. Last winter we needed it. The snow was deep and it stayed cold for weeks. Other ranchers who didn't have hay to feed their cattle lost nearly half their herds." Mariella put a hand on his arm. "The first thing I need you to do as my husband is talk with the cattle buyers. They should be coming through here in the next couple of weeks. Last spring they wouldn't negotiate with me and we had to take less than the other cattlemen. We need to get the same weight on the dollar as the others."

Davis nodded his head. "Do you have figures for me to study?"

"Yes. We keep a ledger of all sales. It will give you an idea of what price we need to get."

"How do you know when the buyers are coming through?" He didn't want this ranch to be bypassed.

"They send a rider ahead of them, saying the day they will be at each ranch." She added. "They like to ride through the stock."

"That makes sense. We'll be ready for them when they arrive."

The grass meadow gave way to trees and soon they were driving in the bottom of a tall narrow canyon. Leaves were unfurling on the aspens and mahogany trees and the juniper trees were replaced with a smattering of pines. Green grass covered the canyon floors and sides up to a point where rocky edges dominated the rim.

"This is beautiful," Davis said. He'd never seen a more rugged or beautiful spot.

"When my pa found this spot, he knew it was the

perfect place for Hugh and me to homestead."

The melancholy in her voice made him wonder about the love and life she'd shared with her deceased husband.

"Your family has been around here a while?" he asked.

"Not really. I grew up in Canyon City. Pa was a freighter. But once Hugh and I married and settled here, he and Ma helped us get the buildings and corrals up." Mariella stared toward the creek.

"What happened to your pa?" She'd only mentioned her ma living with her and the corporal had made it sound like the man had passed on.

"After we had the ranch all set up, he went back to hauling freight. His wagon went over a cliff." She remained staring at the stream, her voice barely carried over to him. "The next year Hugh was bringing us supplies from Winnemucca and he was ambushed by Indians. We hadn't heard about the Indians until after he'd left. There was no way to tell him to stay. He wouldn't have anyway, knowing we were in the path of the renegades."

She pointed to the right. "They camped in the canyon on the other side of that ridge. We still had ranch hands then. Drummond and Porter came riding in like their horses' tails were on fire. They'd been up on the ridge and looked down in the other canyon and saw close to three hundred lodges set up in the bottom. Jedidiah sent a rider to the fort to let them know."

The hair on the back of Davis's neck tingled knowing Mariella and her family had been so close to the warring Indians. "Did you take the kids to the fort for protection?"

"No. We put riders on the ridge to keep track of them. If they said the Indians were coming this way, we'd stored food and water in a dirt cellar. We would have hid out in there."

He shook his head. "The fort would have protected you better."

She finally looked at him. There were traces of tears glistening in her eyes. "We would have been easier to kill out in the wide open flats than hiding back in the canyon."

He wasn't going to argue the point. Bringing up the past had caused her sadness.

The road and stream opened to a small meadow. A long low, stone building with log pillars holding up a porch roof stood in the middle of the meadow. This building had what looked like smaller stone buildings to the right and to the left stood a two story barn. The lower story was made of stone and the upper out of timber. To the left of the barn was a smaller long building with a porch. Behind the barn and other building were corrals made of sticks with rope weaving them together.

"The building left of the barn is the bunkhouse. Right now only Jedidiah is living there. It can hold up to twenty men." The wistfulness in her voice told Davis she wished it held that many men still.

"The buildings to the right of the house are the smoke house and hen house. The cellar I told you about is dug into the canyon wall and is our spring house as well." Mariella pointed to the barn. "Pull the wagon up over there. We'll unharness and put the horses out before going to the house."

Davis reined the horses to the barn and hopped down. Mariella climbed down from the wagon, holding her skirt out of the way. Davis waited for her to open the large, double, wooden doors on the barn. He was impressed with the stone work and the wood working.

"This is an impressive barn," he commented, following Mariella back to the harnessed horses.

She started unhooking the traces from the wagon tongue. "Hugh helped his brothers build their barns and houses when they homesteaded. He learned a lot. But he preferred taking care of cattle."

Davis unfastened the harnesses on the far side and drove the horses into the barn where they continued to remove the harnesses.

After the horses were free of the working tack, Mariella led the two to a small corral behind the barn. She poured grain onto the ground and the two started crunching the oats.

"What about the wagon?" Davis asked, as Mariella exited the barn and shut the doors.

"We'll back it over alongside the barn." She grasped the wooden tongue and started shoving.

"Here, let me do that. You don't want to ruin that new dress." He grabbed the tongue between Mariella and the wagon and shoved, turning the wheels to make the wagon back alongside the barn. He brushed his hands and turned around to find Mariella frowning.

"What's wrong?" he asked, lifting his carpet bag out of the buckboard and walking over to her.

"You aren't going to start pushing me to the side when I have work that isn't women's to do, are you?"

She put her hands on her hips. "If you are, then we won't get anything done around here."

Davis raised the hand not holding the bag with his belongings. "I was only thinking of your new dress."

"Ma!" A young boy came running out of the house. His feet skidded to a stop beside his mother.

Mariella put a hand on the boy's brown hair and smiled. Davis was happy to see a change in her. Her eyes softened and her lips curved into a smile. "Zach, this is Mr. Weston."

"Is he a ranch hand?" the boy asked skeptically, looking Davis over from his dusty shoes to his derby hat.

Davis decided to let Mariella explain this to her son.

Her shining smile disappeared. It was evident she hadn't told her son where she went today.

Mariella crouched in front of her son. She'd only told Jedidiah and her ma what she was up to today. She didn't want Zach thinking she was replacing his father. He may have only been four when Hugh was killed, but he remembered his daddy. Hugh had doted on his son, and his son had thought his father could do nothing wrong. Little Lizzie had been born after Hugh passed.

Her heart squeezed in her chest and her mouth felt as dry as the Alvord lake bed. "Zach, Mr. Weston and I married today. He's Mrs. Mulligan's brother." Zach loved Ernestine like an aunt. She hoped Davis being related to the woman would help Zach accept him.

His little six-year-old mind was humming. She could tell by the way his gaze flashed from Davis to her and back to Davis. Finally he said, "But you're married to Pa."

Tears burned the back of her eyes. He said he understood that Pa was gone and would never come back, like their dog Rusty who had been trampled by a bull. But she now wondered.

"There you two are. I worried you wouldn't get back before dark." Ma hurried across the area between the house and the barn.

Thankful for the distraction, Mariella stood, but grasped Zach's small hand. "Ma, this is Davis Weston. Davis this is my ma, Ethel Simon."

Davis held out his hand. "Mrs. Simon, it's a pleasure to meet you."

Her mother smiled bright and shook hands with Davis. "I'm happy you and my daughter will be working together to save this ranch. It would be a shame to see all her hard work be taken over by Mr. French."

"I agree," Davis said. He picked up his carpet bag and looked at Zach. "Zach, I'm going to put my bag on the porch. Then I'd like you to take me around and tell me all about the buildings on the ranch."

Mariella watched Davis close, wondering what kind of father he would be to children that were not his own. Ernestine said he'd been a good father to his own son.

Zach peered up at Mariella. "Do you want me to?" he asked.

"Yes, that would be a big help to me if you could show Mr. Weston around." Mariella squeezed Zach's hand and watched him posture like a grown up.

"I'll take you around cuz I know everything about

36

the ranch." His young voice held a note of seriousness that tugged at her heart.

Even though he was only six and didn't quite understand all that had gone on, he had stepped in as her protector from the day he'd found her crying over the loss of his pa. She hoped her children would accept Davis as their father. If they accepted him, she would be more open to accepting him as a husband.

"Thank you," Mariella said to Zach and then mouthed the same words to Davis as he walked back to where they stood.

He nodded and motioned to the barn. "Show me what I need to know about the barn," he said to Zach.

Her son released her hand and trotted ahead of Davis, rattling on about the horses and tack in the barn.

Ma put her arm around Mariella's waist and led her toward the house. "He seems like a nice man."

"I knew Ernestine wouldn't have suggested I marry her brother if he wasn't a good man. But I don't know how well he's going to fit in around here." Mariella liked how Davis had taken Zach's mind off who he was and used the boy's pride to strike up a friendship. "He does know how to get along with little boys." She stopped at the porch and picked up Davis's bag. "I told you he lost his wife and son in a boating accident, didn't I?"

"Yes, you did. I hope being around Zach doesn't bring him sad memories," her mother said.

"Me too."

They continued into the house.

Walking toward the kitchen, Ma said over her shoulder, "Lizzie is napping."

Mariella stopped inside the door and stared at the bag in her hand. There were only three bedrooms in the house. Her mother had one, the children had the other, and then there was the one she'd shared with Hugh. She wasn't ready to share her room with Davis. He'd have to stay in the bunkhouse. She placed his bag by the front door and strode across the main room to the children's room.

Mariella tiptoed over to the small bed where her precious daughter lay sleeping. She gently touched the fluffy blonde curls. They were lucky to have Lizzie in their lives. After finding out Hugh had been killed, Mariella had been so overwrought the child came a month early. They'd prayed over her small body that barely breathed and she'd come through. She had a weak constitution, but she was with them. She could see Davis being gentle and mindful of Lizzie's frailness. Mariella kissed her sleeping child's head and left the room.

The daylight was almost gone, but she needed to go for a ride. So much had happened today, she needed to clear her head.

In her room, she took off the pale green calico dress Ernestine had made her. She hung the dress and petticoat in a wardrobe her father had made from hewn alder. The skin under her corset itched. She dug a finger under the edge and tried to scratch. She was the only woman she knew who wore a corset while working cattle. But the bounce of riding a horse made her bosoms and her back ache. She'd rather suffer the confining whalebone than the pain from flopping body parts. She pulled one of Hugh's linen shirts on over her chemise and corset, and buttoned the top. She pulled the wool trousers over her legs and hips, and fastened them. Her mother had altered the waist to fit her more slender one and she'd hemmed the legs. Mariella shoved the bottom of the trouser legs into her boots and left her room, grabbing her wide-brimmed hat and leather gloves by the door on her way out of the house.

She strode across the yard and down the side of the barn to the corral in the back. Her gelding, Dash, stood at the far end of the corral. Mariella whistled.

Dash raised his head, nickered, and trotted to the gate.

Tears burned the back of her eyes. Dash had been her first gift from Hugh. They'd met at a social in Canyon City when she was sixteen. Six months later, he'd shown up at her house with a tan-colored yearling colt and a marriage offer. She'd jumped into his arms and kissed him for the first time.

Dash nuzzled her face. "You, Zach, and Lizzie are all I have to remember Hugh." She stroked his face and looped the rope hanging from the fence around his neck and led him into the barn. All the emotions bombarding her mind needed to be cleared. The best way she knew was to ride up the canyon and check the cattle. That always cleared her head.

Chapter Five

Zach and Davis stepped out of the cellar as a shrill whistle rang through the canyon.

"What's that?" Davis asked Zach. The young boy did know a lot about the ranch and now Davis knew as much as the boy.

"Ma whistling for Dash." Zach waited for Davis to close the heavy wooden door on the dugout cellar.

"Who is Dash? A dog?" Davis asked when the door dropped into place.

"Ma's horse. She must be goin' for a ride."

Davis watched the boy. He didn't seem the least bit worried his mother was riding off by herself. "Where would she be riding to this late in the day?"

"Check the cows. She's pertiklar 'bout the cows bein' watched." He continued to the back door of the stone house.

Davis had noted the precision with which the stones had been cut and laid in all the buildings. He was impressed with the shingled roof on the house and barn, and noted the sod roofs on the other out buildings. The smokehouse was large enough to handle several beef or hogs at the same time. He'd heard hogs squealing as they walked to the hen house and spotted a pen with two hogs farther up the canyon behind the outhouse.

They entered the house through the kitchen. The smell of cookies swarmed his head and Davis was tossed back to before the accident, walking into a kitchen filled with the same scents and seeing Sarah and Christian, heads bent together making cookies. His heart slammed into his ribs and air sucked out of his lungs.

"Mr. Weston? Mr. Weston, are you all right?"

The unfamiliar female voice drew him out of his memory. He focused on the woman with brown hair streaked with gray standing in front of him. Mrs. Simon. Mariella's mother. He wasn't in Michigan and his family wasn't alive.

"Mr. Weston, are you ill?" Mariella's mother led him over to a kitchen chair.

"No. No, I'm not ill. I just…" He shook his head. He didn't need this woman feeling sorry for him because, even after traveling two thousand miles he still hadn't run away from his memories.

"Ma went riding," Zach said, picking up a cookie and eating it.

"Is it safe for her to ride alone?" Davis asked, drawing his thoughts back to the present.

Mrs. Simon studied him. "She knows this canyon,

41

and Jedidiah will be headed back here for supper. He'll run into her."

"I see." He didn't really, but he had no choice than to agree with her. "Where does Mariella keep the ledger? She wanted me to acquaint myself with the prices before the cattle buyers get here."

The older woman studied him a few seconds. "She said you were to look at the ledger?"

"Yes. On our drive here she said the cattle buyers were coming in a few weeks and I needed to know the prices and weights for the cattle to deal with them." He peered back at the woman. "That is why she married me, to act on her behalf as her husband."

The woman sighed. "That's true. She's been beating her head against a tree trying to do business with the weak-minded men around here." She nodded toward the door out of the kitchen. "In the main room is a desk in the corner. She keeps all the ranch records in there."

"Thank you." He headed to the door.

"Wait." She filled a cup with coffee and placed four cookies on a plate. "Supper won't be for another couple of hours."

"Much obliged." Davis took the coffee and plate of cookies into the main room.

The room was a bit larger than the kitchen. The furniture in the room was sparse. Two hand hewn chairs, a chair of the same rough nature that would sit two at once, a small table by each chair, and a braided rug on the floor in front of a fireplace. The main door was a large door of wide thick planks. He noticed his bag sitting by the door in front of a bench under hooks for coats. Several coats of various sizes hung from the hooks.

He spotted the desk far from the fireplace, tucked in a corner alongside the front window. A lantern sat on the top of the desk.

Davis placed the coffee and plate on the desk and lit the lantern. He searched the top of the desk and noted a list of supplies. It looked like a trip to Winnemucca was in the planning stages. He pulled out a drawer on the left hand side and found a ledger. Spreading the book open, he picked up the coffee, sipped the strong brew, and ate a cookie as he read through the numbers.

He turned up the lantern as the light from the window dimmed.

Stomping from the kitchen side of the house, roused him from the calculations he scrawled on a piece of paper he'd found.

A child cried behind one of the doors off the main room. He stood, stretched, and when no one came to the child's aid, he listened at the doors and opened the middle door.

A thin, pale child of about two sat in the middle of a small bed. Her blonde curls were tousled and her face puckered and red as tears slid down her cheeks.

"There, there angel. You're not alone." Davis crossed the room and crouched next to the bed. He rubbed the child's back and spoke quietly. "I'm Davis. Since I've met everyone else, I'd guess you to be Lizzie."

The child snuffled and looked at him with big, round eyes. They peered into one another's eyes for a few moments, and she held up her arms to be picked up.

Davis smiled. This was the first person in this house he'd won over. He picked her up, being careful to cradle her gently in his arms. She wrapped a small arm around his neck and patted his beard with her other hand.

"You like my whiskers?" he asked.

"I imagine your beard is softer than Jedidiah's whiskers."

Davis spun toward Mariella's voice. She stood inside the room. He took in the tall boots, wool trousers flaring at her hips and cinching in at her small waist. His gaze drifted quickly over the man's shirt, billowing out of the waist of her trousers and hiding her bosom. Her brown hair with rust highlights hung down around her shoulders.

"Did you have a good ride?" he asked, crossing the room and handing Lizzie over to her mother.

"I did. Found some strays and headed them back to the herd." She held the child to her and kissed the pale cheek. "Did you have a good nap?" she purred to the child.

After his qualms about whether Mariella could be a good mother as well as run a cattle ranch, seeing her with her children had answered that question. A person would have to be blind to not see her love for her children.

"Supper is ready," she said, watching him over the child's head.

He headed out the door and stopped half way to the kitchen. "After supper, I have some numbers to show you."

She glanced at the desk with the glowing lantern. "Ma said you were looking at the ledger."

"I was. You said the buyers should be coming soon, I wanted to make sure I knew what to say. I found some numbers I don't understand."

Her brow scrunched. He already knew that meant she was thinking.

"I'm sure you'll set me straight after supper." He grasped her elbow and escorted her into the kitchen.

Mariella couldn't miss the expressions on Ma and Jedidiah's faces when Davis escorted her into the kitchen and held out the chair at the end of the table while she sat. Hugh had shown her respect and treated her well, but he'd never held her chair for her.

She placed Lizzie in the high chair next to her and on the same side of the table as Zach. Motioning toward Jedidiah, Mariella said, "Davis Weston, this is Jedidiah Morton. He's been the foreman of the Bar S Ranch since we laid the first stone for the house."

Davis extended his hand and the two men shook.

"Pleased to meet you, Mr. Morton," Davis said.

"No one calls me mister. I'm just plain ole Jedidiah," her foreman said, moving to the seat beside Ma. Since Hugh's death he'd taken to sitting at the head of the table.

Mariella watched as Davis contemplated the only seat left. The one at the head of the table. He pulled out the chair and studied Zach.

"Zach, do you mind if I sit in this chair?" Davis asked.

Mariella's chest ached as she watched her son

think about the question. She glanced at Davis. The boy's answer meant as much to him as it did to her.

"I guess it's all right," Zach said, and glanced across the table at Jedidiah, who nodded slightly.

Davis sat and peered across the table at her. She wasn't sure what he was asking with his eyes. They didn't know one another well enough to know their thoughts, but she had a feeling it wouldn't be long. Not with the way her family was accepting him.

Ma broke the awkward silence. "Better dish up the food before it gets cold."

Mariella watched how Ma and Jedidiah interacted with Davis as he asked questions about the cattle, the ranch, and ultimately, Peter French.

Davis wiped his mustache and beard with a cloth napkin and peered at Jedidiah. "How come no one has sent a petition to the county seat about the way Mr. French is taking over land that isn't his?"

Mariella stood. "Zach, let's check your school work." She plucked Lizzie out of the highchair, tucking her on her hip, and herded Zach into the main room. When the topic of Peter French came up, Jedidiah used colorful language she didn't want her children hearing.

Davis reached out as she walked by, catching hold of her arm.

She stopped and peered down at him.

"How long until you want to go over those numbers?" he asked.

She glanced between the two men. "When you two are done talking, I'll be ready."

He nodded and released her arm.

In the other room, she set Lizzie on the floor to

play and rubbed her hand over the area where Davis had touched her. How could he be affecting her so soon when she barely knew the man?

Chapter Six

Davis walked into the main room feeling as if he'd just been in a boxing match. His ears burned from the language Jedidiah used while talking about Mr. French. It was obvious the foreman of the Bar S had little respect, and even less tolerance for the dandy runt claiming all of Blitzen and Harney Valleys, chasing the farmers off the land that had water.

He found Mariella sitting in one of the chairs, her eyes closed, humming. He didn't know the tune, but it sounded pleasant.

"That's a nice tune," he said.

She jumped and her eyes opened.

"Sorry. Didn't mean to scare you." He stopped several feet from her chair.

"I was deep in thought." She stood. "You wanted to go over the ledger?"

"If you're tired we can do it tomorrow." He'd noticed dark circles under her eyes when she turned to him.

"I am tired. It's been a long and…eventful day."

He pulled his pipe out of his vest pocket. "If someone had told me a year ago, I'd be remarried in a year, I would have hit them in the mouth."

She watched him a few moments. "Why?"

He closed his eyes briefly to wash the pain away and found it wasn't as piercing. "After the accident, I couldn't see myself as a husband to anyone but Sarah or a father to any child but Christian." Davis didn't understand the emotions rolling over him all day any more than he understood the pain and grief he'd endured when he'd lost his family. "But today, seeing my sister, meeting you and your family, I feel like I have a purpose again. Helping you keep the ranch."

Her eyelashes drifted down, covering any thoughts he might have been able to see in her eyes. "I'm glad you're here to help us."

Davis glanced over at his bag still sitting by the door. "Where am I sleeping?" he asked.

Her lashes flew up and she stared at him.

"My bag is sitting by the door. I take it there isn't a guest room in the house." He hadn't expected her to invite him into her bed. He wouldn't sleep with a woman he didn't care for. While he liked her, he wasn't desperate enough to sleep with her and give her the wrong idea about his feelings.

"I thought you could sleep in the bunkhouse with Jedidiah." She played with the sleeve of her shirt billowing over the garter on her arm.

49

"I'm fine with that arrangement." He walked over to the door and picked up his bag. "What time is breakfast?" Davis studied her tired face. He wanted to linger in her presence, not to see if she'd change her mind, but because he still knew so little about her.

"Six. Wear your work clothes. We'll ride the canyon to familiarize you with the area and the cattle."

He nodded and left the house. Jedidiah stood under the porch of the bunkhouse as if waiting for him.

Davis crossed the yard, dropped his bag by the bunkhouse door, and pulled out his tobacco. "Looks like we're bunkmates," he said to Jedidiah.

The old man looked him over from head to toe. "I hope not for long."

Davis snickered and filled his pipe. "What can you tell me about Hugh and Mariella?"

The old man rolled a cigarette and stared up at the moon. He didn't say a word until he'd lit his cigarette and released a stream of smoke into the night air. "They took a fancy to one another. Courted about six months and married. Hugh had his eye on this property even before Bull told them about it. Bull, Mariella's pa, thought a lot of Hugh. The three of them worked hard putting up the buildings, purchasing the right cattle, and making a go of this place."

Jedidiah moved to a bench along the outside wall of the bunk. "Mariella promised Hugh she'd keep this place going for Zach to have when he was of age. Means a lot to her to keep that promise."

"I figured it was something like that. Most women wouldn't take on the work of the ranch or the battle with Mr. French. I knew when my sister sent me the letter there had to be a reason she wanted to hold onto this so badly." Davis wondered at the commitment Mariella had taken on. She toiled to keep a promise to the man she loved. He respected that.

Davis finished his pipe and picked up his bag. "Which bunk do you want me to take?"

Jedidiah pushed to his feet. "The one farthest from me."

***

Mariella stood in the kitchen helping her mother put breakfast on the table when Jedidiah and Davis entered. She smiled at both men and busied herself putting food on the tray in front of Lizzie. Her cheeks had heated from the direct smile Davis sent her way when he walked through the door.

Last night was the first night in months she'd slept clear through and woke feeling refreshed. Having another to help handle the burdens of the ranch had allowed her to drift off without worries banging around in her mind.

"Looks good, Mrs. Simon," Davis said, walking over to stand beside Mariella's chair.

"Mariella made the hot cakes," Ma replied, setting cups of coffee in front of the men.

"In that case, it looks delicious, ladies," Davis said, holding the chair for Mariella as she sat and then walking over and doing the same for Ma.

"Why do you do that?" Zach asked.

Davis moved to his place at the head of the table. "It's showing respect for the women who made this good meal for us."

"Pa never did that." Zach stared at Mariella.

She wasn't sure what to say. It was true. Hugh never held a chair for her. Not even when they were courting.

"Your pa and ma spent lots of time together. Your pa could tell her how he respected and loved her. I'm a newcomer and this is my way of paying my respect." Davis lifted his cup to take a drink and winked at her over the cup.

Mariella's heart thudded in her chest. He'd just saved her from a hard question and winked at her. A silent, yet intimate action.

"My stomach is raisin' a ruckus. Pass the hot cakes," Jedidiah said, breaking the awkward moment.

The breakfast finished without any more questions she couldn't answer.

"Zach work on the numbers I wrote on the slate and read to your sister." Mariella stood, tousled Zach's hair, and kissed the top of Lizzie's head. "I'll see you two tonight."

Mariella grabbed the saddlebag she'd brought in last night and had put sandwiches and cookies in for the mid-day meal in the canyon. "Come on, Davis, we have a lot of riding to do today."

He stood, plucked his derby cap from the peg by the back door, and followed her out of the house.

She stared at his hat. "We'll add a new hat to the list of supplies for Jedidiah to pick up in Winnemucca."

Davis resettled his hat on his head. "Why do I need a new hat?"

"That one tells anyone who can see it, you're a greenhorn. And the brim won't protect your face from the sun. It can burn your skin in one day in the hot summer months."

She noted he had on his fancy shoes. "You should go in the bunkhouse and see if you can find a pair of boots that fit. Riding in those shoes isn't a good idea. You need boots to protect your lower legs from brush and rattlesnakes."

He stopped. "Is anything I'm wearing to your satisfaction?"

She scanned the length of him. While his vest was a mite fancy for a cowhand, she liked how it molded to his form. The long-sleeved shirt underneath would protect his arms from the sun's rays. His trousers were a thinner, finer quality than work trousers. Ma would be sewing leather patches on them soon.

"The rest will work."

He nodded and strode to the bunkhouse.

Mariella hurried to the corral. She whistled Dash over, caught him, and then caught Hugh's gelding, Poker. She led the two into the barn and started saddling them.

Davis entered the barn wearing a well-used pair of boots. "The soles are nearly gone, but they were the only pair that fit."

"We won't be walking much today. We can get them resoled at Fort Harney." Mariella handed the reins to Davis. "This is Poker. He likes to go slow. Just nudge him with your knees to speed him up."

"There a reason you gave me a slow horse?" Davis asked.

"No. He was Hugh's and doesn't get ridden much." Mariella wondered if she'd made the right decision when Davis's eyebrows rose.

They led the horses out of the barn and headed up the canyon. There was a lot of ground to cover today.

She wound them through the trees, up the side of the canyon wall, back down and across the canyon to the south wall. Along the way they encountered herds of cattle grazing on the early spring grass.

"Aren't you afraid they'll keep the grass eaten down and not have enough for the summer months?" Davis asked as they sat watching a herd of thirty grazing.

Mariella smiled. "No. We've only traveled through the lower part of the canyon. As the summer progresses the grass higher up will be available for them to graze. While they are up there, we'll be cutting the hay in the meadow and storing it for winter feed. As long as the other ranchers don't drive their cattle into our canyon we'll have plenty of feed."

"Why would they put their cattle in this canyon?" Davis asked, studying her.

"When Hugh and I first homesteaded we had to chase the P Ranch cattle out several times throughout the summer. When Hugh spoke with French, he denied his cattle being in our canyon. So the next time we found them, we gathered them up and herded them straight to his ranch house. After that they stayed out. But last summer I found several of his cattle mixed in with mine when we did the roundup in the fall." She stared at the upper edge of the canyon. "He probably thought I wouldn't say anything without a man to back me up."

"If it happens again this summer, we'll confront him." Davis nudged Poker, moving him forward.

She liked the idea of Davis standing up for her and her family. In the short time she'd known him, he seemed like a decent sort. His manners and easy way with the children were making her see him as a husband and not just a man to help her get what she wanted.

"Come on, we'll eat at one of my favorite spots." She eased Dash by Poker and headed at an angle up the side of the canyon. She stopped on top where large rocks made perfect chairs and one could see the bottom half of the canyon and the curl of smoke from the ranch house cookstove.

Mariella dismounted and dropped the reins. Dash started eating the grass. While she dug in her saddlebag for their lunch, Davis dismounted and dropped Poker's reins as well.

"Have a seat. It's the best seat on this ranch." Mariella sat on one rock while Davis sat on the other.

"This is quite the view." Davis took the sandwich she offered him.

"You can see the ranch buildings and then this way—" she pointed to the east "—you can't see all the way to the top of the canyon because of that point, but it is a great view."

She bit into her sandwich and studied the movement of the cattle she could see in the canyon. They were lying down, resting from their morning meal.

"We never had the chance to go over the ledger," Davis said, breaking the silence.

"I forgot. Can we talk about it now?" She took another bite of her sandwich.

"The sale numbers last year bounced from twelve

dollars for the first batch you sold and then a second group only brought in nine dollars a head, yet the year before the same cattle brought twenty to thirty dollars a head." Davis stared into her eyes. "Were the prices that much lower last year?"

Mariella shook her head. She'd tried to get the same dollar value as the other ranchers, but the buyers had told her all kinds of lies about things they saw wrong with her cattle to make them feel better about giving her half what they were paying for the other ranchers' cattle. "They cheated me because I'm a woman. They said our cattle were in poor health. That they wouldn't even make it to market and they were doing me a favor even buying them."

"Were they sickly?"

"No! I was thinking about driving them there myself when French up and stole all my ranch hands. I had to get paid even if it was half the amount. We needed money to live on." She hated to admit it, but the price she'd received last year and the buyers coming through any day had been what prompted her to accept the offer Ernestine had made about marrying her brother.

"From what I've seen of the herd so far, they look like prime beef cattle," Davis said, taking a bite of his sandwich.

"They are and they looked the same last year." She couldn't eat any more. It still irked that the men had badgered her into taking half what the herd was worth.

"I'll run through the ledger again tonight and acquaint myself with the words and prices. Hugh kept good records. It makes my learning the business easier."

Davis patted her knee. "Don't worry. We'll get what the cattle are worth."

His words and actions brought tears to her eyes. She'd missed having someone to rely on the last two years. Jedidiah was like family, but the gruff old cowpuncher wasn't much for sentiments. Ma would listen to her concerns but she couldn't help. She only knew housework and raising children. She'd never paid attention to the conversations Mariella and Hugh had about the cattle and the ranch. It was good to have someone to share things with.

"Thank you. I hope you aren't always fighting my battles and can enjoy yourself."

Davis grasped her hand. "Mariella, these are no longer your battles. When I married you yesterday, they became our battles. While we may not consummate the marriage, I believe in the vow I took and will be with you through good times and bad, through sickness and health."

Mariella could see the sincerity in his eyes and once again thanked Ernestine for bringing them together. "Thank you. And because you are doing so much for me, I will do my best to make your life tolerable."

They ate the cookies in silence. Mariella sent furtive glances his way every now and then, still unbelieving that she could have been so lucky to have a man like Davis willing to save her family. But his comment about not consummating the marriage had her wondering if her size was unpleasant to him.

Chapter Seven

That night after dinner, Davis lit the lantern on the desk and spent several hours once again going through the numbers and reading the terms he should use while negotiating with the cattle buyers. It had rankled when Mariella said she was paid half the amount for her cattle last year because the buyers bullied her. He had no respect for a man who would swindle a widow. He noted the names of the two buyers who came through last year. Especially, the name of the one who paid her the lowest amount.

Mariella and her mother sat in the chairs in front of the fireplace. Both were mending clothing.

"Mariella, do we need to have the cattle rounded up when the buyers come?" he asked. It would seem they should have the number of cattle ready for the buyers.

"We usually say we have a hundred and fifty head, take them up the canyon to look at several of the herds and then sign a contract. They tell us what day they'll be coming through to collect them and we have the cattle rounded up then."

"They don't want an exact figure? Do you know you have a hundred and fifty ready to sell?" He didn't understand not knowing the exact number. In his store he kept an exact count of each item he had on the shelf and what he sold.

"We should have that many of sale size by the time we cull out the ones that won't make the drive or we want to keep." Mariella set the mending down and stood. "We butcher two a year for our own needs and swap beef with some of the locals for other goods. If we sell them all, then we don't have barter." She walked over to the desk. "You can't learn it all in a few days."

"I don't plan on it. But I'm used to running a store. You know what merchandise you have on hand down to the last stick of candy. I don't like saying we have a hundred and fifty cattle to sell and not know that is the number." Davis slid the ledger and the papers he was reading into the drawer and reached up to switch off the lantern. "I'd like to ride back up the canyon tomorrow and take a tally of the numbers in the different herd groupings."

"You don't think I know how many cattle I have?" Mariella's cheeks darkened.

"I'm sure you know how many cattle you had the last time they were all gathered. But that's a lot of area for one to get sick and go down, a predator to take down, or even to stray over the canyon wall." Davis stood. He put a hand on Mariella's arm. "You haven't had enough ranch hands the last year to cover the entire canyon and know if there are cattle that have died."

She pulled out of his touch. Her stormy eyes glared at him. "You don't have to tell me my failings."

"I wasn't. I was only—" He cut his comment short when she whirled away from him and marched straight into her bedroom. Davis dug in his vest pocket for his pipe. It always calmed him whether just holding it or smoking it.

"Don't worry. She's having a hard time admitting she needs a man to help run this place." Mrs. Simon motioned to the chair Mariella had vacated.

Davis sat and pulled out his tobacco. "Do you mind?" he asked.

"Go ahead. It's been a while since this house smelled like a man lived in it."

He nodded and filled his pipe. Once it was lit, he asked, "I don't want to stir up bad feelings, but from studying the ledger, I can see her husband—"

Mrs. Simon raised her hand and shook her head. "Her late husband. You're now her husband."

Davis knew legally he was, but he didn't feel like her husband. He felt more like a business partner. "Hugh had the head for numbers."

"That he did. And I think part of Mariella is angry with herself for not paying heed when he tried to show her things in that ledger. My daughter can work a man into the ground, but when it comes to ciphering she's slow and knows it. I blame myself. We didn't push her to enough schooling. The kids picked on her because she was bigger than most of the boys and she didn't want to go to school."

Davis inhaled his pipe and let the sweet-scented smoke curl around his head. "If she's not good at ciphering, why is she teaching Zach? He should be in a school."

"There's no school in this area. The families are too far apart to find a spot that all the children could attend." Mrs. Simon set her mending to the side. "Mariella has done the best she can in this remote area."

"I can see she has. I wasn't criticizing her." Davis stood. "I'll see you in the morning."

Mrs. Simon nodded and he left the house.

The evenings were still cool given it was the end of May and summer had yet to come to the canyon. The breeze blowing down the canyon off the snow-covered peaks of Steens Mountain was cold. He had to admit this canyon and the mountains were breathtaking. When his sister wrote of Harney Valley in her letters when she'd first arrived here, he'd had no intention of ever setting foot in the area. When talking him into marrying Mariella, she'd referred to the Bar S as an oasis in the desert. He'd thought she was just saying that to get him to come out. But it was true. This lush green canyon with the vibrant greens of the trees and undergrowth and meadows of grass was an oasis, considering only a few miles away one wandered through sagebrush that was thigh-high and kicked up dust with every step.

He entered the bunkhouse and found Jedidiah already snoring. They needed to get more hands to work the ranch. The three of them couldn't possibly take on the branding and castrating that would need to be done this fall. He'd forgotten his promise to Mariella to write an advertisement for the newspapers near them.

He had a small pad of paper in his belongings, but what he wanted was the paper he'd seen in the drawer of the desk. Opening and closing the bunkhouse door quietly, he crossed the yard and wondered why they didn't have a guard dog. Another thing to add to his list of items the ranch needed. Not only would the right dog make an excellent companion for Zach, but it could help with herding the cattle. He'd witnessed an exhibition of a dog herding sheep at the World's Fair in Philadelphia in 1876. He'd taken Sarah and Christian to see the event.

His heart ached remembering how Christian had begged for one of the dogs. When they returned home, Davis had purchased a small dog for the boy. The two had been inseparable. He pushed on his burning eyes. He'd given the dog to a friend of Christian's after the accident. Watching the dog stare at the door waiting for Christian to return had only added to his own misery.

Not wanting to startle anyone by opening the heavy door in the front of the house, Davis went around to the side door that entered the kitchen. A faint light glowed in the kitchen window. Believing it was a lantern turned low to aid anyone needing to use the outhouse during the night, he lifted the latch on the kitchen door and entered.

An oath he'd only heard muttered by Jedidiah burned his ears as a glass hurled his direction.

Davis managed to ward off the glass, but not the milk that splashed across his face, hands, and vest.

"What are you doing in here?" Mariella asked in a

sharp tone. The door opening while she was in the middle of pouring a glass of milk had scared the living dickens out of her.

"I remembered I wanted to write up an advertisement for ranch hands." Davis held up hands dripping with milk. "I needed paper."

Mariella picked up a towel and threw it at the man. He'd scared nearly ten years off her life.

"You have a good arm," he said, wiping the milk from his hands, face, and vest.

"Sorry. I've never had anyone come in the door after dark." Which reminded her she was in her night clothes.

Davis's gaze wasn't on her body but rather her bare toes sticking out from under her nightgown.

"I didn't mean to scare you. I didn't think anyone was up."

"I couldn't sleep and came out to make a cup of warm milk." She picked the pitcher of milk back up. "Would you like some?" He was part of the reason she couldn't sleep. After storming out of the main room earlier, she was ashamed of her behavior.

"I'd be happy to join you. First I want to get that paper before I forget again."

She watched him walk out of the kitchen. Most men would have thrown a fit about having milk flung over them. Davis wasn't most men. She was slowly beginning to understand he was a hard man to rile and liked that about him. She had enough temper for them both.

Mariella filled the pan with milk for two cups and placed it on the cookstove. She'd already added a stick of wood to the coals before Davis had scared her.

The milk was steaming when Davis returned to the kitchen with several papers.

"I couldn't remember how many newspapers you said there were." He set the papers on the table and took a seat on the long side of the table.

She poured milk into two cups and set them on the table. When she started to sit, Davis stood up.

"It's silly to be formal when it's just the two of us," she said, waving her hand at him to sit.

"Manners were instilled in me from my mother." Davis picked up the cup of milk and sipped.

"I'm glad. You are so different from Hugh that it doesn't bring back memories having you around." She quickly brought the cup up to her mouth. What on earth had made her say something so bold?

His eyes dulled a moment, before his lips slid into a soft, half smile. "That's good. I came to help not cause pain."

"But being here causes you pain." She'd witnessed the pain in his eyes several times when watching Zach and other times. His loss was more recent than hers. And from what Ernestine said, happened in front of him. She'd had the privilege of not having to witness Hugh's death.

"Not as much as I'd feared, but there are times…" He sighed and took another drink of the milk.

"Is there anything I can do to help?" She did want to help him. He'd in two short days done more for her than she could ever repay him for.

He shook his head. "Not really. Time will slowly make the memories less painful. Some have eased, some have not."

"That's what Ma tells me all the time. When she lost Pa I thought she'd go back East and live with her sister, but she insisted on staying with me and the children. I'm glad she did. I wouldn't have made it the last couple of years without her." Mariella took a sip of the milk. She and Hugh used to talk but it was never about feelings. They talked about the family or the cattle and ranch.

They sat in silence sipping the milk. Mariella finished hers and stood to put the cup on the dry sink. Davis stood as well and followed her to the sink. He placed his cup alongside hers and faced her.

"Mariella, I'm not trying to take over the ranch. I came here to help, not make you feel inadequate."

She stared into his eyes. "I know. I'm sorry I stormed off earlier. It's been a long hard two years. I know I've done many things wrong, but everything I did was for my family."

"I know. That's one of the things I like about you. Family comes above all else."

Her heart stammered in her chest. One of the things he likes. Being a large woman, she never thought she'd find more than one man who didn't find her intimidating.

"Good night," he walked to the table, picked up the papers, and left through the kitchen door.

Mariella's cold toes drew her gaze from the window and had her scurrying to pick up the lantern and head to her room. While she hadn't planned on consummating this marriage by sharing a bed with Davis, her mind was taking her down that path. She missed having strong arms to hold her at night. And the warmth of another body to snuggle against on the cold winter nights.

Chapter Eight

Davis spent the next two days riding the canyon with Jedidiah, tallying the mother cows, calves, and yearlings in each herd. They rode up to the barn around four and were met by Mariella. The worry lines on her forehead and the downturn of her lips had him dismounting and walking toward her.

"What's wrong?" he asked, stopping short of putting a hand on her arm.

"A rider came by today. The buyer plans to be here late tomorrow afternoon. He asked if he could stay the night and go on to Roaring Springs the following day."

Davis stroked his beard. "What's wrong with that? We knew the buyers were coming any day."

Mariella grasped his arm and led him away from Jedidiah, who made no bones about listening in. "You can't sleep in the bunkhouse. That's where we'll put the buyer."

"I don't understand?" Davis thought he knew what Mariella was suggesting, but he wanted her to come out and say it.

She rolled her eyes. "If he sees you sleeping in the bunkhouse, he'll think you don't speak for this ranch. You need to sleep in the house."

"Can we put your mother in with the kids and I can use her room?" Davis wasn't unfavorable to sleeping in the same bed as his wife, but he knew neither of them were ready to take their marriage to the intimacy sharing a bed meant.

"I thought of that. But Ma is too big for both of their beds." She brushed wispy curls away from her face.

"I could sleep on the floor in there." Even as he suggested it, his bones ached at the thought.

"No, there wouldn't be enough room on the floor for you. There's only the one choice. Tomorrow morning bring your things into my room. He'll only be here for the one night."

Mariella turned to Jedidiah. "Tomorrow night Mr. Cassel will be here to look at the cattle and spend the night in the bunkhouse with you." She narrowed her eyes. "Be sociable, but don't say anything about the reason I remarried."

Jedidiah nodded and led the two horses into the barn.

Davis followed Mariella to the house. "What about Zach? What if he asks why I'm staying in your room?" He didn't want the boy to think he planned to replace Zach's father.

"I'll figure out something to keep him from saying anything during dinner or afterwards." Mariella slowed her pace as they neared the kitchen door. "This is only for the one night. I'm not ready…"

Davis put a hand on her arm. "I'm not ready either. But I have to admit, I'm looking forward to not sleeping in an empty bed."

Her eyes softened and her lips curved into a smile. "Me, too." She glanced around as if ready to tell a secret and she didn't want anyone else to hear it. "That has been the hardest part about losing Hugh. The huge empty bed."

Davis smiled and squeezed her arm. "One more thing we have in common." He released her and motioned for her to enter the house.

After dinner Davis retrieved the advertisements he'd written. He handed them to Mariella to read.

"These are good. Do you really think we can keep the ranch hands once they see French will pay them more?" She handed the papers back to him.

"We'll have to make sure they are men who care about integrity." Davis folded the letters and slipped them in envelopes. "What are the names of the papers you mentioned before and what towns are they in?"

Mariella stood by the desk telling him the papers and towns. When the last one was addressed, he peered up at her. "How do we mail them?"

A smile slowly formed on her lips. "Jedidiah can take them to the fort tomorrow. That will have him away while the buyer is here and less likely for him to slip up about our marriage."

"That's a good idea." Davis picked up the letters.

"I'll place them on the table so we can hand them to him at breakfast."

***

Mariella knew Jedidiah would come up with excuses to stay at the ranch today. But in the end, Davis had told him it was important the letters were sent off right away. She watched her foreman ride out and knew he wouldn't be back until late tonight. There was a saloon at the fort and Jedidiah would take advantage of his trip.

After Jedidiah left, Davis came in the back door carrying his carpet bag. Her stomach fluttered leading him into her room.

"That's a nice wardrobe," he said, running his hands over the alder.

"My pa made it. He was handy at making things out of wood. He made all the furniture in the house." Her pa might have made his money driving freight wagons but his passion had been in making things out of wood.

"I could have sold these in my store." Davis opened the door and placed his carpet bag in the bottom.

"You're not going to take your clothes out?" she asked.

He studied her. "There's no need. I'm only spending the one night. And I'm sure Mr. Cassel won't come in here to see if my clothes are hanging in the wardrobe."

He had a point.

Davis faced the bed. "You're right, that is a big bed."

Her face heated at his comment. She and Hugh were large people. Her father had made a bed they would have room to sleep separate or plenty of room to…her body heated thinking of the nights they'd made the bed creak from their love making.

A throat clearing jerked her mind to the present. Davis watched her, his cheeks above his beard were a darker hue than usual. Had his mind gone to similar thoughts?

"I'll be helping Ma in the kitchen most of the day. But when Mr. Cassel arrives I want to ride with you to look at the cattle." She could answer questions about the past year.

"I was hoping you'd say that. I'll negotiate but you know the cattle." Davis moved to the door. "Do you mind if I spend some time helping Zach with his school work?"

"There's work to be done outside," she said, wondering what made him think he was needed to help with school work.

"I'll get to it. I thought if I helped Zach with his work, then he could help me with mine."

She didn't miss the determined glint in Davis's eyes. Why did he want to spend time with Zach all of a sudden?

"I need the three horses I'm training to be brought in. Zach knows which they are and where to find them."

"I take that to mean I can help him with his school work." Davis didn't budge from the door.

Mariella wasn't sure why she wanted to keep him from schooling Zach. But it was clear Davis wasn't budging from the door, which meant she'd have to squeeze by him, or allow him to help Zach.

"You can help him today to make his work go faster and the two of you can get those horses rounded up." She stood straight, showing she was the one in charge. He might legally be her husband and be helping her, but she was the one who knew the most and would be the one to make sure the ranch ran smoothly.

Davis nodded once and stepped out of her room. Mariella let her body relax and sat on the bed. She was fairly certain they could get through the ride, dinner, and negotiations fine. Glancing at the bed, her heart thumped against her ribs. Sleeping in the same bed would be the hardest part of selling the cattle.

***

Davis strolled out to the barn with Zach skipping beside him. He'd helped the boy understand simple addition and was happy to hear the boy read so well. After Mrs. Simon's comments, he'd expected to discover the boy was far behind where he should be at this stage of his learning.

"Ma said I'm to show you where the horses are and help collect the three she plans to train this summer." Zach tugged on the barn door.

Davis grabbed the handle and helped pull it open. "What horse are you riding?" Davis asked, as they continued through the barn to the corral behind.

"Thunder is my horse." Zach whistled. It wasn't the high pitched sound his mother made. But it had the same results.

A small, dark brown horse trotted over to the gate.

"This is Thunder," Zach said, opening the gate and looping a rope around the animal's neck. "What horse are you riding?"

Davis hesitated. What would the boy think of him riding his father's horse? "The one your ma had me ride so far is Poker."

Zach's face lit up. "He's a good one. He's missed having someone ride him."

With that hurdle over, Davis walked into the corral and looped a rope around Poker's neck. Leading the horse back to the gate, he caught Zach smiling.

"What's so funny?" Davis asked.

"You not havin' a whistle to bring your horse to you." He shrugged. "That's the first thing Ma teaches the horses. To come to her whistle or the whistle of the person goin' to ride them."

"Maybe your ma can teach me how to get Poker to come to me." Davis led the horse into the barn and they saddled up.

He let Zach take the lead when they left the barn. The boy knew where they were going and it made sense to let him lead.

They crossed the stream that ran down the middle of the canyon and headed up the north side. They traveled along the top of the ridge.

Davis eased his horse up beside Zachs. "Are the horses up on this ridge?"

"There's a ravine they like to stay in."

Davis scanned the area ahead and noticed a ravine on the south side of the ridge. They rode up to the edge and looked down into the small canyon made by two small ridges running into Blitzen Canyon. He saw horses, but they had riders.

"What are they doin' here?" Zach said at the same

time Davis wondered the same.

The boy yelled and started his horse down the steep side of the ravine.

"Zach! No!" Davis knew he wasn't as accomplished rider as Zach, but he couldn't let the boy confront the men riding on Bar S property.

He urged Poker forward. The big gelding charged down the ravine in pursuit of the smaller horse and boy. Davis held onto the horn and squeezed his legs around the barrel of the horse. He decided to let the animal pick the best course. Zach's brown hat and tail-end of his horse could be seen in glimpses through the trees.

He heard Zach yelling and urged Poker faster. They shot into a small opening and found a man holding Thunder's headstall.

"Let go of that horse!" Davis shouted as he pulled Poker to a stop beside Zach and his horse.

"Who are you?" the cowboy holding Thunder asked.

"Davis Weston. You're on Bar S property. Why are you trespassing?" Davis released his grip on the horn and stared first at the man holding Thunder and then at the other cowboy leaning on his horn and grinning.

"You happen to be on Bar S property, too," said the cowboy, tipping his sweat-stained hat up so all of his face was visible.

"He's married to my ma and you'd better get out of here," Zach said, pulling on the reins and making Thunder back up. The action pulled the man off his feet. He released the reins to catch his balance.

"Why you little runt!" The man started toward Zach.

Davis dismounted and put his body between the cowboy and Zach.

"Who do you work for?" he asked the cowboy.

"None of your business." The cowboy walked back to his horse and mounted.

"If I catch you on Bar S land again, I'll turn you over to the law."

Both men laughed.

"There ain't no law in these parts," the one with the stained hat said.

"Then I guess we'll have to take matters into our own hands." Davis didn't like threatening someone, but it was evident the cowboys had been trespassing for a reason. They were either stealing horses or cattle. He didn't like thieves. And knew not a court in the land would convict him for dealing with horse or cattle thieves. "You might let others know, I'll be carrying a gun from here on out and anyone I see on Bar S land without permission will be shot."

Both men stared at him and he stared back. They, and anyone else thinking to sneak onto this land, needed to know it wouldn't be tolerated.

"You're bluffing," the man who had held Thunder's headstall said.

"I do not bluff. Get out of here." Davis nodded toward the ridge where they came from.

The two slowly turned their horses to the ridge. The one in the stained hat twisted in the saddle. "You're lucky I'm not in a contrary mood."

Davis glared back. He and Zach sat in the same spot until they saw the men crest the top of the ridge.

"You think they'll come back?" Zach asked.

"Unfortunately, they didn't look like smart fellows. They'll be back." Davis scanned the area around them. "Where do we find the horses your ma wants collected?"

Chapter Nine

Mariella heard the horses coming down the canyon and hurried over to the holding corral to open the gate.

Four three-year-olds came into sight. She wondered why Zach and Davis collected four horses when she asked for three. As they grew closer, she saw the extra horse was the last gelding from the dam of her horse. It had the same tan coloring with black stockings and mane and tail.

The geldings ran into the corral, snorting. She closed the gate. A horse slid to a stop so close behind her she felt the animal's hot breath.

"Ma! Ma! There was men. Mr. Weston told them. They were…"

She grasped her son by the shoulders, but stared over his head at the man slowly dismounting and gathering his horse. "Slow down. Catch your breath.

What is all this?"

"There was men in the ravine. Two of them." Zach's brown eyes were round, his face red and animated.

"What do you mean two men in the ravine?" She released Zach and straightened, peering at Davis as he approached.

"We found two men on Bar S land. I'm not sure what they were up to." Davis's derby hat sat at an angle on his head. The slant gave him a more domineering appearance.

"What happened?" she asked.

"I stopped them!" Zach said, his small body moving in agitation.

"Yes. We had a talk about running a horse down the side of a canyon and not waiting for a grown-up before confronting people you don't know." Davis gave Zach a pointed look.

"Zachary Bull Swanson, did you do something that could have caused injury to both you and your horse?" Mariella had instilled in the boy you treated your horse better than you wanted to be treated. In this wide open, harsh land they were your only means of getting to help.

Zach stared at the ground, sliding the toe of one boot back and forth in the dirt.

She turned her attention to Davis. "Who were the men?"

"I don't know. They wouldn't tell me who they worked for and they didn't say any names." Davis waved to the horses. "We found these not too far from where the men were sneaking along the ravine." He shook his head. "I don't know if they were after horses or cattle, but stealing either one is against the law."

"Davis told them he'd be packin' a gun the next time he saw them!" Zach piped up.

Davis cringed and put a hand on Zach's shoulder. "What did I tell you about calling me Davis?"

The boy looked at the ground. "Only when we're alone like today."

Mariella was happy the two were getting along but not about the gun. "What about the threat of a gun?" she asked, staring at Davis.

He returned her gaze. "I think it's best from now on I carry a rifle in a scabbard. The two we chased off today had rifles and holsters with pistols. I noticed the men we encountered on the way here only had rifles in scabbards, no pistols."

"So you think they were looking for trouble?" Mariella didn't like people sneaking in and stealing their stock, but she really didn't like a greenhorn like Davis running around with a rifle.

"I have no doubt." He handed the horses to Zach. "Put these horses up and give them a good helping of grain. They were rode hard."

Zach grabbed the reins and led the horses to the barn.

"You and Zach seem to be getting along," Mariella said, happy and yet sad. She knew her son needed a man around, but having a man meant she'd get to spend less time with him.

"We came to an understanding. I'm not here to replace his father. I'm here to help you and the family keep the ranch." Davis leaned his arms on the top of the corral. "We picked up an extra horse," he said, changing the subject.

Mariella stood beside him, her arms crossed over the top of the railing. "I noticed. Is there any particular reason you brought in an extra horse?"

"I was hoping you'd help me train him and he could be my horse. Zach was laughing at me this morning because I didn't have a horse that would come to my whistle." He twisted his head and stared into her eyes. "I'd like a horse of my own, not one I'm borrowing."

She liked the idea. He needed to feel like a part of the ranch and not an outsider. "I could help you train the horse. Any reason you picked the half-brother to Dash?"

He smiled. "I like the color, and we'd make a striking pair riding up to people on matching horses."

She grinned. "Mr. Weston, I didn't know you were so vain."

His eyes became somber and the smile faded. "I'm not vain. Vanity is for pompous people who don't give a care to anyone but themselves."

Davis paced toward the house. Mariella stared at his back. *What did I say?*

Mariella's comment about being vain had struck Davis like a hatchet in the back. God he'd loved Sarah, but it had been her vanity that had caused both she and Christian to drown. As much as he'd been shoving the thought to the side, each night he relived the event in his dreams, he realized Sarah's vanity had cost him his family. She had insisted she wear her best dress, which meant layers of underskirts and her new wool walking coat. He'd tried to talk her into an everyday dress as they were boating and picnicking. Then she'd dressed Christian in that ridiculous wool outfit. Both had drown because of the weight of their clothing when wet.

Davis walked on by the house and outhouse, and into the trees a hundred feet beyond. He needed some time to himself. "You picked a lousy time to come to this realization," he said out loud. For over a year, he'd been blaming himself, just like all his customers and friends. Why hadn't he swam out to them sooner? Why had he let the two of them drift away from the shore? He hadn't let them. Christian had insisted on showing his father he could row. He'd pleaded to take his mother out and back in the boat.

Davis sat on a down tree and held his head in his hands. He'd tried to please Sarah and Christian and it brought about their deaths. He'd never make that mistake again.

The sound of a buggy and horses caught his attention.

The cattle buyers.

He pulled out his pipe, filled it with tobacco, and lit it. After two puffs, he straightened his hat, stood, and headed toward the front of the house.

A buggy with two men stopped at the house. A third man sat on a tall bay horse. Mariella walked out of the corral which held the four geldings. Davis smiled. She had on her riding clothes. Men's pants tucked in tall boots and her shirt billowed around her upper body. The outfit only revealed her small waistline.

He strode out from behind the house meeting her as both men stood on the ground.

81

"Mrs. Swanson—" The older of the two started to say.

"It's Mrs. Weston," Davis said, extending his hand for a shake.

The man studied Mariella then Davis. "I see." A frown wrinkled his brow.

"Mr. Cassel, this is Davis Weston, my husband." Mariella slipped her arm through his. "We'll both be showing you the cattle."

Mr. Cassel finally shook his hand and turned to the man standing beside him. "This is my new associate, Mr. Gardner."

"Pleased to meet you both," Mr. Gardner said, shaking hands with first Mariella, then Davis.

"Would you like some refreshments before we take a look at the cattle?" Mariella asked.

"That I would. If I remember right, your mother makes a delicious butter cookie," Mr. Cassel said.

"And she has a fresh plate waiting for us," Mariella said.

Davis put his hand over Mariella's where she had looped her arm through his. She glanced at him but fell into step as he led the way to the front door.

"Ray, see to the horses," Mr. Cassel called over his shoulder.

Mariella stopped and turned to the barn. "You can unharness and put them in the corral if you like."

Davis watched the man tip his hat to her before leaning down and grasping the side rein. Did she know the man? A feeling he hadn't had in a very long while landed in his gut.

He held the door open, releasing Mariella to

continue into the house and held the door for the two men. "I understand we are your last stop today."

"Yes. We've made a circle around the Steens Mountain. Yesterday we started at the Devine Ranch near Alvord Basin." Mr. Cassel followed Davis's lead of hanging his hat on the peg by the door.

Mariella stood in the kitchen doorway. "Come along."

"One thing I've learned, keep the women happy," Davis said, motioning for the two men to precede him. The men laughed and Mariella gave him a long look.

Crying came from the children's room. He left the men and walked into the room. Lizzie was sitting in her bed crying. He wondered if always waking and being alone scared her or if something else was wrong.

"Lizzie, honey, I'm here." He picked her up, and she snuggled against his chest. He had a feeling she was just lonely. He'd have to say something to both Mariella and Mrs. Simon. It wasn't good to leave a child alone as much as Lizzie seemed to be.

He carried her into the kitchen. "Someone is awake," he said.

Mariella crossed the room and stroked Lizzie's head. "That's my sweet girl." She took the child from Davis and put her in the high chair.

Mr. Cassel and Mr. Gardner had cookies raised to their mouths.

Davis sat down and handed a cookie to Lizzie. She smiled and stuck the sweet treat in her mouth. He smiled back.

"How long have you two been married?" Mr. Cassel asked.

Davis decided to let Mariella answer. He held a cup to his lips and waited.

"A week," Mariella said.

Davis winked at her and her cheeks grew pinker.

Mr. Cassel chuckled. "I see. Mr. Weston, have you always been a cattle rancher?"

Davis almost choked on his coffee. He knew the man would be curious, but he hadn't expected this question. "Why no. I'm actually a merchant. This cattle business is all new to me." He didn't miss the glint in Mr. Cassel's eyes. The man thought he would get as good a deal as last year.

"I see. Were you a merchant in Winnemucca?"

"Why do you ask?" Davis peered at the man. His past had nothing to do with the business they would conduct.

"I was just trying to figure out how you and Mrs. Weston met." The man's smile wasn't as pleasant as before. He was digging, trying to find a way to get the cattle cheap.

"My sister. Mrs. J.P. Mulligan." That was all the man needed to know.

"Mr. Cassel and Gardner, we really should ride out and see the cattle before it gets any later," Mariella said, drawing everyone's attention to her.

While the two men had their faces pointed toward Mariella, Davis gave her an affirmative nod.

"Yes, I'd like to be on the way to Roaring Springs as soon as possible in the morning." Mr. Cassel stood. "Mrs. Simon, as usual your cookies were delicious. I'm looking forward to dinner."

"Thank you." Mariella's mom blushed and started

picking up the dishes.

Davis allowed Mariella to lead the men out of the kitchen, he hung back. "Your cookies are delicious," he said to Mrs. Simon. "Thank you for all you do for Mariella."

Out at the barn, Davis helped Mariella saddle horses for the two buyers and themselves. Ray, the man who had rode in with the buyers, tightened the cinch on his saddle and swung up on his horse when they walked the horses out of the barn. They all mounted and started up the canyon. Mariella was in the lead with Ray behind her, followed by Cassel and Gardner, and Davis bringing up the rear.

After tallying the herds, he knew where they were but preferred to let Mariella show off her cattle. What he didn't like was Ray moving his horse up alongside Mariella's.

When they stopped to look over a herd of cattle, Davis moved his horse up on the other side of Mariella. He noticed Ray peering at Mariella's chest.

"Mariella, why don't you, Mr. Cassel, and Mr. Gardner go a little closer to the herd? I'll stay here with Ray." Davis didn't glance at Mariella, he had a narrowed gaze on the man.

"I think that's a wonderful suggestion," Mr. Cassel said.

When the three were out of hearing, Davis said, "Ray, I don't know what you got away with last year, but keep your eyes off my wife."

Ray smiled. "That's what eyes is for. To take in the beautiful sights."

Davis's hand shot out, grabbing the man by the

shirt before he registered what was happening.

Ray's eyes widened in surprise before they narrowed. "I know better than to mess with a married woman," he said.

"I don't want you staring at any part of her but her face." Davis tightened his grip. "Do you understand?"

The man nodded his head.

The sound of horses approaching relaxed Davis's fingers and he released Ray's shirt. Davis rode over to Mariella and the others. "Ready to see the rest?"

Before anyone answered he turned his horse up the canyon. Mariella soon rode abreast of him.

"What was going on back there?" she asked.

"Now isn't the time to talk about it." Davis wondered at his inability to control his anger. First with the men trespassing and now Ray ogling Mariella. The ranch and the woman had become his to protect. The marriage that bound him in that commitment now came second to the commitment his heart was making.

Chapter Ten

Mariella couldn't remember when she had been so happy to have a meal end and their visitors head out to the bunkhouse. There had been a change in Davis today. One she couldn't figure out and wasn't sure how to ask him about.

He stood by the door having seen the two men out. Ray had excused himself as soon as he'd cleaned his plate. Whatever he and Davis said when they were looking at cattle had Ray avoiding her. They'd had a pleasant enough conversation on the ride out. She'd been a bit uncomfortable the way his gaze drifted downward so much, but he'd held a good conversation.

Davis turned from the door, a pleased smile on his face. "I think we squeezed every penny we could get out of Mr. Cassel."

Mariella crossed the room, meeting Davis halfway.

"That you did." She giggled. "Mr. Cassel looked like he was going to have vapors when you told him the price we wanted."

Davis pulled her into a hug. She was hesitant at first, but leaning her head on a strong shoulder after having shared a moment, this was the kind of companionship she'd missed the last two years.

"It was smart of you to ask for his offer in writing tonight. Before he slept on it and changed his mind," Mariella said.

"I could tell he didn't want to give us that much."

The chest under her arms vibrated when he talked. He smelled of the sweet tobacco he smoked, earthy horse, and male.

"You saying we had other buyers interested at that price." She pushed away, staring into his eyes. "That was brilliant!"

"It was your response with names that did it. I didn't remember a single one in that ledger." Davis held her upper arms. His thumbs moved back and forth over her shirt sleeves. "Go get ready for bed," he said, releasing her. "I'll read for a while and come in later."

Mariella nodded and pivoted toward the bedroom. Her heart raced in her chest. They'd just shared a triumph for the ranch that was all. She wasn't ready to get intimate with Davis.

She stepped in the bedroom and closed the door without looking back. Staring at the bed, her body warmed thinking about Davis sleeping on one side. She fanned her face and quickly donned her nightgown. She'd only ever bedded with one man—Hugh.

At the wash stand, she splashed water on her face

and washed under her arms. She didn't want to smell like a ranch hand when Davis crawled into bed. Hugh had his own earthy scent she'd appreciated, but Davis smelled as good as he dressed. She'd never met a man that was so contradictory. He dressed and smelled like a dandy, talked like a dandy, and yet, he was ready to carry a rifle with him and had said something to Ray to make him avoid her.

Mariella smiled. Zach and Lizzie were both fond of him.

She dabbed some good-smelling water Hugh had given her after one of his trips, behind her ears and padded across the floor to the bed. Do I leave the lantern on or turn it off? She stared at the yellow flame for several minutes and decided it would be best to lower the flame.

Turning back the bedding, anticipation sparked through her body. Anticipation of what, she didn't know. She'd made it plain they wouldn't consummate the marriage tonight. But a small voice in her head said if Davis made the first move, she wouldn't object.

The door opened. "Are you settled in?" Davis whispered.

"Yes." She wasn't sure whether to look at him or hide her eyes.

"Thank you for leaving some light."

The bed creaked, and she rolled slightly his way as he sat on the side of the bed. Mariella watched his back bend and move as he took off his boots. Two thumps on the floor meant his boots were off. He straightened and stood, unbuttoning his vest. He walked over to the wardrobe and hung his vest and shirt on a peg on the back of the door. He still wore a short-sleeved undershirt. The white cloth hugged his body, showing defined lines in his back.

Her mouth went dry as his hands moved to his trouser waistband. Mariella, rolled to her right side and stared at the wall. The lantern went out, and she felt his weight ease down on the bed.

Lying here, knowing he slept next to her, would keep her awake all night. Her body hummed, and her mind kept telling her all the reasons to stay on her side.

"Good-night." His husky voice whispered, not far from her head rushed memories of nights spent wrapped in Hugh's arms.

"Good-night," she whispered, hoping her voice didn't sound as pained as her heart.

Mariella closed her eyes, willing her mind to conjure up Hugh and their good times. They'd had many, but memories didn't keep her warm at night or help her save the ranch. The man lying within arm's reach could do both. He had worked his way into her thoughts, and she grew fonder of him with each act of kindness Davis bestowed on her family and her. A thought came to her.

"What did you say to Ray?"

The bed bounced and creaked as he moved.

"I told him to only look you in the face."

From the sound of his voice she could tell he'd turned on his side and was facing her. She spun onto her left side and faced him. She couldn't see him in the darkness, but felt his presence. "Why did you say that?"

Air puffed her hair. "When I rode up alongside the two of you, I saw where he was looking. No man is going to stare at my wife's body like he's drooling over candy in a store."

The anger in his tone should have scared her, but it made her body tingle. "I knew he was staring at my chest. Most men do. But I enjoyed his conversation. He was telling me about some of the other ranching families I know."

"He didn't have to stop talking to you. He just had to keep his eyes upward." A hand touched her face. "Go to sleep. I won't let anyone hurt you or the children."

"I know," she whispered and closed her eyes. His warm hand brushed across her cheek and disappeared.

Davis lay awake listening to Mariella breathe. Lying in bed with her, talking in whispers, and then touching her, his need for her throbbed. He'd not had this strong of an urge while dating Sarah. He'd been ready to make love to her when they'd married, but it still wasn't as intense as he felt right now for Mariella.

He knew Mariella was tough, but she was also gentle with her children and loving with her mother. She had qualities he was thrilled to discover. When Ernestine told him about Mariella, he'd expected one thing and had found exactly the opposite. He'd hoped for a woman he could get along with and have a congenial relationship without hearts and desires becoming heated.

The few short days they'd been together, he was becoming more and more aware of her womanly curves, her quick laughter, and even quicker temper, but most of all she was an intelligent woman. Sarah had been intelligent, but she'd lacked the spontaneity that he found refreshing in Mariella.

He rolled to his side, putting his back to the temptation that he could tell was still awake. With his back to her, he'd try and put her out of his mind. A sweet scent lingered in the air. He smiled. Lemon Verbena. She'd put that on before sharing a bed with him.

***

Davis woke from the throbbing in his shaft. He'd not experienced this reaction in his body for years. Drawing his mind awake, he realized an arm draped over his body and soft bosoms pressed against his back. The heat of a woman pressed against his backside.

Opening his eyes, he saw he was on the side of the bed he'd fallen asleep on. Mariella had ventured to his side. He grinned, then sobered. She couldn't see the desire he had for her. While she might be draped over him, she could very well think he was her late husband. As badly as he would like to roll, take her in his arms, and taste her wide expressive mouth, he didn't believe either of them were ready for that.

Instead, he pulled himself to the edge of the bed and rolled to his feet.

Mariella made a sound, and he quickly turned away from the bed. His shaft was making a tent of his underdrawers.

He quickly dressed, pressing his need against his body to button his trousers. It was painful but he could hear Mrs. Simon already preparing breakfast in the kitchen. He'd need a walk in the brisk morning to douse the heat in his body.

Once dressed, he picked up his boots and tiptoed out into the main room. Lizzie sat on the hearth rug playing with a rag doll. She held her arms up to him, but in his state, he didn't want to dally inside.

She whimpered and said, "Peas."

Davis picked her up, carried her into the kitchen, and placed her in her highchair.

"Good morning, Davis," Mrs. Simon said, cheerfully.

He grunted at her and continued on out the door. The crisp air filled his lungs as he walked as quickly has his predicament would allow to the stream. At the stream, he knelt and splashed the ice cold water on his face. After several splashings and lungs full of the air, his need lessened.

The swish of grass and crunch of footsteps prompted him to stand. He turned and discovered Mr. Gardner approached.

"Good morning," the man said, stopping ten feet back.

"Good morning." Davis ran his wet hands over his hair and then sluiced the excess water from his beard. "You're up and around early."

"I could say the same about you." The man stared at him with a faint smile.

Davis knew it was odd for him to be washing up in the stream so early in the morning. "Mrs. Weston was still sleeping and I didn't want to wake her," he said by way of explaining his washing in the stream.

"That's very considerate of you." He continued to stare. "Mr. Cassel finds it interesting that no one along the way knew about this marriage. You would think something like this in such a small community would have been big news."

"My sister, her husband, the Justice of the Peace in Sagehen, and Mr. French's men who tried to keep us from the Bar S, knew." Davis saw a flicker of annoyance in the man's eyes. "And the two men who were trying to rustle livestock from this ranch, knew."

Mr. Gardner straightened. "What do you mean men trying to rustle livestock?"

"Just what I said. Yesterday when the boy and I were rounding up those geldings in the corral, we came across two men on Bar S land. They were up to no good and left once we confronted them." Davis motioned toward the house. "It looks like breakfast is ready."

Mrs. Simon stood at the corner of the house yoo-hooing. Mr. Cassel, Ray, and Jedidiah were crossing the yard to the house.

Without waiting for the other man, Davis headed to the house. He entered the front door, hoping to catch Mariella before she entered the kitchen. She stepped out of their bedroom as he reached for the door knob.

Her golden brown eyes peered into his.

"Did you sleep well?" he asked, noting there were faint gray smudges under her eyes.

"Once I fell asleep."

He nodded. He'd heard her tossing and turning for several hours.

"Where did you go?" she asked, quietly.

"Out for a walk." If she didn't know she was clinging to him in her sleep, he wasn't going to mention it.

"I see."

"Breakfast you two," Mrs. Simon called.

"Everyone else is here." Davis tucked her hand

through his arm and they entered the kitchen together. He held her chair as she sat, then took his seat.

Zach frowned at their entrance, but soon fell upon his plate of bacon and eggs.

Ray kept his eyes on his plate. This morning Mariella was wearing a more form-fitting shirt. Davis liked the vision, but he didn't like the fact the others were given a glimpse at her curves. He noticed Mr. Gardner furtively glancing at her.

"Where are you going this morning?" Davis asked to get the man to look at him.

"We have two small ranches like yours to visit before heading to Roaring Springs." Mr. Cassel said. "I hope they aren't as hard to negotiate with as you two." The man frowned.

Davis bit back a smile. The man knew he'd robbed Mariella last year. What he made off his profits then would have to even out his loss this year.

Mariella smiled at Davis. "I was lucky to find a businessman who knows cattle."

Her compliment heated his cheeks.

"I find it interesting you have a new husband when the rumors about the Blitzen Valley claim you are ready to sell out to Peter French," Mr. Gardner said.

Chapter Eleven

Mariella choked on her bite of bread. Her mother handed her a cup of water. A chair scraped and a hand patted her back. She couldn't see who through the tears in her eyes, but instinctively knew it was Davis.

When she'd controlled the choking, drank some water, and cleared her eyes, she glared at Mr. Gardner. "Who is spreading that rumor?" Davis's hands rested on her shoulders. She had no doubt he was also staring at the little man squiggling in his chair beside Mr. Cassel, who, was studying everything in the kitchen but her.

Mr. Gardner lifted his hands submissively. "It's what I heard from several of the other ranchers."

"No, you didn't." She leaned forward. "The only person who would gain anything from those rumors is Mr. French. He probably sent his ranch hands about telling lies." She shoved to her feet. The chair moved, and Davis stood beside her.

When his arm settled around her shoulders she said, "We will never sell this ranch. It will remain in our family for years. You can tell that to Mr. French when you see him." She didn't feel like eating anymore knowing the largest cattle rancher in Blitzen and Harney Valley was trying to undermine her with all the other small ranchers.

"Davis, will you see that these men leave as soon as they finish eating?" Gazing into his eyes, she felt better. He understood.

"I will."

She nodded, picked up Lizzie, and nodded to Zach. "Come on, you have school work to do."

Mariella didn't feel like sitting at a table with men who were trying to take away everything her family had worked for. In the other room, she started Zach on his numbers and played with Lizzie.

Thirty minutes later, Davis entered from the kitchen. "I just saw them all off." He sat on a chair facing where she sat on the floor playing with Lizzie.

"Thank you." She peered into his eyes. "I'm sorry I left you to deal with them. I was afraid I'd say something to make Mr. Cassel back out of our deal."

"He said his men would be here in one week to gather the hundred and fifty head." Davis patted Lizzie's head. "We need to start rounding them up."

"I agree." She kissed Lizzie's soft cheek. "I'll get some sandwiches made and we can start today." She pushed to her feet.

Davis caught her arm when she walked by his chair. "Don't let their talk worry you. We'll keep this ranch out of Mr. French's hands."

She smiled down at him. "I know. I just don't like my neighbors thinking I've given up."

Davis smiled. "Well, I say we tell then different."

His smile was infectious. "How?"

"While Jedidiah was at the fort, he heard there was going to be a social at the Diamond Ranch a week from Saturday. I think we should attend." Davis slid his hand down, linking their fingers. "What do you say, Mrs. Weston?"

"Can we, Ma?" Zach asked. "I haven't seen Jimmy and Sam in a long time."

Mariella liked the idea of attending a social with a husband again. "I think it's a wonderful idea. We'll all go. It will be a treat after rounding up and selling the cattle."

"I was hoping you'd say that." Davis stood, still holding her hand. "I'm curious to see you fancied up."

Her cheeks heated. "I guess you'll find out in over a week." She slipped her hand from his and strode into the kitchen. Her cheeks continued to steam. What am I going to wear? She only had the one nice dress. The one she'd worn when they were married. How much more fancy did he want to see?

"My, you seem flustered," Ma said, turning from the basin where she cleaned up the breakfast dishes.

"Davis said we're all going to the social at Diamond a week from Saturday."

Her mother smiled. "I saw him when he crept out of your room this morning." Her mother's cheeks reddened. "Are you now truly husband and wife?"

"Ma!" She couldn't believe her mother had asked

such a question. "I was talking about a social, not my marriage."

Ma's glowing face and eyes dulled. "What about the social?"

"Davis said he wanted to see me all fancied up. I only have the one good dress. He's already seen me in it." She couldn't believe she was worrying about a dress when they had a hundred and fifty cattle to round up.

"I'll have a new dress for you before the social." Ma's bright face and smile were back. "Your husband won't be able to take his eyes off you."

Another blush heated her cheeks. "Ma!"

"Are those sandwiches ready?" Davis asked from the kitchen doorway.

"No. Go on out and saddle the horses," Mariella said without turning around.

"Zach wants to come."

"If his work is done he may." She liked the idea of having both Zach and Jedidiah around while bringing in the cattle. They would keep her and Davis from being alone. After sharing her bed with him last night, she wanted to be with him as much as possible, but since he'd slipped out of bed so early, she wondered if he didn't feel the same.

***

Davis and Jedidiah saddled the horses.

"Did you hear any of the rumors Mr. Gardner spouted when you were at the fort?" Davis asked as they led the horses out of the barn.

"Nope. There wasn't nothin' said about sellin' this ranch."

It confirmed what Davis thought. Mr. Gardner had

to be an associate of Mr. French. He was going about spreading the rumors in hope of discrediting this ranch and Mariella with her neighbors.

"We'll be attending the Diamond social," he told Jedidiah. "It will give Mariella a chance to talk to her neighbors and let them know she isn't selling."

"It's a good idea. And if she didn't attend they'd all wonder. She and Hugh never missed a social." Jedidiah swung up on his horse's saddle. "I'll go scout for a herd."

Davis stared after the man. What wasn't he saying?

Mariella and Zach walked across the area between the house and barn. A grin spread across his face. They had as many similarities as they had differences. Both were stealing sections of his heart. He had planned to fight any emotional connection to this family. Not wanting to be hurt again. But this family made him feel needed and that life was worth living.

Mariella tossed the saddlebag with their lunch behind her saddle and tied it on. "Where's Jedidiah?"

"He said he was going to go ahead and scout for the herd." Davis pulled his gaze from her backside that looked even more fetching today in the tight trousers she wore.

She snorted. "We all know where the herds are. He just wanted to get away from you before he said something."

"What would he say?" Davis frowned. What could the old man say that he didn't want to say?

Mariella shrugged and mounted.

Davis mounted and waited for Zach. They all three rode up the canyon single file with Mariella in the lead and Davis in the back.

By noon they'd gathered two herds together. Davis watched Jedidiah and Zach eat their lunch while sitting on their horses and keeping the herd together. He and Mariella sat under a pine tree taking a break from the saddle and watching.

"I don't think I've put this many hours in a saddle my whole life," he said, lying on his side, propping his body up with an arm and holding a sandwich in the other hand.

Mariella laughed. "Getting saddle sore, greenhorn?"

The term greenhorn should make him mad, but the way Mariella said the word, it sounded more like an endearment. "Yes, I am. Do you have a salve you could rub on my sores?"

Her laughter stopped and her gaze held his. Pink started at the neck of her shirt and rose, coloring her cheeks a bright red.

The thought of sleeping in the bunkhouse after sampling the soft bed in Mariella's room had him thinking all morning about how to keep sleeping in her bed. The heat in her cheeks and the way she'd hugged him during the night, he didn't think it would be too hard to convince her.

Davis sat up. "Mariella—"

"Hup! Hup!" shouts from Zach and Jedidiah rang through the canyon.

Mariella leaped to her feet. "The cattle are scattering!"

She was on her horse before Davis could capture Poker's reins. When he was finally mounted he stared in wonder as she and her horse raced through the trees, dodging the trunks and branches.

Knowing he couldn't ride like that to chase strays, he trotted Poker to the bottom of the canyon and started trailing the cows, which were still gathered, back toward the corrals. Jedidiah caught up with twenty head, adding them to the main herd. Eventually, Zach also added ten head to the group moving slowly down the canyon.

Davis spun in his saddle trying to catch a glimpse of Mariella. Why hadn't she returned with cattle? He rode over to Jedidiah.

"Shouldn't Mariella be getting back here?"

The old man stared at him. "She knows what she's doin'."

"I saw her racing through the trees. She could be hurt." He started to rein his horse around.

Jedidiah grabbed the reins. "She'll catch up when she can. One thing about that woman, she's tenacious when she's tryin' to catch somethin'."

"But she could be hurt." Davis glared at the man and his hands still holding Poker's reins.

"She'll be furious if you go lookin' for her and we lose more cattle. She'll come along." Jedidiah released the reins. "Stay with the herd. Don't need them breaking loose again."

Davis didn't like sticking with the herd. His mind was flashing through all kinds of reasons Mariella wasn't catching up to them. All of them made his gut churn.

***

It was late in the afternoon when they spotted the

102

ranch and Mariella still hadn't returned. Davis spun in his saddle every five minutes hoping to catch a glimpse of cattle headed their way. It wasn't until the herd rumbled into the yard and he spotted someone opening the holding corral gate that he realized the tall, curvy body was Mariella.

He left Zach and Jedidiah to shove the last of the cattle into the corral, trotting Poker over to where Mariella stood. Davis swung down off his horse and pulled Mariella into his arms.

"Thank God you're safe," he said, holding her tight and breathing in her scent of horse, dust, and faint lemon verbena.

She pushed with her hands on his chest and stared into his eyes. "What are you talking about?"

"When you didn't come back to the herd like Jedidiah and Zach, I thought…" He couldn't say what he'd thought.

"I caught up to a bunch on the rim and trailed them along the rim." Her eyes sparkled. "You were worried about me?"

"Yes. You went racing through those trees like your horse's tail was on fire." He hugged her close. "Mariella, my heart can't take losing another wife."

Mariella slipped from his arms and looked into his eyes. "I know why you're saying that, but I won't let a cow get away when I can stop it, just because it makes you upset."

Davis took a step back. He wasn't just thinking of himself. He knew losing another wife to an accident would break him. But she had children to think about. "I know you've been the boss and the ranch hand on this ranch. But you also have to think about Zach and Lizzie. What are they going to do if something happened to you?"

She narrowed her eyes. "That's low."

"Think about it. If you go racing off and your horse stumbles and something happens to you, who is going to keep this ranch for your children?"

Her mouth opened, swallowed, and then said, "You," in a hoarse voice.

He blinked at her several times. Yes, he'd married her with the knowledge he would help her keep the ranch, but raising her children, keeping the ranch for them. He knew nothing about that.

"I-I…" He didn't know what to say.

Mariella stared at him. "When you married me you took on my children and this ranch. I don't care if you love me, but you darn well better carry enough feelings for my children to keep them together as a family. Otherwise, this marriage is off." She grabbed Dash's reins from where they were flung over the corral and stomped toward the barn.

Davis stared after her. Not until she disappeared into the barn did he notice Jedidiah and Zach standing by the corral gate watching him.

His backside was sore as hell, but he needed some time to think. He crawled back into the saddle and headed up the canyon.

Chapter Twelve

Mariella fumed and mumbled under her breath as she unsaddled Dash. "Fool man, what did he think marrying me would get him? I have a family. He married me and my family." She huffed and slammed the saddle down on the stall railing.

"Take care of that saddle. It cost Hugh a lot of money," Jedidiah said, leading his and Zach's horse into the barn.

"Why are you taking care of Zach's horse?" she asked, scooping a ration of grain for Dash.

"Thought he didn't need to see his ma mumbling and having a hissy fit."

"Can you believe that greenhorn would walk away if something happened to me? Leave my children and ranch at the mercy of the likes of Peter French." She couldn't stand still. Her anger at Davis hurt more than pure anger. She'd started to care about the man. When he'd swung down off his horse and pulled her into his arms, she'd witnessed his worry and concern for her. She'd felt his heart racing as he held her tight.

"A lot has happened since you two agreed to this marriage." Jedidiah pulled the saddle off Zach's mustang. "You both have some compromisin' to do and some discoveries to make."

Mariella stared at Jedidiah. "What are you talking about? He needs to step up and take the responsibility of the children and the ranch."

Jedidiah slung an arm over the mustang and peered at her. "That man has defended this ranch and your son from intruders. He badgered the best price for the cattle. And I've seen him givin' you a randy eye." He waved his hand. "You can't expect the man to blurt out all he's feelin'. You've been without a husband longer than he's been without wife. His memories are closer, clearer than yours."

The old ranch hand moved to his horse and started loosening the cinch.

Mariella thought about all Jedidiah said. They both had suffered loss. Both to accidents. She didn't see her husband die. Davis had witnessed his wife and son's accident. His fear of losing her was stronger because of that. But that didn't explain why he didn't agree to taking care of the children or the ranch if something happened to her? On their rides he'd made comments about how beautiful it was and he was glad he came.

Davis hadn't brought his horse in to unsaddle. "Where is Davis?" she asked.

"He mounted and headed up the canyon."

"But he said his backside was sore from all the riding." Her cheeks heated at his teasing about her rubbing salve on his sores.

"Guess his mind and heart hurt more and he needed some air." Jedidiah grasped the lead ropes to all three horses, leading them out to the horse corral behind the barn. "I'll toss some hay to the cattle."

Mariella nodded. *How can I make this up to Davis? She didn't think he'd ride too far, not with the soreness in his backside. I can either wait for him to return or try to find him.*

***

Davis stood in the stirrups, giving his backside a rest from the hard seat of the saddle. He stopped up the canyon far enough he couldn't see the ranch house and corrals. Every once in a while the sound of the cattle bawling to gain their freedom filtered through the trees.

He dismounted and paced back and forth as Poker grazed on the lush grass. *Why didn't I readily agree to take care of her children? Because that would mean you'd lost another wife. What would people say then? And how would that affect the children?* He paced and taunted himself for ever thinking he could start over fresh with a new family.

With a reckless wife, like Mariella, it would only be a matter of time and he would be a widower again. He'd spent the whole afternoon terrified she'd been hurt. Believing she lay wounded in the trees and they wouldn't be able to get to her in time. The fear and panic that had sliced through him watching his wife and son drown had visited him again.

When he'd seen Mariella at the corrals, a flood of emotions had raced through him. The strongest had been joy at seeing her unhurt. Holding her, his mind and body had felt at peace. As if he'd found home. That thought circled in his mind as he battled with the insecurity of losing another person he cared about.

Poker nickered and he spun toward the horse.

Mariella walked toward them. She didn't storm forward. Her steps were hesitant, her face apprehensive.

He stood still, watching her approach. His gaze was bold, taking in her curves, her windswept hair with auburn wisps of curls about her face, and her bottom lip held firmly between her teeth. She had the beauty of a woodland fairy, but the build of a lumberjack.

She stopped several feet away from him. Her gaze held his. "I'm sorry."

He didn't understand. He was the one who couldn't give her the answer she wanted. He was the one who rode off. "What are you sorry for?"

"For not thinking about how racing through the trees would scare you."

"It wasn't just the racing through the trees. It was not seeing you for hours and thinking…"

Mariella stepped forward, placing a hand on his arm. "It was inconsiderate of me. I've not had someone worry about me for a while and I've gotten kind of reckless."

"You have to think of your children." He wasn't sure if it made him feel better or worse that she was apologizing. He did feel like a fool.

Her eyes lit with anger. "I do think of my children. That was one of the reasons I wanted a husband. So I

108

knew my children would be provided for if something happened to me. Ma has the love but not the means to care for them."

"Children need a mother." He held his hand out to her. "I knew you had children when I accepted my sister's offer to come here. But I didn't come here to be a father only. I came here to be a husband and a partner in this ranch."

She placed her hand in his. "You've done so much already. Chasing those men off and getting us a good price for the cattle."

"Promise me you won't head off hell bent to do anything. Stop and think of your family." Davis waited, holding her hand, hoping she could give him this small piece of mind.

"I'll try. You may have to stop me a time or two. I've always been a person to act first and question later." She shrugged and her lips curved in an apologetic smile.

"You took off so fast today I didn't have time to stop you." His mind still played the image of her dodging trees and limbs as her horse sprinted through the forest.

She tugged on his hand and scooped up Poker's reins. "Come on. Ma should have supper ready."

Hand in hand they walked back to the house.

Davis glanced sideways and caught Mariella watching him. A sweet, vulnerable smile played on her lips.

"Your bed is mighty comfortable. And a lot more room than the bed in the bunkhouse." He was fishing for an invitation to stay in the house.

Her step stalled for a second and her lips straightened. "I bet it is."

"I think you liked me in your bed. Your arm was around me and your body was pressed against mine when I woke up." He stopped. They were within sight of the house. Drawing her attention to his face he said. "I didn't mind you snuggling. And I appreciated sharing the bed. We don't have to go any farther, but when we start getting answers to the advertisement we placed in the newspapers it would be odd for me to sleep in the bunkhouse."

Her gaze traveled over his face. "That was you I was hugging, not a dream?"

"Yes, it was."

Her cheeks brightened. "I thought I was dreaming."

His vanity had to ask. "Were you dreaming about me or Hugh?"

Mariella's cheeks darkened in color and her gaze flew to his mouth. "You," she whispered.

Davis's heart beat against his ribs and his body came to life. He placed a hand under Mariella's chin and drew her to his mouth. He placed a chaste kiss on her lips.

She didn't pull away, but she didn't flow into his arms either. He kissed her once more and released her chin.

The sound of a dinner bell rang out through the trees.

"I'll tell Ma you're putting your horse up," Mariella said, heading toward the house in long strides.

Davis grinned. Courting his wife would be fun. The dance coming up next week would be a perfect

110

place to show her he believed in her, the children, and the ranch.

After putting Poker out in the corral with the other horses, Davis hurried in to supper. He stopped at the wash basin on the back porch and washed up.

Stepping through the back door, he found everyone seated at the table waiting patiently.

"Sorry I'm late." He hung his hat on the hook by the door and took his seat at the head of the table. Glancing the length of the hand hewn wood, he smiled at Mariella. She blushed and Mrs. Simon started passing the bowls and plates of food around.

The table conversation consisted of separating out the sale animals from the producing stock in the corral the following morning. They'd brought in whole herds and needed to keep only the two-year-olds out for sale.

Davis could see where the process of bringing in the cattle would have been more easily done if they had more men. Ones to separate while others gathered. His ads for ranch hands wouldn't even be seen by potential cowboys until after they'd sold the cattle. But there would be a need for help bringing in the hay later in the summer.

After dinner, he plucked Lizzie from her high chair and wandered into the main room. He sat in a chair entertaining the child and answering Zach's questions until Mariella entered the room.

"I have some ranch questions for you," Davis said, handing Lizzie over to her mother's outstretched arms.

"I'll put the children to bed and you can ask them." Mariella herded Zach into the children's room and closed the door.

Davis rose out of the chair and walked to the desk. He sat down and wrote out his thoughts on the hired hands. He wasn't sure how many were needed year round and if that was enough to take care of the haying needs.

Mrs. Simon sat in one of the hearth chairs and started sewing on a new garment not mending.

Within minutes, Mariella returned. "What questions did you have?" She placed the other hearth chair by the desk.

"How many ranch hands did you have before?" Davis held a pen poised over the paper where he'd written his questions.

"We had five."

"Were they year round and does that include Jedidiah?" He wrote the number down.

"That was besides Jedidiah, and yes, they were year round." She glanced at his paper. "And to answer your other question, we hired a neighbor to cut the hay but we, the ranch hands, Hugh and I, hauled the hay into the barn to feed the horses in the winter, and stacked the rest in the fields. We winter the cattle in the field."

He studied her. "With Mr. French's fences you don't have to worry about them wandering off."

She made a sound in her throat. "We didn't have that problem before his fences. The cattle stay where they have food and water." She stared out the window. "Someone has to go down a couple times a day and break the ice on the edge of the river so the cattle can drink. In the winter the ranch hands keep track of the cattle, keep the horses tended, and clean and repair tack."

"That's what I needed to know. I want to make sure we hire enough men even though we'll have the majority of the hard work done before we even hear from someone.

Mariella shook her head. "The sorting and rounding up for sale is the easy part. We'll have to round all the cattle up in the fall to castrate and brand. That takes many people and many days."

Davis scratched his beard. He'd forgotten about that business. The best way for a rancher to keep track of his stock was by branding.

"I'll take your word for it."

Mrs. Simon stood. "Good night, you two. See you in the morning."

"Good night, Ma," Mariella said.

"Good night Mrs. Simon," Davis said, smiling at the woman.

The older woman stopped at the door of her room. "You didn't take your things from Mariella's room. Does that mean you'll be staying in the house permanently?"

Davis watched Mariella.

She smiled and said, "As long as he behaves himself."

Mrs. Simon's smile crinkled the skin around her eyes. "Good. Behave yourself, Davis." She disappeared into her room.

Davis smiled. "Thank you. After spending all day in that saddle, I need a soft bed tonight."

Mariella's eyes lit up with mischief. "Still want me to rub salve on your backside?"

He knew she was only teasing and not ready to become so intimate, but the idea sent his mind and body to thoughts he'd best beat down before he acted on them.

"Not tonight, but I'm sure by the end of the week, I'll need it." He nodded toward the bedroom door. "Go on in and get ready. I'll be in shortly."

She stood and peered down at him. "Thank you for accepting your sister's offer."

Before he could respond, she spun around and strode to the bedroom, shutting the door.

Davis glanced down at his notes. He hoped they had decent law-abiding men reply to the advertisement. Otherwise, it looked like they'd be doing the work of eight with three people.

He filled his pipe with tobacco and wandered outside. Smoking and watching the sparkling stars in the dark blue night sky, he contemplated the work ahead and the woman getting ready for bed. Both were daunting prospects.

Chapter Thirteen

Mariella enjoyed watching Davis work the gate. His mind was much more active than Hugh's had been. He calculated his moves and acted after his mind had come up with a solution. Which meant, many times when she and Jedidiah pushed a cow toward the gate, if Davis thought one they wanted to keep was too close, he'd not open the gate until it was too late. Which had Jedidiah cursing up a storm and Mariella giggling.

"Dang blame it, greenhorn, even young Zach can work a gate better than you can." Jedidiah stopped at the gate and glared down at Davis. "The way you're workin' that gate we'll still be here sortin' this lot tomorrow."

Davis glared back at Jedidiah. "If you'd cut out one cow at a time instead of a cow and two of the steers were keeping, I could open the gate."

"Boys!" Mariella could tell they weren't getting the job done and needed to placate both of them.

They both looked at her and said, "Boys?" in unison.

"That's what you're acting like. A couple of school boys." She whistled and Zach came running out of the house.

"Yeah, Ma?" He slid to a stop next to the gate where Davis stood.

"Now we'll get some cows sorted," Jedidiah spouted.

Davis glared at Jedidiah.

Mariella shook her head. "Zach, show Davis how to run the gate. Jedidiah, no more cursing or slanted remarks."

The old man mumbled under his breath.

"I really don't think I need someone to show me how to open and close a gate," Davis objected.

"Just stand back and watch." Mariella used the same soft tone she did when trying to get Zach to understand schoolwork. She wanted Davis to learn everything about cattle ranching. She'd planned to have him run the gate even before he volunteered so he could give his backside a rest today.

Davis nodded, but she could tell he wasn't happy with losing his job to a child.

"Come on," she said to Jedidiah and they maneuvered their horses into the herd of cattle. She pushed out two cows and a steer, just so Davis could see how Zach moved the gate to let the cows out and leave the steer in.

She saw Davis shaking his head from the corner of her eyes. She smiled and continued moving the three cattle forward. The cows knew the process of sorting and stayed along the fence. The steer stayed wider. Zach opened the gate to the inside pushing the steer back into the corral and allowing the cows to slide out the opening.

Davis narrowed his eyes at her. "Why didn't you tell me to open the gate to the inside?"

"I thought you'd figure it out. But it also works better with Zach because he is smaller and doesn't scare the cows." She pivoted her horse around and said over her shoulder. "You can take the gate again. Zach, get mounted up."

"Yahoo!" Zach hollered and ran to the barn.

Mariella laughed as Jedidiah pushed three cows and two steers toward the gate. She reined Dash around to see how Davis handled this group. Happiness warmed her chest as she watched Davis maneuver the gate, separating the cows and leaving the steers in the corral. The sorting would go smoother now that he'd mastered using the gate properly.

Ma brought them sandwiches for lunch. They downed the food and drank water before getting back to the sorting.

The business of sorting took concentration, which didn't leave her much time to think about her second night with Davis in her bed. All she could do was grin at how when he came to bed, he'd rolled her way and they'd whispered good night. This morning she'd woke before him and found her arm draped over him and her body pressed to his back. She'd slowly started to pull her hand away and he'd captured it, holding her against him.

"Hey! What're you thinking about? Get that last cow," Jedidiah hollered as he pushed the last cow toward her.

Mariella shook away the thoughts and concentrated on the cow. Between Dash's instincts and Davis's gate work, they finally forced the last cow out. Zach and Thunder chased the cow up the canyon to reunite it with the rest.

Jedidiah rode up to the gate. Davis let him out and waited for her to pass through.

Mariella dismounted and turned to Davis.

"That was cruel bringing a six-year-old out here to show me how to run a gate," Davis said.

She peered into his eyes to see if he was upset with her. She saw a spark of merriment in his eyes.

"I wanted you to see that if a young boy could do the job, you could." She put a hand on his arm. "I'm sorry I waited until Jedidiah was cursing you."

Davis smiled. "I was frustrated the old coot seemed to be having fun cursing me."

Mariella laughed. "That he did!"

Davis leaned his arms over the pole gate and stared at the cattle. "If we'd had the extra hands this process wouldn't take so long would it?"

She stood beside him, watching the steers mull around. "We would have rounded up all the cattle at once and drove them all down here and sorted in one day." She sighed. "With the three of us it just takes longer to do everything."

Davis put an arm around her. "We'll have help for

the Fall roundup. I promise."

She leaned her head on his shoulder. It was good to have his broad shoulders to carry some of the burdens. "Thank you."

"Looks like another day in the saddle tomorrow," Davis said, turning them toward the house.

"Yes. Will your backside take it?" she teased.

"I hope so. I don't want to be crippled this Saturday and not be up to dancing with you."

Mariella sighed. She'd not been this content in a while. Many of her worries had been taken on by the man at her side. It was good to also have someone to talk to besides Ma and Jedidiah. Davis listened and gave her things to think about.

They washed up at the back door and wandered into the kitchen. Mariella sniffed and her stomach rumbled. Ma had a roast in the oven and pies cooling.

"It smells wonderful in here, Mrs. Simon," Davis said, scanning the kitchen and seeing the makings of a full and satisfying supper.

"Thank you. I figured all of you could use a good meal after eating so fast at noon." Mrs. Simon lifted a lid on a pot on the stove and stirred the ingredients, letting even more mouth-watering scents into the room.

Mariella walked over and plucked Lizzie out of the high chair. "Do we have a count of the steers in the corral?" she asked, sauntering into the main room.

Davis followed, enjoying the view of the child balanced on her swaying hips. "No. Would you like me to go out and get a count?"

Mariella smiled. "Lizzie could use some fresh air. Why don't we all three go count those steers?"

Davis agreed. The child was pale and could use a bit of sunshine and fresh air. "That's a good idea." He grasped Lizzie from Mariella's arms. "Come on, Lizzie, girl. You're going to help your momma and I count ornery steers."

The child giggled and pressed her head to Davis's chest. The simple act melted his heart and had him vowing he'd make sure her life was full of love and laughter.

The soft smile and love in Mariella's eyes proved she had the same thoughts.

Davis held the front door for Mariella to exit. He and Lizzie followed. Mariella slipped her hand through the crook of his arm that held Lizzie. Happiness filled his heart. He had a family again.

At the corral, he shifted Lizzie and stared over the upright pole fence. "I can't see them well enough to count everyone." He noticed a platform on the east side of the corral. "Hold Lizzie and I'll go over there, where I can get up higher and count."

Lizzie lifted her head. Her bottom lip protruded in a pout.

Davis grinned. She didn't want to leave him. "Honey, I don't want to scare you up on that platform."

He handed the child over to her mother.

Mariella cooed and told Lizzie to look at a pretty bird in the sky.

Davis hurried to the platform, stepped up and started counting the bawling, restless animals. Once he'd counted the group three times and was confident he had the correct number he returned to Mariella and Lizzie.

The child held her hands out for him to hold her. He glanced over her head at Mariella. She nodded. Drawing the child back in his arms, he said, "I counted twenty-seven."

"I thought it looked like there were about thirty in there." Mariella stopped as Zach and Thunder came racing down the canyon.

When the boy noticed them, he pulled his horse to a trot.

Davis didn't like seeing the boy ride so wild, but it was no different than how Mariella had lit out through the trees the day before. "Like mother, like son," he said.

Mariella's gaze flew from her son to Davis. "Do you think I need to scold him for riding so fast?"

He could tell by her words and the slight raising of one of her eyebrows, she was ready to argue with him.

Shaking his head, Davis said, "No. Because he slowed down when he saw us, he knows he shouldn't be racing his horse like that."

Mariella's gaze softened.

"But it wouldn't hurt to have a talk with him later about safety while riding in the canyon alone."

She nodded and reached out, plucking Lizzie from his arms. "Maybe you should help him unsaddle and have that talk."

Davis stared at Mariella's back as Lizzie waved a small hand at him. Dang if the woman hadn't set him up. He grinned. She was comfortable with him holding her daughter and having a talk with her son.

He spun toward the barn and followed Zach and his horse into the building.

"Want some help putting your horse up?" Davis asked, walking up next to the boy.

"Nope." He didn't look at Davis.

"Want some company while you unsaddle your horse?" Davis could see the boy knew he was going to get a scolding. That wasn't his plan.

The boy shrugged and loosened the cinch on his pony.

"Remember yesterday when I was worried about your ma?" Davis started.

"Yeah." Zach carried the saddle over to a rack low enough for him to put the saddle on.

"I was worried because she'd tore out through the trees riding fast and wild. All I could think of was if she got hit in the head with a limb or if the horse stumbled she could be lying on the ground hurt and we'd have a hard time finding her." Davis leaned against the stall railing.

"Ma wouldn't get hurt, she's a good rider." Zach put a bucket of grain in front of Thunder.

"Even a good rider can have accidents. I bet if you asked Jedidiah, he'd tell you he's fallen off a horse a time or two."

Zach shook his head. "No, he hasn't. He's proud of always stickin' in the saddle."

Davis blew out a frustrated breath. "That's probably what his pride tells you. But I don't think there's a person alive who's ridden horses that hasn't taken a fall at one time or another."

Zach continued shaking his head.

"For your ma's sake. Don't be racing through the canyon when there's no one around to pick you up if you fall." Davis strode out of the barn door. He pivoted and added, "Get that horse put up. Supper's almost ready. You need to get cleaned up."

Davis pulled his pipe out of his pocket as he continued toward the house. That talk hadn't gone at all like he'd planned. He wondered where Zach got his stubborn streak, from his ma or his pa?

He stopped at the corner of the house, savoring his pipe and the peacefulness.

Zach came running over and washed his hands at the basin on the back porch. Before Davis had his pipe put away, Jedidiah wandered over from the bunkhouse. He washed at the basin and entered the house.

Davis stopped, washed his hands, and entered the house. Everyone was seated at the table, waiting for him. Mariella questioned him with her eyes. He gave his head a slight shake and she smiled.

Had she sent him out there knowing Zach would stubbornly ignore his request?

Sitting down, he peered around the table. Everyone watched him expectantly. Not sure what he was supposed to do, he picked up the potatoes and started passing food while Mariella sliced the roast and handed out pieces.

Chapter Fourteen

Mariella sat on the buckboard seat next to Davis.
Ma, Zach and Lizzie sat in the back on blankets.
Jedidiah rode alongside. He'd opened and closed the
gates as they went through the land French had fenced
off. Thankfully, they hadn't encountered any of
French's men. She didn't like the children to hear their
talk.

They were headed to the social at Diamond Ranch
to celebrate the sale of the cattle. They'd rounded up all
the cattle and Mr. Cassel had handed them a bank draft
when he and his drivers came by for the hundred and
fifty head of cattle two days ago.

They were now about a mile from the Diamond
Ranch. Her stomach gurgled and churned. She'd never
been this nervous attending a social before. Given

Diamond Ranch was part of Mr. French's holdings, she worried there would be a confrontation, but more than that, she worried what the neighbors would think of her remarrying.

Ernestine and J.P. would be there with their children. She was looking forward to visiting with her friend.

"Turn down that road there," she said, guiding Davis.

"I can feel your knees shaking," he said softly, placing a hand on her knee.

Her body heated at his touch. Though they slept in the same bed, they were both still hesitant to fully commit to one another. Her body was willing and ready, but her mind was still working through the loss of Hugh and getting intimate with Davis.

"I'm pretty sure Mr. French will be at the social."

"Are you scared of him?" Davis asked, studying her.

"No. I just don't want any trouble." She bit her bottom lip. Did she tell Davis how insulting the little man was to her?

"No one is coming to the social to start trouble. Everyone will be there to have a good time." Davis put his arm around her waist. "I'm sure Mr. French won't want to start trouble at a gathering of so many people."

She wanted to have Davis's optimism, but she'd been on the other end of French's barbs too many times to think he would leave her alone now. "He has a temper and I don't want anyone to get hurt."

Davis peered into her eyes. "What aren't you telling me?"

"His said some nasty remarks to me in the past. I don't want you stepping in and getting hurt."

Davis's eyes narrowed and his arm tightened around her. "No one, I don't care who he is, will get away with saying anything against you."

"Please, don't—"

"Defend my wife? There's not a man there who wouldn't understand."

Mariella was sorry she'd said anything. French's temper and unstable personality were part of the reason people didn't try harder to homestead free land he'd fenced in.

"Just promise me, you won't do anything unless he becomes ornery. If he only says one thing, don't respond."

Davis stared ahead.

Mariella put a hand on his arm. "Please. For me and the children. Try not to take offense if he only says one thing."

"I'll defend you, but I won't do it publicly."

"Thank you, that's all I ask." Mariella still had doubts about Davis keeping still if French was in one of his moods, but she knew he wouldn't ruin the evening on purpose.

Davis would have been impressed with the Diamond Ranch if he hadn't already seen Roaring Springs and knew Mr. French made certain every ranch he owned was well-equipped to deal with cattle raising and keeping his ranch hands happy.

Hearing Mariella's worries about Mr. French, Davis was even more curious about the man. From what J.P. had told him on their ride from the Roaring

Springs Ranch to J.P.'s homestead, Mr. French was a small, arrogant man, who could turn cattle into gold. A buggy and two more wagons rolled up the road toward the ranch. He could already see half-a-dozen wagons parked in the field in front of the barn.

"Put the wagon there, next to J.P.'s," Mariella suggested.

Davis glanced at her. "How do you know that's their wagon?"

She grinned. "Their mules, Jack and Jenny."

He'd sat in the wagon staring at the two animals' backs for several hours, and he wouldn't have been able to pick them out of other mules. He shook his head and pulled their wagon up alongside the Mulligan's wagon.

Zach scrambled out the back of the buckboard.

"You check in with me every once in a while," Mariella yelled at her son.

He waved and continued running toward the barn.

"He must not get to see his friends very often," Davis said.

Mariella sighed. "Only if they visit or we come to a social."

Davis tied the reins on the brake handle and climbed down. He held his hands up to Mariella.

She waved them away. "I'm too big for you to be lifting out of a wagon."

Davis didn't move. This was the first time she'd made mention of her size. He didn't know if it was because they would be around other people who would talk about it or if she was feeling vulnerable thinking about Mr. French.

"Mrs. Weston, you look fetching in that new dress.

The green and pretty flowers is a dress fit for summer."
He wasn't going to mention how the dress fit her full
curves to perfection and was sure to catch every man's
eye when she walked in. Which made him both proud
and jealous.

She continued to wait for him to move.

"If you don't get down here no one will get to see
the pretty dress your mother made."

"That would be a shame after all the work I went
to." Mrs. Simon spoke up from the back of the wagon
where she remained holding Lizzie and waiting for the
two of them to help her carry the food she'd prepared
into the barn.

"See. Your ma wants to show off her handy work.
And we can't leave her and Lizzie sitting in the back of
the wagon all day."

Mariella huffed, sat down on the wagon seat, and
leaned forward, dropping into Davis's arms.

"See that wasn't so hard," he whispered in her ear
while still holding her close. They'd all taken baths the
night before and she'd come to bed smelling of lemon
verbena. From the scent today, she must have dabbed
on a little more after dressing. "You smell pretty too."

She pushed out of his arms, her cheeks red.

Pride hadn't been an emotion Davis had felt in a
while. Today, it nearly burst his chest. He had a
wonderful woman, two beautiful children, and he was
learning a new trade.

Mariella picked up the picnic basket. "Help Ma out
of the wagon, please," she said, plucking Lizzie from
her mother's arms.

Davis walked to the back of the wagon and lifted

Mrs. Simon out the back.

Jedidiah rode up and dismounted, tying his horse to the back of the wagon.

"Fill the bucket with water and give the horses their grain before you come in," Mariella said to Jedidiah.

He nodded and picked up the bucket in the back of the buckboard.

Davis caught up to Mariella, taking the basket from her. She smiled timidly and they continued to the barn.

Ten ranch hands stood outside the barn, talking and laughing. Their gazes one by one took in Davis and then latched onto Mariella.

Davis ground his teeth at the way the men openly gawked at his wife. But having a woman with a body like Mariella's, he was going to have to accept other men would look.

He hustled Mariella and her mother into the barn as quickly as possible. The married men would know better than to ogle another man's wife.

Ernestine met them at the door. "I'm so glad you came!" she exclaimed, hugging Davis, Mariella and Lizzie, and Mrs. Simon. "Zach said you were right behind him."

"It looks like everyone is here," Mariella said, her gaze scanning the room.

"Yes. I don't think there's a homestead or ranch being tended at the moment." Ernestine herded them over to makeshift tables made out of barrels with boards laid across the tops. Potatoes, breads, cakes, pies, and cookies were set out on the tables. The ranch would be supplying the meat for the evening. At the end of the last table was a punch bowl.

"Would you like something to drink?" Davis asked Mariella. He'd spotted J.P. with a group of men. His brother-in-law had waved him over, but he wanted to make sure Mariella was settled first.

"I'm fine. I see J.P. is anxious to introduce you." Mariella shifted Lizzie to her other arm.

"Do you want me to take Lizzie?" he asked.

"No, we'll be fine. Ma or Ernestine will help hold her." Mariella nodded toward the men. "Go."

He glanced at his sister. She was beaming like a proud mother. He grinned and headed across the barn to the small group of men with J.P.

At the group, J.P. made the introductions. "I thought by now Mariella wouldn't have you lookin' like a greenhorn." J.P. glanced up at Davis's derby hat.

He grinned at his brother-in-law. "I think my hat is growing on her."

"I think that's not the only thing." J.P. quipped and the other men all laughed.

Davis glanced over at Mariella. She was listening to Ernestine and two other ladies but her gaze was on him. He smiled and tipped his head. She blushed and returned her attention to the women.

The talk turned to weather, cattle, and how Mr. French was fencing homesteaders out of the valleys.

"We could be a growing community if he hadn't stretched his wire from one end of the valley to the other, keeping people from the open land in between his fences," Allan Gorely said.

"Don't get all het up, Allan," J.P. said. "You have to remember we're on his land for this social and don't need to start anything."

The men grumbled and agreed.

"Is Mr. French here?" Davis asked. He wanted to meet this man and size him up himself.

"Haven't seen him. But he usually only shows when the food is ready, gets a plate, and leaves."

Davis scanned the room again and noticed Ernestine holding Lizzie and Mrs. Simon talking with another woman, but he didn't see Mariella.

"Excuse me," he said to the men he'd been talking with and headed to Ernestine.

"Where is Mariella?" he asked as soon as he was close enough he could ask in a normal tone.

"She went out to the privy." Ernestine studied him. "Why are you so protective?"

"Did you see the dress she has on?"

"Yes, it's a fetching color on her."

Davis frowned at his sister. "And shows off her body too much. The ranch hands ogled her when we came in." He took a couple steps then asked. "Where is the privy?"

"During socials they use the one behind the bunkhouse."

His heart lurched and his feet set in motion. He didn't like the thoughts running rampant in his head.

Outside the barn, he scanned the area and found what looked to be the bunkhouse. There was a small group of ranch hands standing at the end of the building. He jogged over and pushed through them.

His hands fisted as he lunged forward. "Get your hands off my wife!" he shouted, shoving a fist into the face of the ranch hand who had a hold of Mariella's arm. She fell backward onto her backside as the ranch hand went down on his knees.

Davis reached down for Mariella's hand.

"Lookout!" she shrieked.

Davis turned around in time to avoid being hit over the head with a board. He ducked and rammed his head into the man's belly. Knocking the wind from the man and sending him backwards. Davis faced the other men. "I'd like to have a word with your boss. It's apparent he needs to know his ranch hands think it's fine to bother a married woman."

When the men standing around didn't attempt to attack him, he bent down and helped Mariella to her feet. "Are you hurt?" he asked.

She shook her head, but the color had drained from her face and her hands shook.

He took hold of one of her hands and led her away from the bunkhouse and out towards the wagons. Knowing her pride, she would want to be collected before entering the barn.

"Did you get to take care of your business before those men…" He didn't know what to say.

She nodded. "They must have seen me go out there. I opened the door and they were…"

Davis gathered her into his arms and held her shaking body.

"I tried to fight the one who grabbed me, but he was the largest of all of them and had a tight grip on my arm." She raised her head off his shoulder and stared into his eyes. "Hugh and Pa were the only men with enough strength to hold me. I thought I could get away."

"You shouldn't have had to even try. Those men should have left you alone." Anger boiled in Davis's gut. "Were those men Mr. French's ranch hands?"

"Not the one who had a hold of me. But a couple of the others were." Her eyes shifted back and forth as she gazed at him. "Why?"

"The foremen and ranch owners need to know how their men behaved." Davis was going to get the man who touched Mariella and the one who tried to hit him with a board dismissed.

She pushed out of his arms. "Don't cause trouble. I don't want anyone to know what happened."

"Mariella, those men have to be punished for the way they treated you." He placed a hand on her cheek. "No woman should have to worry about a man putting his unwanted hands on her."

"The way you came to my rescue…" She grasped his right hand in her hands. "Oh! Your knuckles are bleeding." She pulled a handkerchief out of her skirt pocket and wrapped it around his fingers. Her gaze took in his hat and she bit her bottom lip.

"What's wrong with my hat?" He pulled it off his head and shoved the squashed crown back out to its round shape.

"Ma! Ma!" Zach ran toward the wagons where Davis and Mariella stood.

Chapter Fifteen

Mariella forgot her fears and worries when she heard Zach's shouts. She ran toward him dropping to her knees in front of him. Grasping his upper arms, she looked him over and asked, "What's wrong?"

Davis had took flight right behind her and now stood to her side.

Zach gulped air and said, "Gran can't find Lizzie."

Davis took off running for the barn before Mariella could stand. She grabbed Zach's hand in one hand and the front of her skirt with the other, jogging toward the barn, conscious of Zach's short legs.

At the barn, everyone seemed to be searching for the child.

Ma ran up to her, tears glistened in her eyes. "I set her down for a moment to help unwrap the food and when I turned back around she was gone."

Mariella gave her ma a one-armed hug and scanned the barn. Davis was questioning everyone. She glanced down at Zach. "Did you see your sister?"

He shook his head.

"Was there anything in the barn you think she would have been interested in?"

Zach's face lit up. "Johnny brought a kitten in."

Ma nodded. "He showed it to everyone, including Lizzie."

"Davis!" Mariella shouted to get his attention.

He stopped his conversation with Ed Prescott and jogged over. "Did you find her?"

"No, but we think we know where she might be." Mariella grabbed his arm. "Zach, go find Johnny. We need him to show us where the kittens are."

"What kittens?" Davis asked as she led him out of the barn.

"Johnny brought in a kitten and showed it to Lizzie." Mariella stood outside the barn waiting for Zach and Johnny to appear.

"You think she followed him back to where he found the kitten?" Davis sounded skeptical.

"Just because you always see her in bed or in a high chair doesn't mean she can't walk and get where she wants to go." Mariella frowned. Did he think Lizzie was an invalid or a slow child?

"I would think someone would have stopped her if she was toddling around." Davis glanced over her shoulder. "See someone did find her."

Mariella spun around ready to thank the person who found Lizzie. Her tongue stopped when she

135

spotted Mr. French carrying Lizzie toward them. Lizzie had her thin arms wrapped around a calico ball of fur.

"Lizzie!" Mariella stepped forward, snatching her daughter from Mr. French's arms.

Davis stepped forward with his hand extended. "Thank you for finding Lizzie." He shook hands with Mr. French.

"Mrs. Swanson—"

Mariella interrupted Mr. French. "Mrs. Weston. This is my husband, Davis. Davis…" she paused. "This is Mr. French."

As she'd expected, Davis's expression went from gratitude to wary.

Mr. French looked Davis up and down. "I'd heard Mrs. Sw—Weston had remarried. Where did she find you?"

Davis bristled at the way the little man asked the question. "She didn't find me. We found each other." Davis put his arm around Mariella's waist, showing they were united in their thoughts and actions.

"I'd heard you were crossing my land earlier in the month." Mr. French's gaze was level with Mariella's bosoms. He didn't even try to look into her face.

"You can't legally keep us from our property," Davis said, drawing the man's gaze back to him.

"Are you a lawyer?" Mr. French asked, glaring at him.

"No, but we plan to hire one to make sure you can't keep us from our land." Davis felt Mariella pull on his hold. He hadn't told her he planned on using some of the money from the cattle to have a lawyer look into Mr. French's fencing people out of their land

and land that could be homesteaded.

Mr. French glared at the two of them. "The child can keep the cat. She's innocent." He walked by them and into the barn.

Mariella leaned against Davis. "Why did it have to be him who found Lizzie?"

Davis shook his head. "I don't know, but I'm glad she's safe." He glanced down at the child, smiling and petting the sleeping kitten in her arms. "It looks like we now have a kitten."

Mariella kissed the top of Lizzie's head. "She can charm even a snake."

Zach and Johnny skidded to a stop.

"You found her?" The disappointment in Zach's voice made Davis grin.

"We didn't. Mr. French did. And it appears he gave your sister a kitten," Mariella said.

"See," Johnny said, bumping Zach's shoulder. "I told you Mr. French wanted to find homes for them."

Zach shoved his friend. "I didn't say you was a liar."

A scuffle ensued. Davis removed his arm from Mariella's waist and cupped her elbow, escorting her, Lizzie, and the kitten into the barn away from the boys. He remembered being that age. If he wasn't rolling around on the ground with a friend, it was an enemy. Boys liked to scuffle.

People were lined up along the tables filling plates.

Davis tweaked Lizzie's nose. "Looks like we found you in time for supper."

She giggled and continued petting her kitten.

"Let me take her while you fill a plate for the two

of you." Davis spotted Mrs. Simon standing by their basket, holding their plates and eating utensils they brought with them. He lifted the child and kitten from Mariella's arms and continued escorting her toward her mother.

"Look who you found!" Mrs. Simon exclaimed. "And what did you find, Lizzie?"

"Kitty," Lizzie said, snuggling the kitten to her cheek.

"I see that. Does your kitten have a name?" the older woman asked.

"Kitty," Lizzie said, peering at her grandmother as if the woman were daft.

"That's a fine name for the kitten," Davis said.

Lizzie shared a wide, happy smile with him.

"Lizzie and I will be right here on this bench," he said to Mariella who looked down at them before following her mother down the tables.

Davis studied the people getting food. It was easy to tell the homesteaders from the ranch hands. There were a tenth as many women as men. From the appreciative looks Mariella received from the single men, he was surprised she hadn't found one to marry, instead of relying on the brother of her best friend. A man who didn't know anything about cattle ranching and whom she'd never met.

She chatted and laughed with everyone who conversed with her. His wife was well-liked in the community. His gaze landed on Mr. French. The man he spoke with had his back to Davis. Mr. French was frowning and his gaze was on Mariella. Did my speaking up about a lawyer make Mr. French even more against Mariella and the Bar S Ranch? Davis continued to watch Mr. French and the other man.

"You're deep in thought," Mariella said.

Davis pulled his attention from the two men. "Not very deep."

Mariella laughed and slipped Lizzie and the kitten out of his arms and onto her lap. "Go get your food before it's all gone."

He picked up a plate and fork and headed to the tables of food. Mariella had been right to send him along. Several of the dishes only had remnants of food they had held. Most of the people were sitting on the benches lining the barn walls.

J.P. walked up beside him. "You just now getting food?"

Davis glanced at his brother-in-law's plate and noticed he was coming back for seconds. "Yes. We had to find Lizzie, had an interesting chat with Mr. French—"

J.P. laughed. "Is that why he came in here with a frown on his face?"

"Probably. He's the one who found Lizzie and gave her a kitten." Davis still didn't understand the man. Mr. French was harsh to Mariella and adamant about taking her land, yet he gave Lizzie a kitten.

"I heard he's good with children, but short with grown-ups."

Davis glanced over where he'd watched Mr. French talk to the man earlier. The man now stood sideways. Anger heated his face. "J.P., that man with Mr. French, do you know who he is?"

J.P. followed his gaze. "Yeah. That's the foreman

of this ranch."

Davis cursed under his breath.

"Why?"

"I caught him and another man on Bar S land. I could tell they were looking for trouble." Davis started to walk toward the two.

J.P. put a hand on his arm. "Not now. Not here."

Davis stared into his brother-in-law's eyes. "I want him and Mr. French to know, our land is off limits to anyone other than our family and hands."

"I understand. But think of the kids and Mariella. If you go over there accusing them of trespassing, it's their word against yours. Over half the men in this barn work for Mr. French. This isn't the time or place to get into an altercation with the man."

Davis glared at the two men.

"Don't. His men are loyal to him." J.P. grabbed Davis's arm, turning him toward Mariella.

J.P. was right. They'd have to use a lawyer to speak to Mr. French and get their right-of-way opened to their land.

Mariella watched him walking toward her. He could tell she had questions. His backside barely hit the bench before she was asking questions.

"Why were you staring at Mr. French?"

"I wasn't. I was staring at the man he was talking to." Davis put a forkful of potatoes in his mouth.

"Why?" She persisted, handing Lizzie a piece of meat to chew on. The kitten woke up and sniffed the meat sticking out below the child's hand.

"Because he looks familiar." Davis took another bite. He was torn between telling Mariella everything

140

and keeping it to himself to not have one more thing ruin her outing.

"From where?" She slipped a bite of cake into her mouth.

Davis watched her lick the sticky frosting off her lips. He stifled the urge to lean over and help her lick the frosting off.

"You're staring at my lips," she whispered.

He smiled. "You want to know what I was thinking?"

She glanced around to see who was close, set Lizzie and the kitten at her feet, and leaned toward him. "What were you thinking?"

He met her and whispered in her ear. "I wanted to lick the frosting from your lips."

Her head turned, putting her lips within licking distance. "This isn't the place," she said, but he could see by the twinkle in her eyes, she wasn't averse to the idea.

"Later, when we're home," he said, feeling his body spring to life at the thought tonight might be their wedding night.

"Do you promise?" she asked, her gaze drifting from his lips to his eyes and back to his lips.

He marked an X across his chest with his finger. "I promise."

"Good." She straightened and put another bite of cake in her mouth.

Davis laughed at how she closed her eyes and savored the bite.

"What are you laughing at?" Ernestine asked from behind him.

Mariella's eyes opened and she stared at her friend.

Davis didn't take his gaze off Mariella. "How much my wife is enjoying her cake."

"You need to finish up. The band will start in a few minutes. I'm sure you want to dance with your wife." Ernestine picked up Lizzie. "I found some girls to watch the little ones while we dance." She pointed to the corner of the barn to the right of the doors. "They'll play games with the kids and if some get sleepy, we've spread out some quilts for the little ones to lay on."

"Thank you, Ernestine." Mariella said, taking Davis's empty plate and putting it in the picnic basket with hers.

Ernestine glanced from Davis to Mariella and back to Davis. "I just want to see you two dancing."

Davis stood. "We will."

"Good." Ernestine carried Lizzie away.

"I could use a smoke. I could escort you to the privy." He held out his hand to Mariella.

"I like that idea," she said, taking his hand and allowing him to lead her out of the building.

Dusk changed the buildings and groves of trees beyond the buildings to dark images on a gray canvas. Davis waited until Mariella entered the privy, before walking behind it and relieving himself.

He leaned against the building, filled his pipe, and pulled out his match safe. Snapping the match to life with his thumb nail, Davis watched the flame a minute before lighting his pipe. Two long draws had the sweet tobacco lit and the smoke satisfying his craving for the smell of the tobacco and the calming effect of smoking his pipe.

The door creaked and Mariella stepped out into the growing darkness.

She sniffed. "That smells so much better than the outhouse."

Davis chuckled, linked his arm with hers, and led her back toward the barn. She stopped them under a tree.

"Did you really want to lick frosting from my lips?" she boldly asked.

Her boldness, and his thoughts, started his body humming. "Yes. I've been thinking about tasting your lips for several days now."

She leaned with her back against the tree. "What are you waiting for? An invitation?"

"Is this an invitation?" He moved closer, pressing his body against hers.

"Yes," she said, soft and breathy.

He didn't wait for the word to vanish before placing his lips on hers. If anyone had told him six months ago he'd desire a woman again so soon after losing Sarah, he would have told them they were crazy. But he did desire Mariella.

Their lips touched tentatively. He brushed softly across her full bottom lip. The one that drove him crazy when she sunk her teeth into it while in contemplation.

Her tongue darted out to lick where he'd touched. He covered her mouth, sucking on her bottom lip and delving into her hot, sweet mouth with his tongue.

She moaned and wrapped her arms round his neck. Her body pressed against him. His mind blurred as his body sprang to life.

Kids shouting, broke his hold on her lips. This

wasn't the place to make her his.

Davis released Mariella's arms from his neck and remained pressed against her until he felt her standing on her own. He took a small step back and then another. He kissed her chastely on the lips. "This isn't the place for us to share heated kisses."

She straightened her skirt and shifted the top of her dress. He didn't think he'd touched her anywhere but her lips.

"Are you ready to dance?" he asked, tapping his pipe against the tree to knock the ashes out.

"I think so." She put a hand up to her head. "What about my hair?"

Davis stared at her in the light of the half moon. "It looks fine to me."

She linked her arm in his. "We should get back. I can hear the fiddle playing."

He listened and was shocked that the music did carry well to their tree. Why hadn't I heard it before? Because your heart was pounding in your ears. He grinned and led his wife into the barn and straight to the dance floor. There wasn't any sense in missing out on holding her in his arms if he couldn't kiss her.

Chapter Sixteen

Mariella had to admit, she'd never had such a fine time at a social as she did dancing around the floor in Davis's arms. The drive home seemed twice as long as the ride to the social. She squirmed on the hard seat of the buckboard. It wasn't the seat so much as the heat pooled in her lower regions and the throbbing in her woman parts. Davis had lit a fire in her that she'd thought would never be lit again when Hugh died.

Davis put a hand on her leg. No one in the back of the wagon could see, but his boldness still thrilled her. Since the kiss they'd shared under the tree, they'd had trouble keeping their touching to what was acceptable in polite society.

She placed her hand on top of Davis's. He turned his hand palm up and they linked fingers. They'd stood together today. Her heart beat rapidly replaying the way Davis had launched himself at the man who caught her when she came out of the privy. He hadn't taken time to size up the man or the situation, he saw her in trouble and acted. And he'd warded off the other man who tried to hit him with a board. She hadn't expected that kind of action from a city fella. Then he'd rallied to help find Lizzie and stood up to Mr. French. That reminded her.

"Are we really going to hire a lawyer?" she asked, keeping her voice low so those sleeping in the back of the wagon wouldn't be disturbed.

"Not just us. I had several conversations with others who are concerned about Mr. French's fences. We're going to pool our money and as a group hire a lawyer to look into whether his actions are legal or not. If not, we'll take measures to get his fences taken down." Davis glanced her way. "We won't be fighting him alone. There are six other families willing to fight with us."

Mariella leaned her head on his shoulder. "I bet it's the folks who homesteaded before Mr. French started putting up his fences."

"I think so from what J.P. said." Davis squeezed her hand. "You have a lot of admirers."

She raised her head and stared at Davis. There was just enough moonlight to see his face but not make out all his features. "What do you mean by that?"

"Many of the men I talked to say there aren't many women who could have kept the Bar S running like you have."

The pride in his voice sent her insides fluttering.

"I didn't do that much. I lost all my ranch hands to

146

that skunk."

"But you didn't buckle under when you could have." He was quiet for a moment. "You had a good number of men you could have married right here. Every man at the social enjoyed watching you. Why didn't you remarry one of them?"

She peered harder at his face. "What do mean they were all watching me?"

"That dress your mother made shows off all your womanly curves. There wasn't a man who didn't have their eyes looking you over today." He cleared his throat. "And I'll admit at first it made me mad."

Hugh never said anything about her body or caring whether another man stared at her. "Why would it make you mad? I don't like it when I see them ogling me, but I can't wear a tent everywhere."

"I wouldn't want you in a tent," Davis said. "I don't know how to explain it, but while I'm proud to be married to a fine woman like yourself, it irritates me that other men stare at you like you're a piece of art on display."

Mariella pulled his hand into her lap. "It's hard for me to hide anywhere with my size. You'll have to get used to the men looking. One thing you can be sure, I'm not looking back." And she meant that with all her heart. Davis may have been a stranger three weeks ago, but in that time she'd grown to respect him and would never do anything to lose his respect.

"I know you wouldn't look back. You have too much integrity and love your family too much to cause any scandal." Davis raised her hand to his lips.

His soft lips combined with the soft tickle of his

147

beard, sent tingles up her arm.

Before she melted onto the seat, she brought her mind back to their conversation. "The reason I didn't marry anyone from around here came down to the fact the single men are ranch hands. I didn't want one of them wooing me only for the ranch. Most of them just want to be hands and like the life, but there are some who want to be the ranch owner and they'll do anything to get that."

"Like the foreman at the Diamond Ranch?"

She watched Davis as he stopped for Jedidiah to open the gate to cross the land Mr. French had fenced off on the road to their ranch.

"Jackson Tucker? Yes, I would say he would do anything to have a ranch of his own. He made it to ranch foreman quick when Mr. French bought that place."

Davis's jaw twitched. He flicked the reins and drove the buckboard through the gate and kept moving.

"Why are you asking?" She touched his cheek, feeling the tense muscle over his jaw.

"He's one of the men Zach and I chased off the ranch."

Mariella stared at Davis. "Jackson Tucker? You're sure?"

"Yes. Do you think he was there at Mr. French's orders?" Davis continued, "I saw the two of them talking for a long time over in a corner of the barn tonight."

Mariella shook her head. "I didn't think Mr. French would stoop that low. But he does allow his men to round up any unbranded cattle and keep them."

Davis stopped the wagon for the second gate and studied Mariella. He'd wondered if the men were rustling at the time but hadn't brought it up. "You think they were coming to take any unbranded cattle on your ranch?"

"Our ranch." Mariella squeezed his hand.

Over the past week, working the cattle alongside Mariella, he'd started thinking of the ranch as theirs, but hearing her say it brought a lump to his throat. He swallowed a couple to times to make room to speak.

"How many unbranded cattle are on our ranch?" he asked.

"Anything that was born since last fall when we brought them all in and branded."

Jedidiah had the gate open. Davis drove the wagon through and headed up the road to the house.

"Could you have missed any when you branded? Do you tally how many are branded?" There had to be an explanation for the men to boldly have ridden onto the property.

"We still had some ranch hands then. They did the rounding up. We were so shorthanded I didn't keep a tally." She huffed and said, "Someone could have kept a small herd hidden away from the rest so those calves wouldn't be branded."

Davis released her hand and put an arm around Mariella's waist. "Tomorrow we'll send Jedidiah to check out every inch of this ranch. If there's a small herd with unbranded yearlings, we'll bring them in and brand them."

"That's a good plan," Mariella said as he pulled up to the house.

"I'll help you carry the sleepyheads in, and then put up the horses." Davis hoped his conversation about the foreman and the cattle hadn't lessened Mariella's desire. He had an ache that would need release one way or another.

He climbed out of the wagon and raised his hands up for Mariella. She was already sitting with her legs dangling over the side of the wagon. She dropped into his arms and didn't push away when he placed a kiss on her lips.

"You get Lizzie, I'll carry in Zach." He turned her to the back of the wagon where Mrs. Simon was rousing from where she'd been sleeping on a blanket in the back.

"I'll get the basket and Zach, go on in, Mrs. Simon," Davis said, picking Zach up in one arm and grasping the handle of the picnic basket in the other. For the most part it had been a good day. He and Mariella had shown they were a couple and a family. He'd met several men who were willing to help oust Mr. French from land he didn't own, and he'd discovered who the trespasser was. A very good day.

He set the picnic basket on the kitchen table and carried Zach into the children's room, placing him on his bed. He started untying the boy's shoes.

"You go take care of the horses, I can get him settled in bed," Mariella said, carrying Lizzie into the room.

"You're sure? It will only take me a minute to get him settled." Davis pulled the first shoe off.

Mariella grasped his shoulders. "Go. The sooner you get the horses put away, the sooner you'll be back."

She didn't have to explain. He kissed her on the lips and headed out the door.

Jedidiah was leading the team toward the barn. Davis grasped the tongue of the wagon and backed it in beside the barn, then entered to help Jedidiah.

"You don't need to help me. You got a family to tend to," Jedidiah said.

"You sure?" Davis asked. Jedidiah was a ranch hand but he was at least twenty years older than Davis.

"I'm sure."

Davis didn't ask twice. He strode out of the barn and straight to the kitchen door. They hadn't lit any lanterns on their return, knowing everyone was tired and would go to bed. He skirted the table without catching a foot on a chair leg. Moonbeams shone through the front window casting enough light for him to find the right bedroom door.

He hesitated, wondering if he should knock. She knows I'm coming back.

Davis opened the door and stopped. Standing in front of the wash stand in the dim light of a lantern was Mariella. Her arms were raised, her fingers plucked at the hairpins. The dark brown curls fell about her bare shoulders.

"Come in and shut the door," she said, not a hint of embarrassment as she stood before him in nothing more than her drawers, corset and chemise. The dress she'd worn draped over the end of the bed.

He shut the door, tossed his hat onto the trunk at the end of the bed, and walked over to Mariella. Running his hands through her curls, he peered into her eyes. "You are beautiful," he said, feeling her silky

151

tresses slide through his fingers. "I didn't realize your hair was so long. You always have it braided." He liked how it fell over her shoulder and curled down around her ample breasts.

The corset she wore wasn't long like the one Sarah wore. This one stopped at Mariella's waist. The garments sole purpose was to cradle her bosoms. Hold them up. In her underclothes, that made a fetching sight.

He swallowed and drew his gaze back to her face. "Would you like me to help you out of that corset?" The contraption had hooks on the front and she could easily get herself in and out of it, but his hands itched to help.

She nodded, her gaze locked on his hands as he reached out, slipping his fingers down between the sturdy garment and the soft cotton of her chemise. His fingers pressed into her soft mounds and his heart raced. Slowly, one by one, he unhooked the corset, setting her bosoms free of their constraints.

He tossed the corset to the trunk and looked his fill of Mariella with her hair down, in her underclothes. She was a sight, with the thin white chemise with a touch of lace around the top held out by her nipples peaking under the cloth.

His body jerked to life at the sight.

"Do you want me to put my night gown on?" Mariella's husky voice whispered.

Davis shook his head. "Get in bed. I'll be there in a moment."

She studied him a moment, then walked over to the bed and pulled the covers back. Instead of crawling under the blankets, she lay down on the top on her side, her head propped on one arm and her legs bent slightly, her hips curving into the air. "Do you mind if I watch?" she asked.

"No." His hands fumbled with the buttons on his vest. Sarah had always insisted they undress in the dark. Having Mariella boldly watch his disrobing had his body buzzing with heat and need.

He tossed his vest, shirt, and undershirt on top of her corset. Sitting on the trunk next to the pile of clothes, he pulled off his boots and then stood, to unbutton his pants. He slid the trousers down and off his feet and stood with his back to the bed in his underdrawers.

"You can take those off too," Mariella whispered from the bed.

His shaft was already tenting his undergarment. She would see his desire whether he had the garment on or not. He hooked his thumbs under the waistband and slid the cotton drawers down and kicked them off his feet.

He walked over to the side of the bed where Mariella lay. Her gaze followed his bouncing appendage. When he stopped at the side of the bed, she reached out, touching him.

"My! I wasn't expecting this," she said.

Her touch after such a long time without a woman, made his body jump and his mind go blank for a second.

He grasped her arms, drawing her to sit on the side of the bed. Sliding his hands under her chemise, he ran his hands up her sides. She raised her arms, and he slipped the garment over her head. He tossed it to the

153

side and cupped her bosoms in his hands. They overflowed his palms and the weight made him wonder how she could walk with such a straight back.

"Hugh said those were my best quality," she whispered.

Davis shook his head. "They are magnificent, but your best qualities are your heart and your mind."

Her eyes lit up. He could tell she was pleased with his answer.

"You going to just hold them all night or are you going to show me your talents?"

He smiled and leaned down, flicking first one nipple and then the other with his tongue. She placed her arms behind her on the bed, thrusting her offering higher for him to reach.

He reciprocated in kind by sucking, teasing, and nipping her nipples until she had the bed creaking and cracking from her gyrations.

"Please, fill me," she pleaded.

He grabbed the waistband of her underdrawers, peeling them down her legs and off her feet. She wrapped her legs around his waist and he didn't wait for another invitation.

Davis plunged into her hot, wetness and barely had time to savor the exquisite tightness and fit before his seed released in an explosion. He couldn't believe all it took was one thrust.

"Don't stop," Mariella growled and grabbed his backside, thrusting him in and out.

He fell into the rhythm she set and found his shaft growing once again.

Chapter Seventeen

Mariella felt the first thrust of Davis's entry clear to her heart. She also felt his early release. She wasn't going to be left out of the pleasure and grabbed his backside, making him keep pumping. She was on the edge of pleasure before he entered her and now with him filling her, rubbing her in a way that had her whole body throbbing, she wanted to feel the full force of their coming together.

He thrust and swirled in a way that lit every inch of her on fire. Her fingers hurt from clenching his backside, but she couldn't let go. Her whole body was clenched—coiled. Something had to give soon.

Davis wrapped his hands around the back of her head. His fingers curled into her hair as he held her tight. His lips came down on hers. His tongue plunged into her mouth in rhythm with his lower body and she shattered.

Blackness overcame her, stars shimmered, and her body quaked. Her woman parts throbbed and continued sending small tremors through her body.

Davis kissed her long, wet, and open-mouthed, as he continued to thrust, keeping her body in a quivering state. Her body clenched and coiled again. Mariella couldn't keep hold of his backside any more. Her hands fell to his hips, and he thrust one more deep thrust and held it. The sensation shook her body, and his seed released again.

They continued kissing as he slowly toppled them to the bed.

When he released her lips and held himself up with his arms, Mariella couldn't stop the smile creeping onto her lips. "I think we just consummated the marriage," she whispered and raised up to kiss his neck under his beard.

"I think so too," he said. His eyes sparkled in the lantern light. "I think we should consummate the marriage every night."

"I like the way you think, Mr. Weston." She wiggled, trying to keep her bottom from sliding off the bed.

"Thank you, Mrs. Weston." He nipped one of her nipples. "Are you squirming because you want more?"

"I'm slipping off the bed."

He stood and slipped out of her before grabbing her legs and shoving her farther onto the bed.

She watched his muscled legs carry his wide shoulders and narrow backside over to the wash basin.

He washed himself then rinsed the cloth and brought it over to her. Instead of handing her the cloth, he spread her legs and wiped the stickiness from the insides of her legs.

His touch and study of her woman parts should have embarrassed her, but she found his interest and caring endearing.

While he carried the cloth back over to the wash basin, she slipped under the covers and waited for his return.

Davis turned off the light. The bed creaked and he slid into bed, pressing his body to hers in the dark. His hand brushed up her leg, over her curls, her belly, between her bosoms, and held her chin. He kissed her.

"Good night," he said.

She raised her head, meeting his lips, and kissed him. "Good night."

He remained on his side, his arm draped over her body just under her bosoms.

She'd never slept naked before. She and Hugh never completely undressed. And Hugh had never taken her to the heights Davis did.

She liked this bold husband. Her heart thudded happily in her chest. *I might just more than like him.*

***

Davis woke to a soft, warm, naked body pressing against his back. He smiled. Mariella had been as passionate and giving last night as he'd hoped. He rolled, pressing his front to her front. Her eyes slowly opened and a smile curved her sweet lips.

"Good morning," he said, wrapping his arms around her and drawing her even closer.

He liked the way her bosoms pressed against his chest and the curls at the junction of her legs nestled his shaft.

Her leg rose, resting on his hip. She'd opened herself to him.

He'd heard Mrs. Simon banging the cookstove lids when he woke. Davis kissed Mariella and loosened his embrace. "We don't have time for that this morning," he said.

"For what?" she teased.

He touched her woman parts and was surprised by the slickness. "For that."

"Ma will understand," she said, wrapping her arms around his neck and kissing him as she rubbed her center against his most vulnerable body part.

He growled and rolled her to her back. One of them had to stay sensible or she'd be jumping him every time they were alone, but she had him throbbing with desire and the best way to take care of it was squirming underneath him.

Spreading her legs with his, he slowly entered, not knowing if after having no relations for two years, the encounter last night might have made her sore.

Her hands went to his backside, once again showing him the rhythm that she liked.

He moved as she commanded and soon they were both panting. Davis had gone with instinct last night when he captured her mouth and thrust to the same rhythm as their bodies. He did the same this morning and within two thrusts, her body exploded around him and in his arms. Happiness exploded in his heart, and he released his seed. Giving Mariella what she wanted would be his pleasure for years to come. He'd never dreamed being intimate with a woman could make her unravel like a ball of wool.

They clung to one another for several minutes.

A rap on the door shot them apart.

"Breakfast is ready," Mrs. Simon called from the other side of the door.

Mariella giggled. "Do you think that's the first time she's knocked?"

Davis sat up and lit the lantern. They'd been so caught up in one another, he couldn't say for sure. "I honestly don't know." He stood and walked over to the wash basin. He rinsed the rag from the night before and cleaned himself. Before he could take the rag over to Mariella her hands landed on his shoulder.

"I can clean myself this morning. If you touch me down there, we might get side-tracked again."

He heard the smile in her voice and handed her the rag over his shoulder. She kissed his cheek.

Davis moved away from the wash basin and started dressing, but his eyes were on his full bodied wife. Now that they were intimate, he could look his fill whether she was dressed or not. He liked this new level to their relationship very much.

She bent, pulling on her drawers and he caught a nice view of her intimate parts. He'd strolled through a museum once that had statues and paintings of naked women. The other men with him had laughed and made off comments about the women, but he'd seen the beauty in their bodies. His wife would make a wonderful model for such a painting. Her round hips, slightly rounded belly, full bosoms, and long curly hair would make a masterpiece.

"What are you looking at?" Mariella asked as she picked up her corset.

"You. You are like a painting I saw in a museum." He smiled at the way she studied him.

"What's a museum?" she asked.

"You've never heard of a museum?" he asked, remembering Mariella was a woman of the land.

"No."

He stepped forward and started hooking her corset. "A museum is a place where painters and sculptors put their work on display for the public, people like you and me, to see. When I was in college, I went to one with some of my classmates."

She stepped backwards when he hooked the last fastener. "You were in college?"

He studied the uncertainty on her face. "Yes. I attended two years of a business college before I started my store." Davis didn't understand her fear. "Is there something wrong?"

She carried her dress to the wardrobe and pulled out trousers and a shirt. "No. I guess not. I've never known someone who went to college."

He grinned. "Yes, you have."

Mariella stared at him like he'd gone crazy. "I would know if I'd met someone who went to college."

"My sister, Ernestine. She attended a college for teachers." He pulled on his trousers and slipped on his shirt.

Mariella stopped buttoning her shirt and stared at him. "She did? She never mentioned it."

"Teaching school was never her calling. Father

made her go to keep her from marrying J.P." He grinned when her face lit up.

"You mean, your father didn't abide by Ernestine marrying J.P.?"

"No. He thought J.P. was a drifter that would never amount to anything." Their father had been hard and cantankerous, thinking he knew what was right for his children. Davis had to admit going to college had taught him things that would have taken him several years to learn had he started the store without the schooling. He'd never have to admit that to his father. He passed away Davis's second year in college.

"I don't see that in him. J.P. has worked hard since he arrived, making a good place for his family down there on the marsh." Mariella shoved her feet into her boots and headed to the door.

Davis pulled his boots on and stepped out of the room behind her, buttoning his vest.

They entered the kitchen and found everyone seated and already eating. Mrs. Simon had a huge smile on her face and a twinkle in her eyes. Davis didn't know whether to blush or expand his chest.

He held Mariella's chair as she sat, then took his seat.

Jedidiah winked at him as a sly grin shoved the creases of his face around.

"You must have been tired Ma," Zach said, slicking up his plate with a piece of bread.

"We were. We stayed awake all the way home last night while you, your sister, and Gran slept in the back of the wagon." Mariella cast a brief glance down the table at Davis.

He didn't know whether she wanted him to say something or keep quiet.

"But Jedidiah had to ride his horse home and he was up early." Zach leveled his gaze on Davis.

Before he could say anything, Jedidiah cleared his throat.

"I'm old and don't require as much sleep as your ma and Davis," Jedidiah said.

From the twinkle in the older man's eye and the snicker he couldn't hide, Davis had a pretty good idea the two oldest people at the table knew what had happened between Mariella and himself last night.

"Jedidiah, Mariella and I would like you to spend the next few days traveling over the whole canyon and checking on herds. We think there's one out there that has yearlings that didn't get branded."

"What gives you that idea?" Jedidiah asked, the merriment leaving his face.

"Zach, go get started on your school work," Mariella said.

"It's Sunday!" the boy protested.

"Okay, then go get the fishing poles ready and we'll go fishing today." Mariella glanced down the table to Davis. "Do you like to fish?"

"I do. Better dig some worms after you get the poles ready," Davis said to Zach.

The boy jumped up, shoved his chair to the table, and lit out the back door with a "Whoop!"

Mariella shook her head and turned her attention to Jedidiah. "Davis said the man he caught on our property was Jackson Tucker, the Diamond Ranch foreman. For him to so boldly come on our property, I-we believe

162

one of the hands last fall must have skipped a small herd when we were rounding up the others and then told Tucker there were cattle without brands over here."

Jedidiah ran a calloused hand over his whiskered face, making raspy noises. "Two of our ranch hands went to Diamond Ranch. Wheezy and Skeeter. I don't see Wheezy bein' that greedy but I can see Skeeter bein' that stupid."

Davis took a drink of coffee and asked, "What does this Skeeter look like?"

"Short and thin. If you don't see his face, you'd take him for a young'un." Jedidiah nodded. "He had the brains of a young'un too. He'd of had to been put up to it."

"How long did he work for the Bar S?" Davis asked, peering down the table to Mariella.

"He came on only a few months before he left." Her eyes narrowed. "It was after he showed up that the others started making comments about getting paid better from Mr. French."

"I'd say he was working for either Mr. French or this Tucker before he hired on here." Davis was getting an even worse feeling about Mr. French and his foreman at the Diamond Ranch.

"Skeeter never said anything to the others when I was around," Jedidiah said.

"I guess he was smart enough to know you were loyal." Mariella smiled at the older man.

"They all knew Bull and I went way back." Jedidiah's gaze wandered to Mrs. Simon's back. She'd started clearing the table.

"I best get started looking for that unbranded herd."

Jedidiah shoved his chair back and carried his dishes to the dry sink.

Davis watched the quiet interaction between Jedidiah and Mrs. Simon. He had a feeling they were more than friends from the way the older man put a hand on her back.

Mariella stood, catching Davis's attention. "You ready to go fishing?" she asked as she picked up Lizzie.

"I do like to fish, but wouldn't finding the herd go faster if we all went looking for it?" Davis asked.

A wide smile graced Mariella's lips. His gaze settled on the full bottom lip. The one he'd nibbled and sucked on last night making himself as needy as the action had made Mariella.

"The stream runs the full length of the canyon. That's where the herds get their water. We'll be catching supper as well as looking for the unbranded cattle."

Davis pulled his gaze from her lips and latched onto her smiling eyes. "While Jedidiah looks up high, we'll look in the bottom of the canyon."

"Yes. It might be Sunday, but we can't play all day." Mariella set Lizzie on the floor. "Come on young lady, you'll need a bonnet to be out in the sun all day." Mariella walked out of the kitchen with Lizzie toddling behind.

It struck him he didn't see the kitten she'd been clutching when Mariella carried her in the house.

"Where's Kitty?" he asked Mrs. Simon.

She turned from the dish pan with dripping hands. "I convinced her Kitty needed to go outside for a while."

His chest squeezed thinking how heartbroken the child would be if the kitten came to harm. "Do you think that's a good idea?"

"She's in the cellar with a nice bowl of milk." Mrs. Simon returned her hands to the dish pan. "There's plenty of mice for her to learn to catch in there."

Chapter Eighteen

Davis sat on the edge of the stream holding a fishing pole in one hand and a sandwich in the other. He couldn't remember when he'd felt this relaxed and content. Zach knelt next to him putting a worm on his pole. Mariella and Lizzie sat a short distance away making a necklace from the wildflowers Lizzie picked.

It was a peaceful June day. They'd spotted a couple of herds, but the cattle over a year old all had brands. There had been sixty of this year's calves that would need brands in the fall.

"When you two finish eating, we'll head on up the stream," Mariella said.

"Maaa, you ain't letting us stay long enough in one place to catch any fish," Zach protested.

Davis agreed but wasn't going to say so out loud.

"Why don't you and the kids stay here and fish. I'll ride up the canyon and check on the cattle."

Mariella studied him over Lizzie's fuzzy blonde curls. "I thought you wanted to fish."

"Zach is more excited about fishing than I am." He didn't want to admit he'd never been good at fishing. Any time he fished with other people they always caught fish and he didn't, making it seem like a waste of time.

"You can all go. I'll stay here and fish." Zach said, holding his pole with crossed legs and leaning back as if to take a nap.

Davis tapped his pole and the boy shot up, grabbing the pole and yanking.

Mariella laughed.

"That's not funny," Zach said, pulling in his line and recasting.

Mariella picked up Lizzie. "We'll head on up. You—" she stared at Zach "—stay put. We'll come back by and get you."

Zach grinned and nodded.

"You might as well keep all the fishing gear." Davis laid his pole on the ground by the boy. "Do as your ma said, stay put." After the mishap with Lizzie at the dance, he didn't want to be looking for Zach here in the canyon.

"I will." Zach waved. "Go on."

Davis glanced at Mariella. She was smiling and climbing onto her horse with Lizzie sitting in the saddle waiting. He mounted and waited for Mariella and Lizzie to get settled in the saddle. Once everyone was ready, he headed up the canyon keeping the stream to his left.

They followed a cow heading away from the stream to a herd of about sixty cattle. They were mostly mother cows and this year's calves. After searching the herd and not finding any unbranded, other than the calves, they wandered back down to the stream and continued up the canyon.

"I saw something moving in the trees over there." Mariella pointed to the trees across the stream. She reined her horse to walk through the stream.

Davis followed, trying to see what she'd seen. It could have been a cow or Jedidiah coming down to get his horse a drink.

They continued into the woods and stopped when the canyon floor gave way to the steep canyon sides.

"I saw something. It was as big as a yearling. Dark colored." Mariella spun her horse around, looking all directions.

Having learned from Jedidiah to look at the ground, Davis had been scanning the forest floor as they rode. "I haven't seen any hoof prints or manure piles." He scanned the area. "I don't know what you saw, but it wasn't a cow."

She frowned. "I guess not." Dash started dancing around. "Whoa, boy. Whoa." Mariella wrapped an arm around Lizzie.

Poker started snorting and prancing in one place like he wanted to flee. "There's something spooking them," Davis said. "Go."

Mariella gave Dash his head and he started through the trees. Davis did the same with Poker. He didn't have the agility on a horse that Mariella had. He found trying to duck limbs and dodge trees, frightening. Not to mention trying to keep in the saddle. He caught sight of the grass and stream in the open area and forgot to dodge. A limb struck him in the head, knocking him off the back of the horse. His back hit the ground, shoving air out of his lungs moments before his head struck something that shot pain through his head and cloaked him in darkness.

Mariella glanced over her shoulder. Davis lay on the ground as Poker raced toward her. She pulled back on the reins, sitting Dash on his haunches. "Davis!" she shrieked, racing back to where he lay motionless on the ground.

She dismounted and plopped Lizzie on the ground beside Davis. His forehead was skinned and had small pieces of bark embedded. She put a hand on his chest and leaned down to feel if he was breathing. Her heart stopped when she didn't feel his chest move or a puff of air on her cheek.

"No!" She didn't want to lose another husband. Raising a hand, she thumped him on his chest. Damn him for making her care about him.

He sucked in air and coughed.

"Davis? Davis?" she leaned toward his face as he sucked in air. His eyes didn't open.

Lizzie walked to Davis's head and reached down. She came up with blood all over her little hand.

"He hit his head!" Mariella reached out with shaky hands and raised his head, feeling under it. She pulled out a rock about the size of a horse's hoof. Blood and some of Davis's hair clung to the rock.

I have to get him home. Ma will know what to do.

She'd patched up more ranch hands than anyone else Mariella knew. The only doctor in the area lived in Canyon City. Mariella put Lizzie up on Dash. "Hold tight to the horn. Don't kick your legs or do nothing to make him think you want him to go," she told her daughter.

Then she gathered up Poker and led him over to Davis. "You would have to be the tallest horse," she muttered, studying Poker's tall back and Davis sprawled on the ground. It would be easier to get him on Dash, but she trusted Dash to not hurt Lizzie. Poker had always been a man's horse and had a bit of spirit. Dash had hauled both the kids around since they were big enough Mariella could take them with her.

"Boy, you're going to have to stand still." She dropped the reins and bent to grasp Davis under the arms. She heaved him up alongside Poker. He was heavier than she remembered when he'd settled on her this morning, making them late for breakfast.

She shoved his front up against the horse, grabbed a leg and shoved him up and over the horse, like a dead deer. Blood dripped from the wound on the back of his head. She tore off the bottom of her shirt and wrapped it around his head. Then used the rope hanging from her saddle to tie Davis to his saddle.

She jiggled him to make sure he wouldn't fall and grabbed Poker's reins, climbing up onto Dash.

"Daddy dead?" Lizzie asked

Mariella hugged her daughter. "No, Daddy's not dead. He's hurt bad. We need to get him to Gran."

"Go!" Lizzie exclaimed.

Easing the horses forward, Mariella kissed the top

of her daughter's head. She didn't know how the child knew to call Davis daddy. No one at the house had called him that. It could just be because Davis was close to daddy and daddy was easier for the child to say. For whatever reason, it filled Mariella with happiness to hear Lizzie's concern over the man.

Zach saw them coming. He grabbed up the poles and climbed onto his mustang, racing toward them. "What happened?"

"Daddy hurt!" Lizzie said, pointing to Poker and Davis.

"Something spooked the horses and Davis didn't duck under a tree."

Concern etched Zach's young face.

"Race ahead and tell Gran. She'll have everything ready to help Davis when we get there. Tell her he hit his head and it's bleeding."

Zach whirled his pony around and raced down the canyon.

Mariella wished she could at least trot, but she didn't want Davis falling off or making his wound worse. Dangling his head as it was, couldn't be good, but she had no other way to get him to help.

What usually took an hour to ride, felt like it took several hours. Her heart soared when she caught sight of the ranch house. Mariella stopped the horses at the back door. Ma stepped out and took Lizzie, setting her down and moving to Davis. She pulled off the cloth wrapped around his head.

"Has he woke up at all?" she asked.

"Not that I know of." Mariella quickly unknotted the rope and slid him down with his feet touching the ground. "I'll grab him under the arms if you and Zach can take hold of his feet."

She slid her arms under his arms and started backwards into the house. Ma and Zach each grabbed a leg and staggered in behind her.

"Put him on the table," Ma instructed.

The table was cleared and a cloth was folded at the far end. Mariella huffed and grunted and managed to get him lifted onto the table. Ma placed his feet hanging over the end of the table.

"What can I do?" Zach asked.

"Put the horses up." Mariella pushed Davis's hair off his skinned forehead. "This is where he didn't duck."

Ma glanced at it. "That's nothing. We need to check the bleeding from the back of his head. Help me roll him to his side."

Mariella pushed on Davis's right side, rolling him up onto his left side.

Ma dabbed at the spot bleeding on the back of his head with a rag and a basin of water. She shook her head. "I'll have to stitch it. The cut is too long and pulling apart." She set the rag and basin to the side. "I'll get blankets to help keep him propped on his side."

She scurried out of the kitchen.

Mariella stared at the wound. I should have kept Dash to a slower pace. I knew Davis wasn't a good rider. She mentally lashed herself for not thinking of the consequences when the horses took off. She'd decided while racing through the trees, she must have seen a bear. And the horses caught its scent. That was why they'd spooked.

She touched Davis's hair. He'd become an essential part of this ranch in a short time. And he'd worked his way into her heart. The love she had for Hugh was genuine, but the love she felt for Davis was stronger. He respected her and her opinions. Hugh would ask her questions, but more to hear himself talk and not really because he wanted or needed an answer. And Davis's respect was more than the ranch. The way he held her chair for her to sit at meals, and the way he helped her out of the wagon. He treated her like she was special, something she hadn't received since she'd started growing bigger than most men.

Ma returned with two blankets. She rolled one and tucked it under and in front of Davis's chest and belly. She came around behind and did the same at his back. "Let go and see if he stays."

Mariella slowly let go and he remained on his side.

"Roll up that towel and stick it under his neck to keep his head still."

She did as Ma asked.

Zach burst through the door. "Now what can I do?"

Mariella knew he wanted to help, but he was too small and young to be of help with Davis. "Keep your sister busy. She's scared and worried. Play with her to take her mind off what's happened."

Zach opened his mouth to protest.

"Zach, it would be the biggest help you could give me and Davis."

He closed his mouth and spun around, heading back outside.

"You're a good mother," Ma said, tears glistening in her eyes.

"There's days I don't think so." Mariella confessed.

"There'll be lots of them as that boy grows. Good thing you have a good man to help raise him." Ma nodded to Davis.

"Yes, it is." Mariella stroked Davis's arm. "What can I do?"

"Cut the hair away from the wound while I get the needle and string ready."

Mariella picked up the scissors Ma had placed on the table. Her fingers shook as she clipped the bloody hair around the two-inch long cut on Davis's head.

"That's good. I'll clean it good and then start stitching." Ma stared at her. "If he comes around, you'll need to hold him down."

Chapter Nineteen

Pain in his head pulled Davis out of the blackness. Sparks of light went along with the pounding. The more awake he became, the more his gut wanted to empty. He tried to roll to his stomach, instinct telling him to not swallow the bile. Something next to his body kept him from rolling. He reached under his belly.

"Lay still, Davis."

Mariella's husky voice sounded close to his ear.

"Have to," he couldn't get the words out for the bile rising in his throat. His body heaved twice, and he couldn't keep his stomach contents from coming up.

"Oh no!" Mariella exclaimed.

"Sorry," he whispered, fearing if he said more, he'd make more of a mess. A tug on his head sent a shard of pain to his toes. "Ow!"

"I'm almost done, Davis. Hold still," Mrs. Simon's voice came from behind him.

"Ma is sewing up your scalp." Mariella said.

He felt her hand rubbing up and down his back. Another heave squeezed his stomach, and he spewed again. Damn! He wished he wasn't making a mess.

A cold hand touched his hot brow. "Ma's just about done. We'll bandage your head and you can sit up."

"No. Don't want to sit up," he whispered.

"Okay, then we'll leave you on your side, though it will make dinner a bit hard to eat."

The humor in her voice eased the tension of having vomited and being unable to think clearly.

Cloth wrapped around his head. Pressure on the back of his head brought on a stinging pain to add to the pounding in his head.

"You're stitched up and bandaged," Mrs. Simon said.

He opened his eyes. The world in front of him was blurry and swirled a bit. He closed his eyes again as his stomach started to heave. This time when it erupted there was very little to spew. But that didn't keep his stomach from tossing about several more times.

He heard movement around him, banging of buckets and the door opening and closing. The state he was in, he couldn't do anything but lie on the table and wait for his stomach to settle and the throbbing in his head to ease.

Listening to the sounds around him, he realized the women had cleaned up his mess. He wondered where the children were. The idea of them coming in and seeing him in such a vulnerable way didn't settle well.

Finally, his stomach stopped heaving. He wanted to try sitting up. Pushing off the table with his shoulder on the table and his other hand, Davis slowly sat up, swinging his legs over the edge of the table.

"Take it easy." Mariella was by his side.

He sat on the edge of the table waiting. His stomach didn't heave, but he feared opening his eyes. That had started the second round of heaving earlier.

"You took a bad fall," Mariella said, holding his arm. "I looked back and saw you on the ground. When we got to you, you weren't breathing. I smacked you in the chest and you started breathing, but didn't wake up. Then I saw the blood and found a rock the size of a hoof under your head." She squeezed his arm. "You cut the back of your head good."

Davis slowly raised his eyelids. The room didn't swirl, but it was a bit blurry. "How did I get home?"

"I lifted you onto Poker and led him back. Ma and Zach helped carry you in here." Her voice started out quiet, he could barely hear her.

"You lifted me onto Poker?" He wasn't sure he could lift her onto the horse's back. Especially if she was unconscious.

"I did what had to be done. There wasn't any other way to get you help." The indignation in her voice said she wasn't proud of her strength but rather hated the fact she was strong.

"Thank you." He raised his arm, finding her hand and bringing it to his lips.

"You able to walk to the bedroom? Ma wants to get supper cooking." Her tone said his kiss had restored her assurance.

"I'll try." He slipped his feet to the floor and shuffled his feet so as not to make his head pound more than it already did.

Mariella walked close beside him, taking smalls steps. She walked through the doorway first, then moved beside him again crossing the main room to the bedroom. At the bedroom, she stopped him by the side of the bed. "Sit. I'll take your boots off."

He'd not been treated this special in a very long time.

She grasped his foot and pulled, a steady tug that didn't jar his head too much. When the first boot was off, she grabbed his other leg and managed to get that boot off without too much yanking as well.

"Thank you. If you'd have jerked my legs I might have vomited again."

She giggled.

"That's funny?" he asked, leaning back on the pillows she'd placed against the wooden headboard.

"I've only taken boots off someone who's liquored up. And Pa and Hugh never thanked me."

"I can promise you, you'll never have to take my boots off because I'm liquored up." Davis felt his eyelids growing heavy. "I'm going to take a nap."

"Do you want to lie on your side?" Mariella's voice came from beside his head.

"I'm good," he whispered, being pulled into sleep.

"But if you slide down your stitches are gonna hurt."

"Okay." He slipped into blissful sleep.

Mariella studied Davis's sleeping face. Did he say

okay to put him on his side or okay about sliding? She pulled a blanket over his clothed body and pulled up the chair. He was pale, and she didn't like how he'd vomited until there was nothing left for him to vomit. He must have hit his head awful hard.

Ma brought in her dinner and she ate watching Davis sleep. After dinner, the children came in and she read to them while they sat at the foot of the bed watching Davis.

Mariella closed the book. Both children had their gazes on Davis.

"He gonna live, Ma?" Zach asked.

"Yes. He only hit his head. When a body takes a hit like that it needs to rest." Her heart swelled at her children's concern for Davis.

"Daddy wake?" Lizzie asked.

"He isn't Daddy." Zach said. He remembered his father and wasn't ready to replace him.

Mariella stood, picked up Lizzie and put a hand on Zach's head. "If your sister wants to call Davis daddy she can. He's the only daddy she's known. You can call him Mr. Weston or Davis if you like, but I know if there comes a day you'd like to call him daddy, he'd like that." She sat on the bed next to Zach. "Davis had a son about your age. He lost his son and his wife in a boating accident. So I know he'd welcome calling you son when you're ready."

Zach stared up at her. "He lost family like we lost family?"

"Yes. That's why he came out here and married me. To help him get over his loss." Mariella peered at Davis. She hoped they were helping him, he'd done so much for her family.

Ma poked her head around the door. "Time for you two to go to bed."

Zach hopped off the bed and Mariella put Lizzie on the floor. The child walked over to Davis's hand lying on the bed and kissed it. "Night, Daddy," she said softly and scurried across the room to her grandmother.

Tears stung the back of Mariella's eyes. Not only had Davis won her heart, he'd won that of her daughter. And given Zach's concern, she had no doubt he'd have the boy's affection before too long.

She made a trip to the outhouse and spotted the light on at the bunkhouse. Wanting to mention the bear to Jedidiah, she crossed the yard and knocked on the bunkhouse door.

"Come on," Jedidiah called out.

Mariella entered and held her breath a minute. Smelly feet, liniment, and horse odors mixed to make nauseating air. "Want to come outside," she said, backing out under the porch roof.

Jedidiah wandered out, his big toe sticking out of his sock. Other than his boots missing, he was still fully clothed, right up to the hat on his head. "How's that man of yours?" he asked.

"Sleeping off a head wound."

"Thought he was a better rider than that." Jedidiah chuckled.

"We think a bear spooked the horses. I thought I saw a yearling. We followed and a ways into the trees the horses spooked. I let Dash go not thinking Davis and Poker were taller. Poker must have followed me and Dash and a limb caught Davis in the forehead, knocking him off. That wouldn't have hurt him, but his head landed on a rock."

"Where abouts were you?" Jedidiah asked, leaning against the doorframe.

"I'd say a mile or so before the canyon ends."

Jedidiah nodded his head. "Saw sign of a couple cats hanging out in that area."

Mariella peered at Jedidiah. "What about new calves?"

"Most of the mother cows with newborns stay down closer to the water, but that don't mean a cat won't decide that's where it's gettin' a meal."

Mariella didn't like the idea of a couple of cougars lessening their herd. "When Davis is up to it, we'll go hunting for those cougars."

Jedidiah nodded. "Think we'll have more help by the time we need to cut hay?"

"Davis sent advertisements for help to all the closest papers. I hope so."

"Did he tell you it was Tucker who was on Bar S land?" Jedidiah narrowed his eyes and watched her.

"Yes, he did. We can't do more than make sure all the yearlings and older are branded. Davis has a plan to work with others to get French to take his fences down." Mariella was proud of how Davis had rallied the other small ranchers.

"French know this?" Jedidiah asked.

"Davis told him we were getting a lawyer."

Jedidiah snorted and shook his head. "Shouldn't tell the enemy your plans."

Mariella was of the same thought, but she wasn't going to say anything against her husband. "See you tomorrow." She sauntered back to the house, wondering if French would try to do something to stop them from getting a lawyer.

Ma was in the kitchen punching down dough. "Figured the kitchen was already hot from cooking dinner, I might as well get some more bread made."

"Good idea. I'll take some water in for Davis and go to bed. See you in the morning."

Ma nodded and continued her war with the dough.

Mariella dipped water from the bucket and filled a glass. In the bedroom, she placed the glass on the table by the bed and studied Davis. His eyes moved under his closed lids. Was he dreaming or did the pain of the wound cause that?

She slipped out of her clothes and into her nightgown. Her gaze landed on Davis's clothes. He'd be more comfortable in his underdrawers. She unbuttoned his trousers. Her fingers skimmed his soft male parts and her heart raced. Keeping her mind on the task, she slid the pants down his hips and grabbed the bottom, tugging them off his legs.

Kneeling on her side of the bed, she leaned over Davis, unbuttoning his vest and shirt. She grasped his hand to maneuver his arm through the armhole of the vest.

His hand grasped her and his eyes opened.

She stared into his glassy eyes. Several seconds ticked by before his gaze registered who she was.

"Mariella, what are you doing?" Davis asked.

"I wanted to make you comfortable." She waved his unbuttoned vest. "Can you lean forward to take this off?"

He sat up straight and she removed the vest and pulled his shirt over his head. Today he didn't wear an undershirt. His chest, sprinkled with brown hair, met her gaze. She'd noticed the defined muscles last night when he'd pulled her to the edge of the bed and shattered her body.

"Would you like some water?" she asked, leaning across him to pick up the water.

"Please. My stomach doesn't seem so upset." He took the glass and sipped.

"Sorry for the mess in the kitchen," he said softly.

She smiled. "You couldn't help that. Your body was knocked around and that can upset things."

"I can't believe I didn't dodge that one limb." He rubbed a hand across his forehead. "Can you bring me a wash cloth?"

Mariella backed off the bed and brought him a wet wash cloth.

Davis scrubbed at his beard. "When something like this happens it's the only time I regret having a beard." He held the cloth away from him. "Whew, that stinks. How could you sit so close to me?"

She laughed. "You don't smell near as bad as that bunkhouse. If we do get more ranch hands, we'll have to make Jedidiah clean it, and himself up or no one will want to stay there."

"What were you doing at the bunkhouse?" Davis asked.

"Thought Jedidiah should know there was something that spooked the horses. He says it's a couple of cougars. He'd run across their tracks."

"That's why the horses were nervous. I didn't think

183

of that." His mind must have registered the same thing she had at the mention of cats. "What about the calves? Will the cats kill them?"

"Jedidiah wasn't too concerned, but when you're up to it the three of us will hunt them. We can't afford to lose any calves to wild critters or two-legged critters."

Mariella put the cloth and the cup back and turned out the lantern. "Night Davis." She kissed his cheek above his beard.

"Good night, Mariella." His hand touched hers, and he laced his fingers with hers. "Thank you."

"You're welcome." She closed her eyes and lay on her side, holding Davis's hand. Mariella couldn't remember the last time she'd felt this content. But knew it wouldn't last. Not with Peter French trying to take her land, Tucker trying to take their cattle, and cougars taking the calves.

Chapter Twenty

Davis felt like himself several days after the accident. While he'd still been a bit dizzy when standing and moving too quickly, he'd sat at the desk and wrote up correspondence to a lawyer in Canyon City that Mariella knew of and a lawyer in Winnemucca that J.P. had mentioned. There had to be one who would help the small ranchers find a way to get Mr. French from fencing off land that wasn't his and using it.

At breakfast that morning, he'd asked Jedidiah to post the letters at the fort.

"You feel up to riding?" Mariella asked him when she came in from working with the young horses he and Zach had rounded up.

"As long as we don't go over a walk." He still

became dizzy at times.

"I'd like to ride down and make sure the hay ground is getting water."

"Can I go?" Zach asked from where he sat doing his lessons.

"No. This will just be Davis and I." Mariella nodded to Davis. "You ready?"

"Just need my hat." He walked to the door and grabbed his derby from the peg.

She smiled and shook her head. "We really need to make a trip to Winnemucca and get you a real cattleman's hat."

Davis grinned. "I like this hat."

They left the house and he noted Dash and Poker were already saddled and waiting.

"You were being optimistic," he said, walking over to Poker.

"No. You showed you were feeling better this morning when you woke and couldn't keep your hands to yourself." She smiled and her cheeks deepened in color.

He mounted. "That's because I have a beautiful, caring wife."

She huffed and mounted Dash. "Come on, charmer."

Davis laughed and urged Poker to walk beside Dash.

The meadow land owned by the Bar S spread across the opening of Blitzen canyon. Mariella had said this was hay ground when he arrived, but he didn't realize how large the meadow and marshland was until they rode the perimeter of the ground. Two sides were partitioned off by five strand wire fences.

"Are those fences on the property line?" Davis asked, noting the lines in conjunction with the canyon walls.

"I think so, but I'm not sure. Hugh and my pa stepped the boundaries off when we bought the homestead." Mariella dismounted and dug the heel of her boot into the ground. "We either need some rain or we'll have to divert the water from the creek into the fields. All that snow we had this winter has already soaked down."

"How do you divert the water from the creek?" His father had irrigated crops from a stream on their property, but he'd been too busy going to school and avoiding farm work to pay attention. He had to admit, now he wished he'd paid more attention.

Mariella mounted Dash and rode back toward the canyon. "The stream that flows down the canyon is the snow melt from the mountains. There are a couple of springs that also feed the stream."

"Where does the stream go from here?" Davis had seen the stream farther down in Mr. French's fenced in land.

"It flows down to the big lake. That is what's left after the P Ranch takes water out for irrigating the marshland and hay fields."

Davis nodded. That was why French was fencing off so much land, he was keeping others from the water. This land and water grew good grass for cattle.

At the stream, they dismounted. Mariella stopped beside a board sticking out of the side of the creek. A small hand-dug ditch meandered away from the outside of the board. Mariella grabbed the board and pulled it out, setting it on the ground beside the notch in the creek bank. Water rushed into the hand-dug ditch and spread out over the ground.

"How long do you have to run the water here to get it all the way to the end?" Davis watched the water soak into the ground rapidly. The wind blew down here on the flat more than up in their secluded canyon, drying out the dirt fast.

"I usually start these two—" she pointed to another notch on the opposite side of the stream bank "—let the water run a couple of days then every two days I open up the next notch until they are all running and I leave it that way unless we get a lot of rain." She kicked at the dry soil making dust fly up and catch on the wind. "The wind here dries the dirt almost as fast as you can put water on it. That's why I keep the water running."

"That makes sense. You'll get more grass if it has water." In the distance dirt swirled into the air, growing, moving, and then dissipating.

Davis stared over at the land beyond the fence. "Does Mr. French water like this too?"

"Yes. Hugh watched his hands doing this and put in the notches in the stream banks to water our land and get more hay."

Davis smiled. "I think I would have liked Hugh. He was smart enough to follow Mr. French's actions and to marry you."

Mariella smiled. "So does that make you smart as well?" She swung up onto her horse.

"I would say so." Davis mounted. They reined their horses to head up the road leading to the canyon and ranch.

Boom! Boom!

Davis reined his horse around toward the shots. Mariella did the same thing. A cowboy on a horse held a rifle in the air on the other side of the fence. He motioned with the rifle for them to come to him.

Davis put a hand on Mariella's reins. "You stay here."

She glared at him. "I'll not stay here. This is my ranch, we'll go together."

They walked their horses toward the cowboy. Davis could see the man was agitated, but true to her word not to jar his injured head, Mariella kept her horse at a walk.

Still a good twenty feet from the fence, Davis only caught every other word the cowboy said as the wind whipped up.

"Why did you call us over here?" Davis asked when they were ten feet from the fence.

"Mr. French said if I seen you I was to tell you he expects you to come to dinner at his place this Friday. No kids." The cowboy turned and loped his horse on down the fence line.

Davis glanced at Mariella. "What do you think that is about?"

"You telling him we're getting a lawyer." Mariella turned her horse and trotted up the road.

"Well, don't that beat all?" Davis smiled and kept his horse at a walk. Mariella was upset that he mentioned the lawyer to French and now she was mad because they would have to dine with the man.

***

Mariella pushed Dash into a lope. She didn't care that she'd told Davis they'd walk. The man had spouted his mouth and irritated Mr. French, the one man everyone in the Blitzen and Harney Valleys knew you didn't make mad. He had a temper that had made fodder for many a story. And the man said not to bring Zach and Lizzie. That meant he planned to get angry. She shuddered at the thought. Hugh may have followed Mr. French's cattle and hay raising practices, but he was smart enough to not set off the cattle baron's temper.

At the barn, she unsaddled Dash and went straight to the pen of four-year-olds. She liked working with the horses. Right now she needed to make herself calm down. Working with the red roan would make her calm because he picked up on her moods and behaved accordingly, making him a challenge.

She'd haltered, led, and saddled Red when she heard Davis in the barn unsaddling Poker. She hadn't told Davis, but she planned to give him Red. The horse wasn't as tall as Poker and had a smart sensibility to him. He'd make a fine horse for Davis. A better horse than the one he'd picked out.

"I see you needed to get back to work with the geldings," Davis said, leaning on the uneven tops of the corral fence.

Mariella glanced over at him. His hat shaded his eyes. All she could see was the pinched way his lips appeared. She led Red over to the fence. "Did you ride faster than a walk?" She noted his face was pale. "You did, didn't you?"

"I don't understand why you're mad at me for

standing up for what's yours." His words were quiet. As if speaking hurt.

"I won't talk to you about this now. I don't want to upset Red and you need to rest. You're pale." Mariella waited for him to turn and head for the house.

He didn't. "We don't need to talk about this now. I just want to watch you work with the horse." Davis put his hand out. Red sniffed his hand.

"When your head's better I want you to work with him. He's your horse."

Davis snapped his gaze to her. "I picked out the one that looks like Dash."

"I've worked with him. He's not as intelligent as Red. This horse will be better." Mariella patted the horse's neck.

Davis stroked the horse's nose. "You called him Red. That's a good name. I like it."

"Red seems to like you." She smiled. They would be a good match. "Go on to the house, I don't want you fainting on me. I can't carry you into the house from here."

Davis smiled. "I still can't believe you put me on that horse. But they say when a herculean effort is needed, our bodies take on new strength."

Mariella liked that. It didn't make her sound like some man-woman because of her strength.

Thinking the phrase made her shudder. The boys in school had called her that more times than she cared to think about.

"What's wrong?" Davis put his hand on her arm, rubbing up and down.

"Nothing." She stepped back. "I need to work the

horse. Go to the house and rest."

Davis could tell something was bothering Mariella. But his head was pounding and he couldn't think much past the moment. Following her instructions, he headed to the house. He smiled. She was training a horse for him. He liked the idea of having a horse that wasn't so tall and one of his own. The two of them could bond and work together like Mariella and Dash, and even Zach and his pony, Thunder.

He entered the front door not wanting to answer any questions from Mrs. Simon. Lizzie was playing with a rag doll on the rug in front of the fireplace. She was so careful with the toy, Davis thought she deserved a nice doll. When they made a trip to Winnemucca for supplies, he was going to buy her a pretty porcelain doll. And Zach something nice as well.

"Daddy!" Lizzie exclaimed when she looked up.

His heart expanded and sung at the small child calling him daddy. He hadn't heard that endearment in over a year. He'd been so proud to be a father when Christian was born. He hadn't even minded taking care of the baby while Sarah napped and asked to be left alone. The doctor said Sarah's not wanting to hold her baby was something some mothers went through after giving birth.

Davis walked over to the chair near where Lizzie played. "That's a pretty dolly. What's her name?" he asked.

Lizzie climbed onto his lap, bringing the doll with her. "Sally. You like Sally?"

"Yes, she's a nice doll. Where is your brother?"

She snuggled her small head against him and said,

"He done school. Went ride." She hugged Sally to her and closed her eyes.

Davis wished he had a more comfortable chair and they both could take a nap. Instead, he held the sleeping child and closed his eyes hoping to ease the pounding going on inside his head.

Chapter Twenty-one

Mariella wasn't sure what to wear to dinner with Mr. French. They needed to leave in an hour to get to the P Ranch by six.

Davis walked in from working with Red. She'd been right. The two were a good match. Red was responding to Davis, and she could see he enjoyed working with the gelding.

"Why do you look confused?" Davis asked, hanging his hat on the peg by the kitchen door.

"I don't know what to wear to dinner with Mr. French." She waited for his answer. He knew more about this type of thing than she did. She knew what to wear to a social, but not a dinner with a cattle baron.

Davis walked over, wrapped his arms around her, and kissed her neck. "You should wear the dress you had on when I first met you. You were beautiful and the neckline didn't show too much."

She spun in his arms. "You don't like it when the tops of my bosoms show?" Hugh had liked it. Preferred she wore those kinds of dresses.

"No. I mean, I like it when it's just you and me, but not when other men gawk at them. They aren't treating you with respect when they are staring at your chest." Davis drew her close. "I want other men to see what a smart, feisty woman I married, not look at you like you work in a saloon."

She pressed her bosoms against his chest. "They're kind of hard to hide."

"You don't have to hide them, just cover them up." He kissed her neck. "Your creamy skin is enough to drive a man crazy, show him skin on a handful of bosom and his mind can't work."

His words made her feel soft and womanly. She whispered in his ear. "Come help me dress."

His lips curved against her neck and he kissed her again. "I like the way you think." He released her. "Go ahead, I'll be right in."

Mariella's skin tingled thinking about what they were about to do in the daylight. Ma had the kids outside, helping her work in the garden.

She entered the bedroom, tugged off her boots, and shucked out of her clothes. She stood naked in the middle of the bedroom waiting for Davis. This would be their first coming together since he had the accident.

He bumped into the room carrying a bucket of steaming water. His eyebrows rose at the sight of her standing by the bed without a stitch of clothing. He kicked the door shut with his foot and set the bucket by the wash stand. "I thought I'd help you wash before getting dressed."

The sparkle in his eyes told her it would be a bathing she wouldn't soon forget.

"What do I need to do?" she asked.

"Come stand over here."

While she walked over to the wash stand, Davis shucked out of his vest and shirt and down to his drawers. "I'll wash you, then you can wash me," he said, pouring the warm water from the cookstove's reservoir into the wash basin. He dunked a cloth into the water and washed her face. His soft touch and kiss after her face was cleaned, started a flame of heat lapping at her insides.

He rinsed the cloth and washed her neck, shoulders and each arm. The coolness from the moisture on her skin tingled after the heat of his touch.

After washing each arm, he kissed her, long, wet, and knee buckling. Her body sagged and Davis caught her around the middle with one arm, drawing her against his body. His need for her pressed against her backside. Knowing washing her made him as excited as it did her, added to her need.

Next he washed her bosoms, kissing her neck and sucking on her ear lobes.

Mariella's body tingled, and she could feel wetness between her legs. Davis hadn't even washed there yet. Her body was ready for him to take her and spill his seed.

"Please, take me to bed," she whispered, as he ran the cloth over her belly and down to the curls at the juncture of her legs.

"Not yet, I haven't finished washing you." Davis rinsed the cloth and washed her back, starting at her shoulders and kissing her backbone as he ran the cloth down to her buttocks.

"My legs are wobbling," she whispered.

The sensations sent tremors through her body and caused her woman parts to throb as they had the first night he bedded her.

"Davis! Please!" she begged, knowing only him filling her would ease the need quivering her insides.

"Wash me." He handed her the cloth.

Mariella dunked it in the bucket of water, wrung the cloth out, and washed his face, his neck, shoulders, chest. Glancing down, she stared at the way the front of his drawers tented. "You'll need to get rid of those," she said, rinsing the cloth and preparing to touch him intimately.

Davis slid the underdrawers down and kicked them off.

Mariella's hands shook as she took his member in her hands and stroked the cloth up and down the length.

Davis groaned.

"Am I hurting you?" she asked.

"No. I'm ready." He took the cloth from her, dropped it in the bucket, and kissing her, he danced her to the bed.

The moment their bodies landed on the mattress, Davis thrust into her and she exploded with a thousand lights dancing in her head. He continued thrusting, bringing her smaller bursts of light and vibrations. When she thought she couldn't take anymore, he released, pulsing inside her and sending waves of sensations to her toes.

Davis lay on her for several minutes before raising up, capturing her mouth, and kissing her until she was dizzy.

Three knocks on the door, stopped the kiss.

"You two getting ready to leave?" Ma called.

"Yes," Davis replied, shoving off Mariella. He stood beside the bed, leaned down and kissed her on the lips again, and padded to the washstand.

She watched him clean his private parts, rinse the cloth and bring it back to her. As before, when they came together, he washed her woman parts, and the inside of her legs.

"We better get dressed," he said, tossing the cloth in the wash basin and walking to the wardrobe. He handed her the under clothes and dress she would wear and then started putting on his good suit.

Davis watched Mariella dress as he donned his best suit. He liked how his wife had suggested they change together. He'd never bedded a woman in the middle of the day. There was something wicked about doing so that made the encounter all the more enjoyable. His idea to wash her had been his way of putting his hands on every inch of her. The plan had worked and made them both more heated because of the contact. He'd remember it for future use.

Mariella brushed her hair. He loved the long, curly tresses. Tonight, he'd ask her to leave her hair unbraided so he could feel the silkiness of her hair.

"I'll get the wagon ready," he said, kissing her cheek.

"I just have to finish putting my hair up." She moved her head and caught his lips before he moved away.

Smiling, he caught Mariella around the waist and pulled her up tight against him. "Mrs. Weston, you look beautiful. I doubt Mr. French will carry on with such beauty in his presence." He kissed her on the lips and released her as pounding on the door started.

Davis walked to the door and opened it.

Zach stood with his fist raised to pound some more. "Gran said to get out of there or you'll be late."

Davis ruffled Zach's hair, the same color as his mother's. "We're ready. Your ma is fixing her hair. I'm headed to get the wagon ready."

"Jedidiah has the wagon in front of the house." Zach put his hands on his hips. "If you weren't takin' so long to dress, you'd know that."

Chuckling, Davis walked into the main room.

Lizzie stood up from where she was playing on the floor and hugged his leg. "Daddy, pretty."

He patted her soft, golden curls. "Thank you, Lizzie, but wait until you see your ma."

Mariella stepped out of the bedroom at that moment. Her eyes sparkled, her cheeks were pink, and, the lips he'd just kissed were red, plump, and looking good enough to kiss again.

"Mama!" Lizzie ran over to Mariella and hugged her legs. "You bootiful!"

"Thank you, Lizzie baby." She picked up Lizzie

and kissed her pale, thin face. "You're beautiful too."

"You two need to get going," Mrs. Simon walked briskly into the room, plucking Lizzie from her mother's arms. "You don't want to keep Mr. French waiting."

Davis crossed the room and cupped Mariella's elbow, escorting her out the door and helping her up on the seat of the buckboard.

As they pulled out of the yard and under the sign with Bar S carved into it, Davis said, "We need to get a buggy for paying visits to neighbors and going to socials. Beating our backsides on a wood seat while all dressed up for a special occasion kind of takes the special out of it."

He glanced at Mariella. Her lips curved up into a slight smile.

"I suppose we could get one for special occasions and keep it in the barn so it doesn't get ruined by the weather."

He reached over, claiming her hand. "We'll get one the next trip to Winnemucca."

The horses stopped at the gate. Davis climbed down and opened the gate while Mariella drove the horse and buckboard through. He fastened the gate and climbed up onto the seat.

"They invited us to dinner, you'd think they could have left the gates open. It's not like they have cattle in here right now." It burned him to know the man they were having dinner with kept homesteaders from getting good land, by fencing them out. Illegally. He was sure it was illegal. He was anxious to get his responses from the letters he sent to the lawyers.

***

Mariella enjoyed the ride to the P Ranch, but as soon as she saw the big ranch house and all the outbuildings, her nerves started dancing. She'd heard Mr. French hosted dinners with influential men and didn't want to have him look down on her because she was unsophisticated.

"You'll be fine." Davis grasped her hand and gave it a gentle squeeze.

"There has to be a reason for him inviting us to dinner." She shook her head. "I don't think he wants to be friends with us."

Davis stopped the wagon and grasped her chin, making her peer into his eyes. "We will be congenial and not bring up his fences. But if he brings it up, I will discuss it with him."

She liked that Davis was willing to go against the cattle baron, but she feared retaliation. "I'll try to keep my mouth closed and not say something wrong."

"I'm not worried you'll say anything wrong, I just want you to know I won't start trouble." He kissed her on the lips and started the wagon moving.

The wagon pulled into the ranch compound and two vaqueros grabbed the horses' headstalls.

"Señor French is waiting for you," one of the men said. "We will tend to your horses and wagon."

"Thank you." Davis climbed down and raised his hands to help her.

Mariella sat on the edge of the seat and dropped down into her husband's waiting arms. She'd lost the fear of knocking him down with her size. He'd proved he could handle her.

Once her feet were solidly on the grown, Davis crooked his elbow and she slipped her hand through. They walked up to the door of the house. The door swung open and a small Chinese man ushered them in.

"You're late," Mr. French said, standing by the door to what appeared to be a dining room.

"We had some gates to open and close to get here," Davis said.

Mariella cringed. He'd said he wouldn't start trouble or talk about the fences, yet the first words out of his mouth were conflict.

Mr. French didn't say anything. He tipped his head as if to say, nice barb. "We're eating in the dining room." The small man led them into a room twice the size of her kitchen. A long table sat in the middle of the room. Three places were set on the far end of the table.

Mariella's stomach churned. The places for her and Davis were set on either side of the end. Mr. French walked to his place at the head of the table and stood by his chair.

Davis held her chair. After she sat, Mr. French did as well and Davis sat once he was on his side of the table.

The Chinese man who had answered the door, appeared with a large bowl. He placed it in front of Mr. French and handed the cattle baron three bowls. French filled a bowl and handed it to Mariella.

She placed the bowl on her plate and sent a pleading glance across the table to Davis. He placed the bowl Mr. French handed him on his plate and picked up a large spoon beside his plate. Mariella scanned the utensils by her plate and picked up the corresponding spoon to the one Davis picked up. The soup was tasty with a bit of a bite to it.

As the meal progressed, she mimicked what Davis did and listened to the two men talk about politics and the cattle industry. She voiced her opinion a couple of times. Davis smiled and asked a question that kept her in the conversation, but Mr. French frowned when she spoke up and turned all his attention to Davis.

After a nice dessert of peach pie, Mr. French rose from his chair. "Mrs. Weston, you may sit in the parlor while I talk with your husband."

Davis had come around the table to pull out her chair after the man stood. He stopped at her side. "If my wife isn't allowed to be part of the discussion then we'll take our leave." Davis pulled out her chair, holding her arm as she stood.

"Now see here, Mr. Weston. Women don't understand the details of business."

A ball of indignation rolled up Mariella's throat. She opened her mouth but was cut short before any words burst out.

"Mariella ran the Bar S for two years before I came along. She knows more about the ranch business than I do. I insist she be included in whatever you want to talk about." Davis had pulled her hand through the crook of his arm. He stood beside her straight and unmoving.

Her heart thudded in her chest at the way he stood up to Mr. French.

The little man's glare darted back and forth between them. Whatever he wanted to talk about must be important because she could tell he didn't want to give in to Davis's demand.

Chapter Twenty-two

Davis didn't let Mr. French's glare, or his firm declaration he didn't want Mariella present, make him back down. What he'd said was true. Mariella knew some aspects of the ranch better than he did, and he wasn't going into a talk with this man without her by his side.

"Then we'll all go to the parlor," Mr. French said, motioning for them to exit the dining room.

Davis assumed the room they walked by on the way to the dining room was the parlor and escorted Mariella into that room.

Mr. French followed and motioned for them to take a seat on a small divan. Mariella sat and Davis took a seat beside her. Mr. French didn't sit. He remained standing which gave him his first height advantage since they'd arrived.

"The reason I asked you to dinner was to sort out our differences," Mr. French started.

"Differences?" Mariella questioned sarcastically.

Davis grasped her hand and squeezed, hoping to keep her from saying any more.

Mr. French's face grew red and his eyes widened. "This is exactly why I didn't want her in this conversation. Women don't know when to keep quiet and listen."

"Mariella can keep quiet while we hear you out. But once you've had your say, both, she and I will be allowed to say our piece." Davis squeezed her hand again and stared at Mr. French.

The smaller man's gaze wasn't on Mariella's face. It was on her chest.

Davis had to hold his tongue. It wasn't Mariella's comments he didn't like, it was being distracted by her body.

"Mr. French, what do you consider are our differences?" Davis asked, drawing the man's attention to him.

"I've heard from my men that you don't like opening gates to go to your property. That can't be helped. I have to keep squatters off my land." Mr. French slammed a fist into his palm.

"But from what I've heard not all the land you have fenced off is yours." Davis challenged him.

"I can't have squatters in the middle of land my cattle need."

Davis noticed he'd skirted the business about it being his land. "There is plenty of land in the Harney and Blitzen Valleys for anyone who wants to live here. You can't keep people fenced out."

Mr. French's face darkened as Davis continued to harp on the fact he wasn't allowing people to homestead land that wasn't taken, only fenced off.

"I will do what is best for my cattle. And if you smaller ranches don't stop causing trouble, I'll see that you go out of business!"

"Like sending your foreman to steal our yearlings?" Mariella asked.

Davis glanced at his wife. Her narrowed eyes, pinched mouth, and red cheeks proved her anger at the thought of anyone stealing their cattle.

"I don't send my men to steal cattle!" Mr. French charged forward.

Davis stood, blocking the man from Mariella. "I witnessed your foreman Tucker and another man on Bar S land. They'd come in from over the rim toward Diamond Ranch."

"Did they have your cattle?" Mr. French asked.

"No. We caught them before they had a chance to take anything."

"Then how do you know they were there to steal cattle?" Mr. French shoved his fisted hands onto his hips.

"Because we found a small herd with yearlings who weren't branded in that same area. One of the hands you lured away from us must have left that group when the Bar S rounded up for branding last fall. That person told your foreman and he came to steal them."

206

Davis wasn't backing down on this. He had the same reaction to having cattle stolen as Mariella did.

"That is hearsay and if you spread the rumor around my men are stealing cattle, I'll see that ranch of yours is taken from you."

Mariella popped up behind Davis. Her hands raised as if to choke the smaller man. "You can't threaten us! And we'll see to it you never get your hands on our ranch!"

Mr. French took two steps back and glared at Mariella.

Davis put his arms around Mariella, calming her. "Mr. French, I don't know what you hoped to gain by having us for dinner, but I don't think we have anything more to discuss." Davis spun Mariella toward the hallway and door to the house. He grabbed his hat from the rack where the Chinese man had put it and led Mariella out of the house.

The vaquero who had said he would take care of the horses, hustled out of the barn with the horses and attached them to the buckboard.

"Thank you," Davis said to the man as he helped Mariella up onto the seat. He climbed up beside her and flicked the reins heading the horses out of the P Ranch compound and on the road to their ranch.

"Can you believe the nerve of that man!" Mariella's hands were fisted in her lap. "He wanted to talk about our differences. What do you think he even meant by that?"

Davis smiled. He had a pretty good idea. "I think he wanted to convince us we didn't need to get a lawyer involved. He knows he's in the wrong. But thinks his money makes him above the law."

Mariella shifted, bumping her knees against his leg and facing him. "He's scared of us?"

"That's what I think. He knows if we get authorities looking into his fences, he'll be in the wrong." This bit of insight made him hope one of the lawyers he contacted would take on their inquiry.

Her eyes lost their light and her mouth turned down at the corners. "Do you think he can really take the ranch away?"

Davis wrapped an arm around her, drawing her close. "He has no way of taking the ranch. The only way is if he illegally keeps us from taking cattle or supplies across his property." And that wouldn't happen. Davis knew enough about the law to know no one could keep them from their property. The first thing he would make sure the lawyer they hired did was draw up an easement for them through Mr. French's property. No court in the land wouldn't give them the easement since Bar S Ranch was established before French put his fences in.

"Don't worry about his threats. That's all they were. He can't legally do anything to us." He kissed the top of Mariella's head.

"Legally. What about illegally?" she asked.

"We'll deal with that if it happens." He didn't want to think about getting into a range war with Mr. French and all his ranch hands, but they didn't have a choice if that's how far the man was willing to take this.

"What about the children?"

Davis gathered Mariella closer. "They'll be fine. Nothing is going to break up this family. We won't lose the ranch."

"But he's rich and I've heard he's shot at people who make him mad."

"We'll be fine. Once we get the law behind us, he can't do anything. All hands will point to him." Davis stopped for the gate to cross French's property. He hated the gates keeping them from their land, but he also respected a man's right to fence off what belonged to him. It just seemed with all the fencing material he had, he could have run fences down both sides of the road allowing them to enter their property unhindered.

He climbed down from the wagon enjoying the evening air. The days grew longer, giving them plenty of light for their drive home.

Mariella drove the horses and wagon through the gate and waited for Davis to climb back up. He took the reins from her, clucking to the horses, heading them to the next gate. She didn't want to worry about Mr. French and what he might do. They had enough worries about having enough feed through the summer and not such a brutal winter as the last one.

"I wondered if you thought it was too soon for me to sit in the saddle on Red," Davis said, drawing her thoughts from the bad to think about the good.

"You've been working with him every day and he is a quick learner. You can give it a try tomorrow. I'll watch. If he looks skittish, I'll let you know." She wrapped an arm around Davis's arm and leaned her head on his shoulder. Thoughts of this afternoon flashed in her mind. She smiled. "I had fun getting ready for our dinner."

He chuckled. "That was the best part of the

invitation."

She laughed. "Yes, I'd say so." Mariella tipped her head and nuzzled his neck underneath his cropped beard. She'd watched him trim his beard twice. She found the precise way he handled the scissors and studied the beard in the mirror funny. She'd giggled the first time and he'd studied her for so long before clipping at his beard again, she had to leave the room to laugh.

"Why do you wear a beard?" she asked.

He stopped the wagon and climbed out to open the second gate. Mariella drove the wagon through. She watched him fill his pipe while waiting for her to drive through.

Davis climbed back onto the wagon, lit his pipe, and took the reins from her.

"You going to answer my question?" She nudged him with her shoulder.

"I wear a beard because when I finished school and wanted to start a business, no one believed I was old enough to give a loan to start a business." He glanced at her. "I have a baby face." He puffed on his pipe and stared ahead.

"So you wear that neatly trimmed beard so people respect your ability to do business?" She sort of understood what he was saying. It was kind of like how men didn't take her serious because they were too busy looking at her bosoms. They were eye level to most men.

"Yes. And I've had a beard for so long, I don't think I would like not having one."

She inhaled the sweet scent of his tobacco smoke.

The cigarettes Jedidiah rolled always gagged her, but the smoke from Davis's pipe was soothing.

The barn and house came into sight.

"What are we going to say about dinner?" she asked, chewing on her bottom lip. She didn't want to give Ma or Zach anything to worry about.

"The meal was good. The company not so good."

Mariella laughed. "That is the truth!"

Davis pulled the wagon up to the house and jumped down. He held his hands up to her.

"You could have stopped at the barn and I would help you unharness," she said.

"Get down here. You can go in and say good night to the children."

She slid down into his arms.

Davis kissed her briefly on the lips. "I'll be in shortly." He released her and walked to the horses, leading them over to the barn.

Mariella sighed, watching him lead the horses to the barn. A woman couldn't ask for a better partner. She pivoted and entered the house through the front door.

"Mama!" Lizzie exclaimed, toddling toward her with her arms outstretched.

Mariella picked her up and hugged her tight. Davis and I will do everything in our power to keep you safe and the ranch.

"How was the dinner?" Ma asked from the chair by the fireplace.

"Yeah, was it fancy?" Zach asked. He sat on the floor spinning a wooden top.

Mariella smiled thinking of Davis's words. "The food was good, the company not so much."

211

Ma laughed and Zach stared at her.

"What do you mean?" Zach asked.

"The food was good, tasted wonderful and was served nicely by a Chinese man. However, Mr. French wasn't pleasant to talk with." Mariella carried Lizzie to the bedroom. "Who would like a bedtime story?"

"Me, Momma, me!" Lizzie said, hugging her neck.

"What about you, Zach?" Mariella asked, watching her son spin the top.

"I'll wait. I have something to say to Davis." Zach didn't look up from his top.

She glanced at Ma. Her ma shrugged and continued mending.

"Come in when you finish talking." Mariella carried Lizzie into the bedroom and helped her into her nightdress. "What do you suppose your brother wants to talk to Davis about?" Mariella muttered.

"It's a secret," Lizzie said, squirming down into her little bed.

Mariella peered down at her daughter and touched the end of her nose with a finger. "You know what the secret is?"

She grinned and nodded.

Mariella smiled. Tricking the child into telling her would be wrong. If Lizzie knew what Zach was talking to Davis about then it couldn't be anything bad. "Which story tonight?"

"Puss 'n Boots," Lizzie said, clutching her rag doll to her chest. She listened intently as Mariella read the story to her.

Just as she closed the book, Zach walked into the room. His face held a half smile.

"How was your talk with Davis?" Mariella whispered.

"Good." Zach started shucking out of his clothes.

Mariella picked up his night shirt and held it out to him. "Anything I need to know or can help you with?"

"No." He ducked into the shirt, and she buttoned the three buttons at the neck.

"You like Davis, don't you? You're all right with him being your new dad?" Zach hadn't acted up or been sullen since Davis came, but he also wasn't one to show his feelings. He was more like his father.

"I like him." Zach crawled into bed. "Good night."

She leaned down and kissed his forehead. "Good night, my little man."

Mariella stepped out of the children's room and found Ma and Davis leaning toward one another chatting in low voices. Ma saw her and sat back in her chair.

"What are you two whispering about?" she asked, sitting in the chair next to Davis.

"I was telling your ma about dinner and didn't want the children to hear," Davis said, watching Ma.

"Yes. Being served by a Chinese man and everything." Ma didn't lift her gaze from the pants she mended.

The two were talking about something they didn't want her to know about. First Zach and now Ma. She stared at Davis.

He winked and yawned before asking, "Ready for bed?"

Mariella shook her head. She wasn't ready to go to bed. Her mind was still circling the threats Mr. French

213

had spouted. "I'm going outside for a bit." She stood and headed for the door.

"I'll go with you." Davis was by her side in three strides.

She wasn't sure she wanted him along. He'd distract her and she wanted to think. "I'd like to go out alone," she said.

Davis peered into her eyes. "Don't dwell on it. We can't do anything with threats." He cupped her chin. "When we hear back from the lawyers we'll know what to do. In the meantime, Mr. French can't do anything to us. We need to continue as usual."

He kissed her lips and laced his fingers with hers. "Come on. Let's go for a walk."

Mariella walked beside Davis. He knew what to say and how to get her mind thinking of things other than trouble.

They sauntered out to the corral that held the geldings they were working with. They leaned on the corral watching the horses.

"When did you start working with horses?" he asked, rubbing her back with one hand.

"Pa always trained his freight horses to harness. I helped him. When I married Hugh, he was breaking horses. Bringing in the three and four-year-olds and throwing saddles on them and riding them until they stopped bucking. But I noticed they didn't always settle down into a good working horse. But the horses I had trained and used, anyone could ride and they responded." Mariella sighed. "I had to get Pa to help me persuade Hugh to let me work with the horses and train them." She smiled. "After the first ten I trained were given to the hands and they commented on how well the horses responded, Hugh had to admit I knew what I was doing."

"The little I've seen of you working with these horses, I'm a believer in your training." Davis hugged her to him. "You have compassion. Animals and people respond to that."

Mariella snuggled into his embrace. She'd never had a man compliment her as much as Davis did. And it wasn't her curves he complimented, it was her mind and her heart.

"What did Zach have to talk to you about?" she asked, hoping to catch him off guard.

He didn't say anything and she feared he wouldn't.

"Zach wanted to make sure I knew some things." Davis kissed her Tucker. "Don't ask him what. It was important to him that I knew."

Mariella leaned back and peered into Davis's face. "You won't tell me because you want to keep Zach's trust."

He nodded. "It's hard to get the trust of another man's son. I won't risk hurting him to satisfy your curiosity." He kissed the tip of her nose. "But I will tell you that you were part of the conversation."

"Then whatever you talked about couldn't have been too bad." She laughed. "Now I'm ready for bed."

"Good. Our little tryst this afternoon only made me want more time with you." Davis captured her mouth with his.

Mariella pressed against him, savoring the way his lips moved over hers. He nipped at her bottom lip and sucked gently, buckling her knees. She'd never had a man's kiss weaken her like Davis's did.

He held her tight, pushing her up against the corral.

A horse nickered and Davis's lips left hers. "Let's head to the house."

She clung to his arm, making her wobbly legs carry her by the barn. They started across the area between the barn and house.

Davis stopped. "Go on to the house." His voice held an undertone she'd heard once before.

Her needy body instantly went on alert. "Why?"

He nodded to the bunkhouse. "We have visitors."

Mariella glanced over her shoulder and saw two strange horses tied to the hitching post in front of the bunkhouse. "I'll go with you." She stood straighter but kept her arm looped through his.

The sun had set, throwing the ranch into gray hues with a background in the sky of blue, violet, pink, and gold. They walked to the bunkhouse.

Davis stopped at the hitching rail. "You stay here until I see who it is." He unhooked his arm from hers and stepped under the porch roof and up to the door. Without knocking he walked in.

Chapter Twenty-three

Davis didn't think the visitors were trouble, but it set a bad precedent for Mariella to walk into the bunkhouse. He shoved the door open and found Jedidiah sitting at the table drinking coffee and talking to two cowboys.

"Jedidiah. Men." Davis walked farther into the bunkhouse.

"Mr. Weston, these here men answered your advertisement," Jedidiah said, tipping his head toward the two cowboys. "I told them to bunk here and talk to you in the mornin'."

"Thank you, Jedidiah. Mrs. Weston and I were out for a walk and noticed the horses." Davis studied the two men as he talked. They were both young, but he didn't hold that against them. He had a list of questions he'd ask them tomorrow.

"We didn't want to bother you tonight. That's why we came straight to the bunkhouse," said the one who appeared a couple years older than the other cowboy.

"You're not bothering. Jedidiah was correct in having you wait until morning. Bring them over for breakfast. I'll let Mrs. Simon know we'll have extras. I'll conduct the interviews after breakfast." Davis heard the door opening behind him. "I'll be out in a minute, Mariella," he said, smiling at the men and spinning to the door.

Davis faced Mariella who stood in the doorway as he attempted to walk out.

"What's going on?" she asked, peering over his head.

"A couple of cowhands arrived." He pivoted her around, ushering her out from under the porch. "Jedidiah will bring them in for breakfast with him. We need to let your mother know." He escorted her across the barnyard and passed the house so Mariella could use the outhouse.

"Did they look like capable hands?" she asked, stopping in front of the small building.

"I'd say they could work circles around Jedidiah, but we need to know their loyalty and how much they know about cattle. We'll interview them after breakfast tomorrow." Davis waved her into the building. He used a bush not too far away to relieve himself.

Mariella stepped out of the privy and headed to the back door.

Davis hurried ahead of her, opening the door. One low burning lantern sat on the kitchen table.

"Ma's gone to bed already," Mariella said, staring at the lantern.

"We'll have to get up early and let her know about the extras for breakfast." Davis picked up the lantern, clasped Mariella's hand, and led her into their bedroom.

Out by the corral, he'd used kissing her to take her mind off their dinner and why Zach had insisted on talking to him. The young boy wanted Davis to know his mother's birthday was coming up and she loved to celebrate the day of her birth. He'd wanted to make sure Davis made the day special.

Right now, Davis wanted to make Mariella's night special.

***

Mariella slipped out of the bed early to let Ma know there would be two extras for breakfast. She quickly dressed in trousers and a blouse. Glancing back at the bed where Davis still slept, her body warmed and her skin tingled remembering how he'd pleasured her last night. She'd never questioned the way Hugh bedded her, but she loved the way Davis made her feel special and gave her such pleasure her body quivered and shook several minutes after each encounter.

Tiptoeing out of the room, she closed the door gently and walked into the kitchen where Ma was mixing biscuits.

"We had two men come in last night. They'll be here for breakfast," she said, picking up the coffee pot and pouring a cup.

"I know. Jedidiah has already been here and told

me." Ma glanced at her, smiled, and said, "You didn't have to get up early to tell me."

"I'm up now, I might as well help." Mariella set the large cast iron skillet on the stove and started slicing ham to warm in the skillet.

They worked together in a rhythm they'd grown accustom to having fed the family and ranch hands the last eight years. Since Davis started sleeping in her bed, there had only been a few mornings Mariella was up early enough to help with the morning meal.

The children wandered in. Zach was dressed, but Lizzie was still in her nightdress.

Mariella picked her up, hugged and kissed her, and set her back down. "Go wake up that lazy daddy."

Lizzie giggled and took off running into the other room.

"You know she's gonna start tickling him," Zach said.

"Then he should wake up in a good mood." Mariella knew he would be gentle with Lizzie and make a big deal out of her waking him up.

Stomping at the back door drew her attention to the possible new ranch hands.

Jedidiah entered, taking off his hat and hanging it on the pegs by the door. The two young men behind him did the same.

"Mornin'," Jedidiah said.

"Morning," Mariella replied. She nodded to the two young men. "Pick a seat on that side of the table."

They both stared at her a moment before dropping their gazes and sitting.

Squeals and laughter entered the kitchen. Davis,

carrying Lizzie over his shoulder, entered the room with a huge smile on his face.

"Who sent this tickle bug in to get me up?" he asked, walking over and kissing Mariella on the cheek.

Zach pointed to Mariella. "Ma sent her in."

Mariella started to respond. Davis plopped Lizzie in her high chair and spun toward her. The mischief in his eyes had her skin tingling. But this wasn't the time and place for any shenanigans.

"Breakfast is ready." When he took a step toward her, she said. "And everyone is here." She moved her eyes to signify 'look at the table we have company.'

Davis grasped her silent communication and leaned against the dry sink, studying the young men.

Mariella set the platter of ham and eggs on the table. Davis held her chair then moved to his.

He started passing the platters of food and asked, "What are your names?"

"I'm Abe and this is my brother, Skip." The older of the two said, staring at Davis.

Mariella asked, "Where are you from?"

Abe continued to look at Davis. "We grew up in Montana. Heard they needed hands to drive cattle from Winnemucca to Denver. Got to Winnemucca too late to hook up with a drive and saw your advertisement."

"Why didn't you go back to Montana?" Davis asked.

"Our family has a cattle ranch. We also have four older brothers who all think they should have the ranch when pappy dies. We decided to strike out on our own."

Mariella liked the gumption shining in the young man's eyes. "Are you looking to make quick money and buy your own cattle?"

Abe glanced her way and spoke to Davis. "We know it takes years to save up for cattle and a ranch. But we're young and willing to work at it."

"What about rustling? That's a quick way to make more money and start a herd." Davis said.

Abe stood up, his eyes narrowed at Davis. "Rustlin' is stealin' and we don't do that. If that's how you add to your herd, we're not workin' here." He tapped Skip on the shoulder. "Come on."

"Sit." Jedidiah said.

The two gaped at him.

"Your foreman said sit." Davis stared at the two.

Mariella understood what Davis was doing. He was checking their character, but it was kind of a cruel way to go about it.

"We've had trouble with ranch hands hiding our cattle to keep them from being branded and then sneaking back and taking them. I was testing your moral character," Davis said. He smiled. "You passed. Welcome to the Bar S."

Abe stared at Davis a minute. Skip knocked his shoulder into his brother's and nodded.

"Jedidiah can show you around today and let you know what to expect as part of your job." Davis dug into his food.

Mariella wasn't ready to let it go at that. "Have either of you put up hay?"

They glanced her direction and then said to Davis. "We have a gist of what it is but we've never actually done that."

Frustrated they spoke to Davis when she asked the

questions, Mariella said, "When I ask the question I would appreciate you look at me."

Abe's face turned red as he focused on her. Skip's cheeks darkened as he glanced her way.

"Mrs. Weston and I have a partnership. She knows more about the cattle and I know more about the business side. When it comes to the cattle, she is the person you'll be talking with." He paused. "If you have a problem with that then you may not be right for the Bar S."

Abe swallowed. "We'll be fine. Just take some getting used to."

Skip nodded his head. "W-we ain't … w-with girls."

Mariella smiled. "You're bashful?"

"No, ma'am, we ain't been around them much. It's always been Pa and our brothers, no girls at the ranch." Abe's cheeks grew redder, if that was at all possible.

"Just think of me as another ranch hand and we'll be fine," Mariella said.

Their gazes dropped to her bosoms and then they took concentrated interest in their plates. "Yes, Ma'am," they both said.

She glanced down the table at Davis. The twinkle in his eyes and the way Jedidiah was smiling had her feeling sorry for the two young men. She had a feeling her husband and foreman were going to tease and torment the youngsters over her.

***

Davis was pleased with the two new ranch hands. They were capable and trainable. He still chuckled every time Mariella talked to them. They didn't stare at her bosoms, but they didn't look at her either, which was bothering Mariella. He told her being their age and having not sewed any oats, they were probably growing hard every time they looked at her. She scoffed but he was pretty sure, having been raised on an all-male ranch they hadn't had too much contact with women and therefore hadn't learned how to control their body's response. He was leaving all of that up to Jedidiah.

A knock on the door startled Davis. He'd been caught up in his thoughts and hadn't heard anyone approach. Mariella was riding with Zach. Lizzie and Mrs. Simon were in the kitchen making cookies from the scent of vanilla and cinnamon.

Davis answered the door. A tall thin man of about thirty stood on the porch. "May I help you?"

"I came answering your advertisement in the Baker City Herald."

Davis held out his hand. "Davis Weston, my wife and I own the Bar S."

"Len Smith." The man shook hands.

"Come in. I have some questions for you." Davis opened the door wide, inviting the man in.

Once they were settled in chairs, Davis asked, "Why are you looking for a ranch hand job?"

The man stared at the hat in his hands. "To be honest, I had to leave the ranch I was at. Me and the rancher's daughter became closer than the boss liked."

The sadness in the man's eyes told Davis he hadn't left on his own. "I see. Are you a ladies man?" He didn't need someone flirting with Mariella.

"No, sir. Polly was the first and only woman for me. Just my boss didn't see it that way." He ran a hand through his hair. "I didn't want to stay in the area and run into her all the time."

"And Polly? How did she feel about you leaving?" Davis didn't want some lovelorn woman showing up here or Len getting a letter and heading out when they needed him.

"She cried, but wouldn't go against her daddy." Len stared him in the eyes. "I won't be going back and she won't be showing up here."

"We've had a run of bad luck with our ranch hands being lured away by more pay while my wife was a widow. The ranch hands, all but the foreman, didn't like taking orders from a woman. Which if you take the job, you'll have to do. My wife and I run this ranch together. She knows more about the cattle and I know more about the business. We make a good team."

Davis continued to study the man. "We are looking for loyalty and will treat you with respect. We don't ask our hands to do anything we won't do ourselves. And you'll see our family working beside the ranch hands."

"I respect a man or woman who works," Len said. "And loyalty. If I'm treated right, I'll work till I drop for my boss. I would have stayed on at the last place if the memories hadn't been so raw."

Davis nodded. He had a good feeling about Len. "We can pay you thirty a month. You stay in the bunkhouse and eat in the house."

Lizzie came scampering into the room. "Daddy, Gran cookies!"

Gathering Lizzie onto his lap, Davis made introductions. "Lizzie, this is a new ranch hand, Mr. Smith. Mr. Smith, this is Lizzie our youngest."

"Hello," Lizzie said, leaning her head on Davis's chest.

"Hello, Miss Lizzie."

Stomping at the back door had Lizzie wiggling off his lap. "Zach, my cookie!" she yelled running into the kitchen.

"Davis!" Mariella entered the room and stopped at the sight of Len.

"Mrs. Weston, we have another ranch hand," Davis said, standing and motioning for Mariella to sit in his chair.

She did and Davis watched Len as Mariella came into his view and sat. The man's eyes widened a bit as he looked up at her. But in his favor, he looked her in the face and not the bosoms.

Len stood and held out his hand. "Mrs. Weston, I'm Len Smith."

They shook and Davis could tell by Mariella's soft smile, she liked him.

"You answered our advertisement?" she asked.

"Yes, Ma'am. I was in need of new sights."

When Len didn't say more, Davis stepped in. "I've been talking with Len, I believe he will make a good ranch hand."

Mariella gazed into Davis's eyes for several seconds, then smiled at Len. "Mr. Smith, welcome to the Bar S. Jedidiah, the foreman has two new hands that arrived yesterday out showing them around. Has Davis told you the extent of what we expect from our ranch hands?"

"No, Ma'am."

Davis smiled. "I'll go see where that cookie is

Lizzie said was mine." He held out his hand to Len. "Welcome to the Bar S." He shook and left Mariella to fill Len in. Three hands in two days. If they had three more good men wander in they would be in good shape for haying and the fall round up.

Chapter Twenty-four

Davis sat on Poker watching Mariella, Jedidiah, Len, Abe, and Skip brand the herd Jedidiah and the two young cowhands found the day before when Jedidiah showed them the canyon. After they established what each was better at, the group set to work.

Skip and Abe turned out to be a good combination with their ropes. Skip caught the calf around the neck, and Abe caught a foot, stretching the calf out while Len held it down and Jedidiah and Mariella castrated the bull calves and branded all the calves. They had the twenty head finished by noon.

"Good work!" Davis said to the brothers as they rode their horses out of the corral. "You'll have to give

Zach lessons on roping!"

Abe grinned. "We'd be pleased to teach Zach."

"Get washed up. Mrs. Simon will have dinner ready."

Len walked out of the corral, he was dusty from head to toe. He slapped his hat on his thigh and dust danced in the air. "Those young bucks sure can rope," Len said, stopping beside Poker.

"Yes, they can. And I appreciate you taking the calves to the ground. Next time you can show me what to do." Davis argued with Mariella that morning. He'd wanted to help with the branding. She'd told him he would only be in the way having not participated before. He was to watch today when they only had a small group to work.

Len nodded. "It's a deal. I'm going to knock more of this dirt off."

Davis dismounted to close the gate behind Jedidiah and Mariella. Their hands were full with the supplies and bucket of testicles.

Jedidiah headed to the barn with his supplies. Mariella carried the bucket.

Davis peered down at the oval shaped organs. "Your Ma is really going to cook those and we'll eat them?"

Mariella grinned, her eyes twinkling with mischief. "Greenhorn, you can't call yourself a cowboy until you've eaten calf oysters."

Davis shook his head and held the back door open for her. He'd never heard of such a thing, but everyone at the table during breakfast smacked their lips when Mrs. Simon said to be sure and bring her the testicles.

They entered the kitchen and racing hooves thudded in front of the house. Davis exited out the back and hurried to the front.

J.P. was dismounting. He turned and shook hands with Davis. "How're things going out here?" he asked.

"Learning how to be a cattleman. What brought you out here? Is Ernestine all right?" Davis was happy to see his brother-in-law but worried the visit was because of trouble with his sister.

"Ernestine is right as rain. She sent me out here." J.P. pulled two letters from his vest pocket. "We were at the fort yesterday and she asked for mail for the ranch."

Davis took the letters and patted the man on the back. "We're just sitting down to dinner. Come on in." They entered through the back door.

"J.P.! What a surprise. Did Ernestine come with you?" Mariella looked behind them.

"No. She sent me alone. Said she had too much to do for a social call today." J.P. snatched his hat from his head. "Mrs. Simon. Good to see you again."

"You too, Mr. Mulligan." Mariella's mother put a bowl of steaming potatoes on the table.

Zach walked into the kitchen. "Hi, Mr. Mulligan."

"Zach, go tell the hands we're ready to eat," Davis said.

"Yes, sir." Zach ran out the back door.

"Hands?" J.P. asked.

"We have three new hands. Young men I believe are loyal and will stick with us." Davis poured coffee for him and J.P., while Mariella and Mrs. Simon continued putting platters and bowls on the table.

"That's good news." J.P. sipped his coffee.

"This morning we branded some cattle that went missing last fall," Mariella said. "They all did a good job."

Zach ran in through the kitchen door and stomping sounded behind him. Jedidiah entered followed by the three new hands.

Davis made the introductions and held Mariella's chair as she took her place at the head of the table.

"Why did you ride out here?" she asked, J.P.

"He brought our mail," Davis said, patting the letters he'd placed in his vest pocket.

"Who are they from?" Mariella asked.

Davis pulled the letters out as everyone else started passing the food. The first one was addressed to Mrs. Simon.

"This one is for you." He handed the letter to his mother-in-law.

"Oh, it's from your aunt Fern. I haven't heard from her in a while. Thank you for bringing the mail, J.P."

Davis glanced at the other letter. It was from the lawyer he'd contacted in Winnemucca.

"Who is that one from?" Mariella asked.

He glanced at her, then J.P. "The lawyer in Winnemucca."

Both watched him. "I'll read it after the meal." He shoved the letter back in his vest pocket and tried to forget it through the meal.

***

After the meal, Mariella hurried helping Ma with the dishes. J.P. and Davis had moved into the other room. She was itching to know what the lawyer had to say about Mr. French. Finally, the dishes were washed and she'd helped Ma make a batch of rolls to go with supper.

She walked into the main room and found J.P. and Davis in a discussion.

"That letter doesn't tell you any more than we all know," J.P. said.

"He won't commit to any information without meeting me." Davis ran a hand over his beard.

She'd learned that was his action when he was thinking.

"What did the lawyer say?" she asked, standing next to the chair where Davis sat.

"Not much." Davis's frustration came through in his words.

"Let me see the letter." She held out her hand.

Davis put the letter in her hand.

Mariella read what sounded like a lawyer just trying to get them to come see him so he could make them pay for his time. "He didn't answer a thing you asked."

"I know." Davis slapped his thighs with his hands. "We'll have to make a trip to Winnemucca and see him." He stood. "You were saying we need to lay in some more supplies. We could make the trip, just you and me."

Mariella hadn't been to Winnemucca since losing Hugh. She'd sent Jedidiah to get all the supplies. "I guess we could go."

"Your ma and Jedidiah can handle the children and the hands can take care of the cattle and chores." Davis put a hand on her arm. "We can call it our honeymoon."

She peered into Davis's eyes. The love shining in

his eyes, told her she'd be treated like a princess on the trip.

"I-I—"

"Say yes. It will be good for both of us to get away and talk to this lawyer."

"Okay, I'll go."

Davis grabbed her, lifting her off the ground, then kissing her. "I promise you'll be happy you went."

She laughed. "Put me down."

A throat cleared and she remembered J.P. was in the room. Davis set her on her feet but kept an arm around her waist as they turned to J.P.

"Ernestine will be delighted to hear how well you two are getting along." He raised an eyebrow.

Davis laughed. "You can tell my sister she did a fine job of match making."

"I will. I best be going." J.P. walked toward the kitchen. "You two be careful on your trip and let me know when you get back and what you hear."

"We will," Davis said, still holding her around the waist.

J.P. disappeared. Mariella could hear him saying his goodbyes to Ma.

Davis faced her. "Can you be ready to leave tomorrow?"

"Tomorrow? This is fast. I need to make a list, pack clothes, and food for the four days it will take to get there." Her mind was reeling with all that she would need to do before they left.

"Pack the dress you wore to the social. I plan to take you to a nice dinner while we're there." Davis sat down at the desk.

"What are you doing?" She glanced down at the paper he had a pen poised over.

"Writing down our concerns about Mr. French and his fences. I want to be able to put this list in the lawyer's hands and have him tell me what is legal and what isn't."

She shook her head. He only had a list to make. She had to pack clothing and food and give Jedidiah orders. Mariella huffed and walked into the kitchen.

"What's wrong?" Ma asked.

"Davis has decided he and I are headed to Winnemucca tomorrow." She stared at Ma. "I can't get clothes and food packed and get Jedidiah straightened out with what needs done in half a day."

"Did you tell him that?" Ma asked.

"No. He's too excited about us taking this trip together and seeing the lawyer about Mr. French." She poured a cup of coffee. "I'll need your list of food supplies we need. I'm heading out to the barn to see what we need out there."

Ma grasped her arm. "This will be a good trip for the two of you. You've never had time to really get to know one another."

"I know. I just feel overwhelmed with the short notice." Mariella was warming to the idea of spending over a week with Davis.

"You take care of Jedidiah and your clothes and I'll take care of the food." Ma hugged her. "Enjoy yourself. You haven't had a carefree time in two years."

"Thank you, Ma." Mariella exited the kitchen in search of Jedidiah. She found him in the barn showing Skip the tack that needed repaired.

"This saddle has some stitching coming loose and this headstall needs this piece replaced." Jedidiah handed the tack to Skip.

Mariella noticed the headstall and saddle were her father's. She'd forgotten about the pieces. "Where did you find those?" she asked, walking up beside Jedidiah.

"Been holding it for Zach. Once Davis gets that red roan ready, he'll need his own saddle."

Mariella's chest ached with gratitude for the older man. "Thank you, Jedidiah." She sniffed and hugged him.

"Don't go getting me wet," he said, slipping out of her embrace.

She shook off the emotion that had bubbled up and shifted her attention to Skip. "You know how to do leatherwork?" she asked.

He nodded.

"I appreciate you taking this on. Thanks." She smiled.

Skip ducked his head and his cheeks reddened.

"Jedidiah, Davis and I are going to Winnemucca tomorrow." She led him over to the feed room.

"Kind of a quick decision. This have anything to do with that letter Mr. Mulligan brought?" Jedidiah followed her into the room.

"Yes. Davis wants to talk to the lawyer about Mr. French fencing land he doesn't own. And we do need supplies." She made a mental note to get five more sacks of oats. "Do we need any more rope or wire?"

"Wouldn't hurt to get some wire and more rope now that we have some hands. Also need more coffee for the bunkhouse." Jedidiah put a hand on her arm.

"Don't worry about anything while you're gone. These new boys are good. They know cattle and know how to work. We'll be fine."

"I know you will. With you in charge of the hands and Ma with the children, I won't have anything to worry about." Mariella left the feed room. "I have a list to make. See you at supper."

She returned to the house and sat down at the kitchen table with a paper and pencil. She listed the ranch items they needed to pick up and then had Ma tell her what was needed for the house. "Anything you want me to get for you?" Mariella asked Ma.

"I need more tooth powder and would like several yards of a blue calico to make a new dress." Ma's cheeks flushed.

"You deserve a new dress, Ma. I'll get you something pretty." Mariella tapped her chin with the pencil. "You think Lizzie would like something pretty?"

"Yes. And Zach said something the other day about he'd like a new hat. His is getting too small for his head and doesn't stay on when the wind blows."

Mariella added a hat for Zach to the list. "I'll measure his head tonight."

Davis walked into the room. "I set out the clothes I'd like to take on the chair in the bedroom." He crossed the room and placed his hands on Mariella's shoulders as he leaned over and read her list.

"Looks like we'll be busy when we get to Winnemucca." He kissed her temple. "I'm going out to check on the wagon. Make sure the wheels are greased and everything is in shape for the trip." Davis squeezed her shoulders and walked to the door.

"You couldn't have found a more conscientious husband," Ma said, nodding toward the door.

"Yes, I have to admit, Ernestine knew what she was doing when she suggested we marry." Mariella folded the paper and headed to the bedroom to put their clothes in a satchel.

Chapter Twenty-five

Davis glanced sideways at Mariella. He didn't mind she'd dressed for the trip in trousers and a blouse. He knew she'd packed two dresses in the satchel. One for day and one for their dinner. The past three days and nights, they'd talked, sat in companionable silence, and made love under the stars.

Today they'd pull into Winnemucca. He was excited to show Mariella the better things in life.

They traveled along the river for several hours before seeing the buildings of Winnemucca.

Mariella sat straighter and stared ahead. "It looks larger than the last time I was here."

"When was that?"

"Three maybe four years ago." She glanced his way. "Hugh wanted me to stay home with Zach and not be gone for more than a couple of days."

From things Mariella said on this trip and before about her dead husband, he was beginning to think the man was controlling and wondered how such a strong-minded woman had tolerated it.

"Your ma knows how to care for the children and it's good for a mother to get away now and then." He thought a minute. "I think after we hay, we should have Jedidiah bring your ma to Winnemucca. Give her a break from all she does for us. What do you think of that?"

Mariella's eyes filled with tears and she flung her arms around him. Davis didn't mind, he enjoyed when Mariella showed her softer, woman side.

"That's a wonderful idea. She hasn't had time to herself since she and Pa moved to the ranch."

Davis kissed her temple. "Then we'll make sure it happens."

The railroad tracks followed the river down into Winnemucca and out the other side. Davis maneuvered the wagon into the busy streets.

"Which way to a hotel?" he asked.

"Hotel?"

"Yes. I plan to treat you to a hotel stay." Davis picked up her hand and kissed it. "I plan to show you new things."

Her cheeks reddened and her eyes sparkled. "I like how you treat me special."

"That's because you are." Davis scanned the streets and spied the Grand Hotel. The regal front and two story building appeared to be a nice hotel. He reined the horses to the front of the building.

Mariella scanned the front and tipped her head back to look at the second floor windows. A balcony ran across the second floor with doors opening onto it. "This is too expensive," she said.

"Let me treat you. I'll use money from the sale of my business, not Bar S money." Davis grasped her hands. "Let me do this for you."

She peered into his eyes. The softening of her golden brown orbs told him she wanted to be pampered.

He hopped down from the wagon and raised his hands to Mariella. In the weeks since they'd first met, his desire to make her happy had grown. He wanted her to trust him completely and be proud of him.

She slid to the edge of the seat and dropped into his arms. Davis held Mariella close for two heart beats, before releasing her and grabbing their satchel out of the back. He extended his elbow to her and she slid her hand through the crook of his arm.

The hotel had fancy trappings and a dapper looking man with a mustache behind the registration desk.

Davis marched up to the desk. "Mr. and Mrs. Weston. We'd like a room with a balcony and a bathing tub brought up and filled."

The man's gaze took him in briefly and scanned the length of Mariella. Davis knew when she wore the trousers it accentuated her hips, and when she wore a woman's blouse, like she was today, it accentuated her other attributes.

"Will finding us a room be a problem?" Davis asked, bringing the man's attention back to him.

"No. No, sir." The clerk spun a large black book around on the desk. "Sign here." He dabbed a quill in ink and handed the pen to Davis.

After signing their names, Davis exchanged the pen for the key to room 105.

"I'll send the Chinaman up with a tub and water right away." The clerk smiled at Mariella.

Davis tucked her hand in the crook of his arm and led her up the stairs.

"You're being rude," she whispered in his ear.

"That's because he's being rude by staring at you." Jealousy and anger roiled in Davis's gut. He'd never felt jealous about Sarah. But she didn't dress in distracting clothes or catch the attention of men. With her tall stature and curves, Mariella caught mens attention without trying.

"I've learned to ignore it when men stare at me. Most of them are eye level so it's easier for them to stare there than look up."

Davis stopped at the top of the stairs and spun her in front of him. "No. It isn't right for them, no matter their size, to stare at your chest, or your backside. You deserve respect." Staring into her eyes, he could tell she didn't understand how disrespectful the men were being.

He continued down the hall to their room. Unlocking the door, he pulled her inside and pushed the door shut with his foot. Davis set the satchel on the chair inside the door and captured, Mariella's face in his hands.

"When men stare at your body, they aren't respecting your mind. They only think of you as a conquest."

Her eyes searched his, but he could still see she didn't understand. He'd noticed her mother never said anything when a male was caught staring at Mariella. Had her father allowed men to ogle his daughter? He shook his head.

"Mariella, you are beautiful inside and out. A man doesn't need to gawk at your body to see the beauty inside. They need to look into your eyes and see your heart."

Her eyes softened the way he enjoyed. But he wasn't going to kiss her, even though his lips ached to make contact. He had to make her see she should stand up for herself.

"When a man is staring at your bosoms and not into your eyes, you should call him on it."

"Pa told me to just ignore it. That it wasn't worth making an enemy." Her brow wrinkled as she concentrated on the conflicting information.

"If some man is staring at your body, he is an enemy. Have you caught Jedidiah staring at you? Or J.P.? Or even our new hands? They all respect you and don't stare at you." He rubbed his thumbs at the corner of her wide, soft lips. "I respect you and want you to stand up for yourself."

"The next time a man is staring at your body, do you think you could say something to get their minds back on how smart you are?"

She nodded even as her eyes locked onto his lips.

Davis pressed his lips to hers. He kissed her open-mouthed as he'd learned lately was the way to quickly light her fire.

Two knocks on the door made him ease out of the kiss and lower her to the bed.

He opened the door.

A small Chinese man stood at the door with a long deep bath tub. "You bath?"

"Yes. In here please."

Mariella sat on the bed staring at the large metal bath tub the small man dragged into the room. She'd never had a bath in a tub she could sit in and stretch out her legs. All they had at the ranch was a round tub that she couldn't even sit in. She usually knelt and had ma pour water over her.

Davis directed the man to put the tub in the only space large enough. The spot happened to be in the corner near the window and balcony door.

The little man left, but Davis left the door open.

"He'll be back with buckets of hot water to fill the tub. I'm going to take the horses and wagon to the livery." He leaned, kissing her cheek. "I'll be back as quick as I can. Don't get in the tub until I get back."

Davis disappeared through the open door. The Chinese man appeared carrying two steaming buckets. He smiled, nodded, and poured the buckets into the tub before leaving again.

Mariella stood and unpacked her dresses from the satchel. She shook them and hung them from pegs on the wall. She also hung up Davis's nice suit.

The Chinese man returned ten times with steaming buckets. "Last," he said, setting the last two buckets on the floor beside the tub.

Davis hurried through the door. He handed a coin to the Chinese man and thanked him, shutting the door behind the little man.

"What's that in your hands?" Mariella asked, noticing the small package in Davis's hands.

He grinned and walked over to her. "For you."

She unwrapped the package. A bar of flowery soap and liquid in a bottle that said hair soap lay in the brown paper.

"I thought since you were having a nice bath you should have nice things to go with it." Davis tossed his derby to the chair and started unbuttoning his vest.

Two knocks at the door caused him to frown. He went to the door, conversed, and shut the door. He turned from the door with towels in his hands.

Mariella stood in the same place staring at him. He planned to take a bath with her. That was evident by his unbuttoning his vest. Her cheeks heated and her body quivered. It was one thing to be naked when they were bedding and getting dressed. This. This was a whole different kind of intimacy.

"Don't stand there. Get undressed." He shucked out of his shirt and undershirt, standing by the bathing tub in low riding trousers, suspenders draping at his hips.

Her gaze traveled across his flat stomach, following the sprinkling of brown curly hair on his chest. It was a wide, strong looking chest. How many times had she seen her frail daughter cradled against that chest? Each time she witnessed his gentleness with her daughter, Mariella's heart soaked in more love.

"We both won't fit in that tub," she said. "You go first."

He shook his head and took the soap and hair soap

from her hands, setting them on the floor by the tub. "You are going first and I'm going to help you with your hair." He pulled the tie on the end of her braid off and ran his hands through her curls.

His fingers eased the braid loose before unfastening the row of buttons on her blouse.

Mariella stood mesmerized by his methodical work. Once the buttons were loose, he slid the blouse down her arms. Then he unbuttoned her trousers and slid them down her legs. Davis grabbed her right foot and pulled off the boot. Then her left. When she no longer wore boots, he relieved her legs of the trousers, drawers, and stockings. She sat on the edge of the bed with only her corset and chemise.

Davis put both hands on either side of her on the bed and leaned down, kissing her open-mouthed, tangling their tongues, and sending heat through her body. Pulling out of the kiss, his eyes danced with good humor. His fingers unhooked her corset, adding it to the pile of clothes at the foot of the bed. Last he drew her chemise over her head.

He held out a hand to her. She took it and he led her over to the bathing tub.

"Step in," he said, still holding her hand.

Mariella stepped into the tub and eased down into the long metal vessel. Having hot water encompass most of her body was a wonderful feeling. She bent her knees and slid down, covering her body as far as she could. "This is wonderful," she whispered.

"Scoot forward and I'll pour some water on your hair."

Davis's husky tone made her look into his eyes.

The heat swirling in his gray eyes made her wish he was in the bathing tub with her.

She slid down more, holding her upper body on her forearms and tipping her head back, so her hair dangled in the water. Water splashed over her head and she closed her eyes. Hands gently massaged her head and worked her hair. More water poured over her head.

"You can sit up now," Davis said.

She slid up, sitting on her backside. Davis dunked the soap into the water and started rubbing the bar all over her body, massaging and cleaning every inch of her. His touch had her breathing rapidly and her body quaking with need.

"You're clean," he said, after driving her crazy massaging her feet. "Stand up."

She put her hands on either side of the tub and pushed up. Davis grasped her hand as she stood and steadied her as she stepped out of the tub. He wrapped a towel around her and peered into her eyes.

Placing her hands on his shoulders she leaned into him, initiating the kiss. Something she hadn't done before. The heady feeling of taking charge surged through her and she mimicked the kisses he'd bestowed on her. Opening her mouth and darting her tongue into his mouth.

Davis groaned, wrapped his arms around her, and kissed her until her knees were weak. His arms loosened their hold and he peered into her eyes. "My turn."

Mariella nodded and stepped back, looking for the satchel.

"Oh no. I washed you, you are going to wash me,"

he said, shucking his drawers down off his feet and stepping into the tub.

She shoved the wet strands of hair out of her face to get a better look at his naked body. His need for her was evident in the way his member stood out in the water.

"Do you want your hair washed with this soap, too?" she asked, picking up the bottle of liquid soap.

"If that's what you want to do," he said, dunking his head under the water.

When he came up, she dolloped a blob on his head and massaged. While having him massage and scrub her hair had started warm feelings in her body, doing the same for him warmed her heart with a feeling much like she had when helping her children. She poured water over his head to rinse and then started scrubbing his back, chest, and the area of a man only a wife can touch. And touch she did. With soap slick hands she grasped the member with her hands and slid them up and down the shaft. Davis moaned and raised his hips.

Startled, she glanced at his face. A smile tipped his lips and his eyes were closed. She rinsed the soap from the member and ran her hands down his muscular thighs and calves, finishing with his feet.

"I'm done," she said, watching Davis.

His gaze held hers for several moments before he shoved to stand in the tub. She handed him a towel when he stepped out.

"You know, we are missing an opportunity," he said, stepping close and wrapping his arms around her.

"We are? What kind of opportunity?" She didn't know what he was talking about.

"We both are naked and there's a big bed sitting right there." He tipped his head toward the bed.

She smiled, liking his way of thinking. "It would be a shame to miss this opportunity."

Davis covered her mouth with his, deepening the kiss, and moving them to the bed. They both fell across the mattress, still kissing and hands roaming to touch and feel every inch of naked flesh.

Chapter Twenty-six

Davis whistled as he climbed the stairs to the hotel room. After a romp in the bed, they'd dressed and had a wonderful dinner in the hotel restaurant before returning to the room and taking their intimacy to an even lengthier level. He'd never dreamed a wife could want him with the eagerness Mariella did. He'd hold his seed as long as he could to give her the most pleasure. Once she exploded around him, he couldn't hold it any longer. When he thought he was through for the night, she'd kiss him and run her hands over him until he'd be rigid and ready for more. And her body. He'd never tasted anything so intoxicating. They'd torn up the sheets three times last night.

When he woke, Mariella had her arms and one leg wrapped around him. He'd been tempted to wake her and go another round, but she'd looked so peaceful, he'd slipped out.

He balanced the tray of food in one hand as he unlocked the door with his other. Pushing the door open, he stopped and stared.

Mariella sat in the middle of the bed, the covers pooled around her waist, her large bosoms in full view for him to see. He kicked the door closed, walked to the bed, and placed the tray on the table.

"Good morning," he said, leaning down and kissing her luscious lips.

She kissed him back, wrapping an arm around his neck. His body fell to the bed, covering her.

"Why did you sneak out this morning?" she asked when he came up for air.

"You looked so peaceful, I wanted you to get plenty of sleep." He kissed the bosoms bulging up from his weight on them.

Mariella giggled. "More sleep so we can have more fun tonight?"

Davis glanced up and raised an eyebrow. "Woman, if we have more fun than last night, you may need a new husband."

She giggled again. "You seemed to keep up just fine."

"I enjoy it when you are bold." He captured her lips, kissing her with the passion they'd shared the night before.

Her body moved, wiggling and pressing against his growing shaft. They had too much to do today to spend the day in bed. He rolled to his feet.

Mariella's wonderful full bottom lip stuck out in a pout.

Davis groaned. He'd never wanted to kiss away a pout as badly as he did right now. He pivoted, marching to the pegs by the door and depositing his hat. "Get dressed. Then we'll eat, see the lawyer, and get our supplies. We'll head back first thing tomorrow morning."

When he faced the bed, Mariella stood in all her naked glory beside the bed. She ruffled her hair with her hands, tossing long locks forward to hide her breasts.

Need ripped through his body. He'd never witnessed a woman who flamed his body with desire before. His hands shook as he turned his attention to the people and traffic in the street.

He heard her dressing and didn't turn around until he heard the dishes on the tray clank.

Mariella sat on the side of the bed dressed in her nicest day dress, eating a piece of bread. With her dressed his mind could work as it should.

"Do you get all your supplies in one place or do we need to go to several?" he asked, picking up a plate with two eggs and a slice of ham.

"Feed at one spot and household supplies at another." Mariella pulled a slip of paper out of her pocket. "Here's the list."

Seeing the list he knew why the buckboard was needed to bring the supplies back.

"We'll see the lawyer then collect the horses and wagon and get our supplies," he said, dragging the chair over near the bed and sitting down.

***

Mr. O'Reilly, the lawyer, turned out to be more interested in keeping them in his office to collect a nice fee than actually helping them discover whether or not something could be done about Mr. French building fences to keep people out of property he didn't own.

"He was no help at all," Davis said, escorting Mariella down the street to the livery to collect the horses and wagon.

"He certainly talked a lot without saying anything that made sense," Mariella commented.

Davis stopped. He stared into Mariella's eyes. "That is true." He glanced up and down the street. "There has to be another lawyer in this town. Do you mind gathering the supplies while I see if I can find another one and talk with him?"

Mariella rubbed a hand up and down his arm. "We came here to talk to a lawyer and find out something. It would be a shame to go back without finding someone who can give us direction." She nodded. "Go. I'll get the supplies and meet you back at the hotel."

Davis kissed her Tucker. "Thank you. We do need to get some answers. I'll see you at the hotel."

Davis decided the best way to find out if there were more lawyers was to go to the courthouse. He found the building and entered. A man of average build, with shaggy blond hair and faded blue eyes behind round spectacles sat behind a desk.

"May I help you?" he asked.

"I'd like to know how many lawyers are in this town, their names, and where I can find them," Davis said.

The man looked him up and down. "You a lawyer looking for a town to settle in?"

"No. I'm a cattle rancher looking for some legal advice."

The man scoffed. "You don't look like a rancher."

Davis sighed. "I am. Could you give me the names and where I can find them?"

The man wrote down three names. One was the lawyer he'd already seen. The other two were not far from the courthouse.

"Thank you." Davis held the paper in his hand as he exited the courthouse. He spotted the streets he needed. Walking along, he noticed the streets were cleaner and better kept than the hotel street.

Several blocks from the courthouse he spotted the shingle for Alford Taylor, Lawyer. Davis walked into the small building. Two chairs and a small table crowded against one wall of a small room. A tall thin man walked out of an open door in the back of the room.

"May I help you?" he asked, extending his hand.

"If you're Mr. Taylor. That's who I'm looking for." Davis clasped the man's hand. "I'm Davis Weston of the Blitzen Valley."

"Mr. Weston, come into my office. I am indeed, Mr. Taylor."

The man's office was lined with bookshelves filled with books and a large desk that took up most of the room.

"Have a seat." Mr. Taylor sat behind the desk and picked up a pencil. "Why are you seeking a lawyer?"

"About two hundred miles from here in the Blitzen and Harney Valleys there is a cattle baron who has been fencing off land that isn't his. We, the smaller ranchers and homesteaders of those valleys, wonder if there is any legal action we can take against him."

Mr. Taylor leaned back in his chair. "Tell me more about this fencing."

Davis told him how Peter French was building miles of fence starting on his property and running the fence to another property he owned and fencing in everything in between. Even fencing people from their own land.

"I don't understand how he can legally keep the people from land he doesn't own," Davis said.

"He can't. It does sound like you have cause to bring actions against him." Taylor leaned over his desk. "I can't help you with this as I am a Nevada lawyer, but I do know a lawyer in Canyon City who can be of service to you. They'll need to know the names of the people he's fencing out and the acreage that he is not allowing people to homestead."

"I can get the information written up," Davis said, wishing he'd gone to Canyon City rather than Winnemucca.

"Fine. I'll send a post to William Hachett, the lawyer in Canyon City. He'll know we spoke and help you."

"Thank you. I appreciate your help." Davis shook hands with the man and left the office.

Wandering back toward the hotel to see if Mariella had finished purchasing the supplies, he saw a livery that sold buggies.

***

Mariella sat beside Davis on the wagon. The back was full of the supplies. Their time together at the hotel had been wonderful. She'd never felt so cherished. What she and Davis had shared had deepened her emotions for him and showed her there was more to a man and woman coming together than what she'd experienced before.

She could sense Davis had experienced the same. However, he'd been quiet since leaving Winnemucca three days ago.

"Are you still worrying over what the lawyer told you?" Mariella asked.

"Yes, and other things." Davis stared forward not looking at her.

"What other things?" She slid her arm through his and waited.

He pulled out his pipe, stuffed tobacco in the bowl, and pulled out a match, lighting the pipe.

Mariella inhaled the sweet scent. She'd become fond the scent that lingered in Davis's clothing and beard. However, she knew right now he was using it to stall his reply. Knowing that made her uneasy. What could he have to say that made him hesitant?

He glanced her way. "We're going to have to round up the other folks who wanted to fight Mr. French and collect some money. We're going to need funds to pay a lawyer. We can't afford to pay for it all."

She stared at him. "I agree. We aren't the only people Mr. French is blocking from their land or pushing out. We can send Jedidiah around to invite the folks who spoke up at the social to come and we'll discuss it with them."

Davis nodded. "But not everyone will be able to contribute the same amount, I fear." He studied her. "I've found when people start talking money they are either too prideful to say they can't afford to pay or they refuse to pay their share. I've been trying to figure out a way to consider everyone's circumstance." He shook his head. "And so far I can't figure it out."

Mariella hugged his arm. "Maybe we need to ask them and see what they think is best."

"I just thought if I could have something already figured out it would be easier than wasting time with several people talking it over."

She saw the reasoning behind that. "True, but if you don't give them their say, they may think you are as bad as Mr. French."

Davis stared at her. "Do you think I'm as bad as Mr. French?"

The sadness in his eyes made her heart ache. "No! Never. I'm just saying if you push people into doing things, they'll think of you like they do Mr. French who has been pushing them around since he arrived in Blitzen and the Harney Valley. She kissed Davis's cheek above his beard. "You are nothing like Mr. French."

Davis turned his head and captured her lips, kissing her. "Thank you. I thought maybe you were thinking I was getting too bossy."

"No. I like when you tell me what to do when we're in bed." Her cheeks and woman parts heated thinking of the things he'd directed her to do their last night in Winnemucca. She'd never have dreamed the things they did, could be so arousing.

"But you prefer I don't boss you around during the day." His eyes gleamed with mischief.

"Yes, unless we're in bed during the day."

Davis laughed and grasped her behind the neck, pulling her face close to his. "You are a wicked woman, Mrs. Weston." He kissed her open-mouthed, tangling their tongues, until her body melted against his.

He drew out of the kiss but kept his arm around her waist, holding her close. "Don't you tell Ernestine, but I'd planned to come here and become your husband in name only." He kissed her temple. "But the moment I walked into her house and saw you, I had a feeling my plan wasn't going to stick."

Mariella sat up and studied him. "Why a marriage in name only?"

Davis stared down the road. "I didn't want to have another family ripped from me. I figured if I stayed detached, whatever happened couldn't hurt as much as the last time."

She rubbed a hand up and down his back. "Nothing is going to happen to us. We're strong."

What would he think if she told him her fear of something happening to him?

Chapter Twenty-seven

Jedidiah returned from spreading the word about the meeting to form a committee to seek justice for homesteaders.

Davis walked over to the barn as Jedidiah dismounted. "Were you able to talk to each family?"

"Yes. They'll all be here tomorrow afternoon." Jedidiah led his horse into the barn.

"You told them families were welcome?" That had been Mariella's stipulation. There was no reason the children couldn't play while the parents conducted business.

"Yes, most asked if they should bring something. I told them no." Jedidiah stopped. "You really think a handful of homesteaders can do something to stop Mr. French?"

Davis had asked himself the same thing many times. "We aren't going to know if we don't try."

Jedidiah nodded. "That's true."

Mariella and Len were sharpening the sickle blades on the hay reaper. Davis shook his head. He was surprised each day by the things his wife knew. She was instructing Len, who said he was willing to learn how to do it. Skip and Abe tended to prefer working with the cattle but would help when it came time to hay.

Davis stood out of sight watching Mariella instruct the ranch hand.

"Hold the stone like this. It gives the best edge to the blade." She made a downward stroke along one of the blades. The high pitch of the stone sliding across the blade signaled she was making progress. "Slide the length of the stone down the blade, then move a bit farther down the point of the blade until you've sharpened both sides of a blade," she said above the shrill sound of her work.

Davis smiled and pivoted. He had things to do as well, like write up the agenda for the meeting tomorrow. Back in the house, he found Lizzie playing with the new porcelain doll they'd bought for her in Winnemucca.

"Do you like your new doll?" Davis asked, crouching next to her.

"She's bootiful." Lizzie hugged the doll tight.

Davis's heart squeezed with happiness. This fragile child had become important to him. He'd fallen in love with the entire family and he'd be damned if he'd let anything take them away from him. He'd lived an honorable, thrifty, unselfish life. Losing this second family would tear him apart.

He kissed Lizzie's blonde curls and stood. The meeting tomorrow had to lift the threat on their ranch and many others.

***

Mariella decided to dress like the other women who would be present today for Davis's meeting. She had on her good dress and had wrapped her hair in a bun. Davis had commented on how pretty she looked and patted her bottom as she walked out of their bedroom. Her heart sung with happiness. She couldn't remember ever being this happy. She'd had a good life with Hugh, but he'd never complimented her or asked her opinion or even discussed things with her that weren't cattle related. She enjoyed the talks she and Davis had in the evenings about everything other than cattle. And she enjoyed the pleasure he gave her in the bedroom. If she were to die today, she would go with a happy, happy heart.

She and Ma had roast beef and a ham to serve cold today along with bread, jam, and pies. The families attending the meeting were all friends, except for the Farleys. They were a new family who'd homesteaded land inside Mr. French's fences. According to Jedidiah, Mr. French's hired hands had been harassing them.

Davis had read the agenda for the meeting to her last night. She loved how his logical mind had put things in a list. All the points were necessary to know from each of the families.

The jangling of harnesses and Zach shouting, told

her the first of their visitors had arrived.

Mariella wiped her hands on her apron and untied the garment, peeling it from her body and draping it over a chair. She walked into the main room and crossed to the door as Davis opened it.

Ernestine and J.P. walked to the house as Skip led their horse and wagon to the barn.

"It's good to see you two," Ernestine said, giving them both hugs.

J.P. and Davis shook hands.

Mariella wrapped an arm around Ernestine leading her into the house. "I wish we were getting together for a better reason, but I'm glad you're here."

Ernestine stopped and peered into her face. Her friends eyes lit up and her lips spread into a wide grin. "You and Davis must be getting along even better than at the social."

Mariella glanced at her husband. He winked and grinned. Her heart thumped so hard in her chest she thought everyone must be able to hear it. "We make one another happy," she said.

"That's wonderful!" Ernestine hugged her again, smiled at Davis, and turned to J.P. "Didn't I tell you they would be good together?"

J.P. nodded. "That's all you talked about once you got the notion."

The sound of more people arriving put a halt to the family conversation. They ushered in four more families, including the Farleys.

"Now that we're all here and the children are busy playing, I think we should get down to why I asked you all here." Davis stood in front of the fire place. They'd brought in the chairs from the kitchen, giving every wife a place to sit with their husband standing behind them. Except for Mariella who sat to the side of Davis. She noted a couple of the women had bored expressions on their faces. Their gazes slid over the furnishings and corners of the room.

"We are all having troubles with Mr. French and his ranch hands. He's either blocked us from our property with his fences or has told us our property is his because it is within his fences when he hasn't properly filed the papers." Davis peered at each family. "I visited a lawyer in Winnemucca when Mrs. Weston and I traveled there for supplies." His gaze rested on her a moment.

She could tell by the gleam in his eyes, his thoughts had strayed to their nights in the hotel.

He continued, "The first lawyer was of no help, but the second one said we had legal means to do something. He gave me the name of a lawyer in Canyon City. We need a lawyer from our own state. He has sent a letter of introduction to this other lawyer, stating what he felt we needed. My plan is to go to that lawyer after I have each one of your claims written down."

Mariella noticed the men were paying close attention and nodding.

"But we, the Bar S Ranch, can't pay for all the legal costs. We also need to decide how each family can contribute to the legal funds."

This started a rumble of voices.

"We shouldn't have to pay. Why don't we all just go confront French?" Mr. Gorely demanded.

Davis held up his hands. "Because that is a good

way to either get killed or let him know we have a plan."

"I don't have a problem helping pay for a lawyer if it will get French to leave us alone," Mr. Farley said.

"I agree," J.P., Ralph Emmet, and Jim Smith said.

"Mr. Gorely, do you agree to help pay for a lawyer?" Davis asked.

Mariella studied the man then scanned the wives. Only Ernestine, Mrs. Farley, and Mrs. Smith appeared interested in the conversation.

"I don't have much I can put into a pot to pay a lawyer. I've stretched myself to get the supplies we need for planting," Mr. Gorely said, not looking at anyone in particular.

Mariella glanced at Davis. She'd seen him scribbling on paper for several hours yesterday.

"I've calculated the lowest amount we can start with having discovered the price lawyers ask to help." Davis handed a piece of paper to each of the men.

J.P. and Mr. Smith nodded. Gorely, Ralph Emmet, and Mr. Farley all frowned. Mariella had a feeling these men were stretched as far as their pocketbooks could go.

"This would be enough to get the lawyer to look into laws and get a letter written up and sent to Mr. French." Davis shook the paper he held. "We may not need to put in more than this."

"What if that pint-sized jack-n-apes gets his own lawyer?" Mr. Gorely asked.

"Then we will need to come up with funds to counter." Davis studied Mr. Gorely. "If a family can't come up with the funds, you can pay with a steer or hog." His gaze scanned the families. "Or whatever you can spare that would cover your share."

Mr. Emmet and Mr. Farley nodded. Gorely was still grousing.

Mariella decided it was time she said something. "I know paying money to someone to keep our own land seems unjust, but we can't have anyone harmed. Going through the law is the only way we all remain safe and get our land." The women all nodded. The men watched their women.

She and Davis had discussed how they had to make everyone understand this was the best way to keep people from getting hurt. Everyone knew of Mr. French's temper. At several socials the women had discussed fearing for their husbands when he ranted about talking to Mr. French. Men felt the need to confront problems head on. Over the years, she'd learned a little quiet shifting of ideas from her to her husband could keep him safe and make him think it was all his idea.

"I think we could spare a beef or milk cow to pay our portion," Mrs. Smith said.

Mrs. Gorely eyed her husband shyly and said. "I've some preserves and could sew for you."

"No wife of mine is going to pay for my family's well-being." Mr. Gorely shifted his body to hide his wife. "I'll bring hay when I cut this summer."

Davis nodded. "Mariella, is all this acceptable to you?"

She peered up into Davis's eyes. "Yes. Mr. Gorely bringing hay and the Smith family will provide a beef or milk cow to match their portion of the lawyer fees."

"Why don't you show our guests to the kitchen and the food you and your mother prepared? Gentlemen, I'd like you to sit with me one at a time and tell me your grievances against Mr. French. I'll write those up and the contracts to pay for the lawyer."

Everyone started filing into the kitchen.

"Mr. Emmet, I'll start with you, if you don't mind." Davis sat at the desk and motioned for Mr. Emmet to pull up a chair next to him.

Mariella led the rest into the kitchen. The children were already grabbing food and running out the back door. Ma stood by the table, greeting each person who entered.

Ernestine locked her arm through Mariella's and led her to the back door and out into the brilliant June sunshine.

"Tell me more about your trip to Winnemucca." The sparkle in the woman's eyes crept heat up Mariella's neck, blooming in her cheeks.

"There's nothing to tell. Davis talked to lawyers and I picked up supplies." Mariella glanced over her shoulder. "I should get back to our guests."

"Your mother can handle the guests. You are glowing. Have you and Davis consummated the marriage?"

Thinking of all the ways Davis pleasured her and how many times he'd spilled his seed, her lips curved into a smile.

"You have!" Ernestine hugged her. "I'm so happy for both of you."

Mariella hugged her friend then stepped back. "He makes me feel special. I've never felt that before. Pa always said nice things and complimented me, but Davis makes me feel…" Cherished and loved. The thought hit her and she stared at her friend not really seeing her. Loved. Does he love me?

"What's the matter? You look stunned." Ernestine grasped her arm.

"Nothing. I really need to get back in there." Mariella shifted out of her friend's grasp and headed in the back door. Tonight she needed to have a talk with Davis. To see if he loved her. She'd been holding back her feelings, thinking she was being disloyal to Hugh, but her heart had never been lighter or happier.

Mr. Emmet was now in the kitchen and Mr. Farley was missing. Mariella moved about, visiting with each couple, reassuring them this was the best way to keep their land.

Mr. Farley returned and Mr. Smith went to talk with Davis. She noticed as each man returned Mr. Gorely became more uneasy. What didn't he want to talk about? Was he spouting against Mr. French when he didn't have a claim to spout about?

When Mr. Gorely left the room, she walked over to J.P. "Is there a reason, Mr. Gorely is so sore about Mr. French? I mean more than claiming his land?"

J.P. cast a glance toward Mrs. Gorely who was visiting with Ma. "I'm not sure he's fully claimed his land. It's down in the marsh that French has a lot of claims on. I've heard French has offered Gorely a lot of money. Most think he's holding out for more. It might not be in his best interest to sic a lawyer after Mr. French." J.P. picked up a slice of ham. "I doubt you'll see that hay he offered."

Mariella understood they'd see no compensation for Mr. Gorely's portion of the lawyer fees. And most likely the man would back out of the petition. He was wasting Davis's time. She spun to head into the main room and put a stop to Davis helping the man.

Davis entered the kitchen. He walked straight to Mrs. Gorely and spoke quietly to her. The woman's eyes widened and she scurried out the kitchen door without so much as a good-bye.

Mariella strode over to Davis. "What was that about?"

"During my discussion with Mr. Gorely, I discovered he is getting ready to sell to Mr. French. I asked him to leave." Davis stared into Mariella's eyes and saw she already suspected the man of bailing. He turned her to the rest of the room and studied the rest of the men. He didn't want to put any more financial strains on these families. He'd already decided to use his savings to help pay for the lawyer.

"Mr. Gorely just informed me he plans to sell his claim to Mr. French next week. I asked him not to mention our plan, but from the look in his eyes, if French gets wind of this and asks, I have no doubt Mr. Gorely will give us up for a few dollars in his palm."

The other men started talking at once.

Davis raised his hand. "That's why, I'll finish writing the grievance up tonight and stop by each of your homes tomorrow for your signatures on my way to Canyon City."

Mariella opened her mouth to speak and for the first time in their marriage, he talked over whatever she was about to say.

"The sooner we can get this paper in the hands of a lawyer the better. Mariella and the hands can tend to the ranch while I carry this letter to the proper authorities."

The men all nodded and agreed. Each one shook his hand and took their leave.

Davis could tell Mariella wasn't happy with him. She went to work helping her mother clean up the food and barely said good-bye to Ernestine when she and J.P. left.

She had something she wanted to say, in private, but he had a grievance to get written. Davis exited the kitchen and went straight to the desk. Each man had given him the information he needed for the lawyer.

The kitchen door banged open, and Mariella stalked across the room toward him.

"I don't have time for you to give me what-for," Davis said, hoping to deflect her from laying into him.

"You better make time for me, your wife." She stopped beside the desk and stared down at the paperwork covering the top.

"Mariella, this—" he waved his arm over the papers "—has to be done. We need to get the information to a lawyer before French finds out."

"How do you know he doesn't already know? What if he has someone waiting for you? He could have asked a hired hand to take that from you however he wants."

Her large, worried eyes belied the anger in her words.

He stood, pulling her into his arms. She was worried something would happen to him like with her first husband. "I'll be fine. I'm taking Jedidiah with me to show me the way. We'll ride horses so we can travel faster." He rubbed his hands up and down her back. He'd miss sleeping beside her. These days he counted the minutes until the sun went down and they could snuggle together in their big bed.

Chapter Twenty-eight

Mariella kept busy the last four days, falling into bed so exhausted she didn't miss Davis until morning when she tried to snuggle and there wasn't a warm, male body. It brought back memories of the first months after Hugh's death. She'd ached for arms to hold her and someone to help with the ranch. Now she ached for the smell of Davis's tobacco, his strong arms, and calming voice. Even though he was only on a trip to Canyon City, missing him ached more than losing Hugh.

Today, she and the three ranch hands were headed to check on the herd. The thunder and lightning last night could have frightened them over the edge of the canyon wall, putting them on the Diamond Ranch land or if they stampeded up the canyon, they could be strung out along the top of the mountain range and mingling with French's cattle and Judge Ridley's cattle from Barren Valley.

She and Len took the north canyon wall while Skip and Abe took the south canyon wall. Mariella stared at the ground, checking for track to give her an idea if cattle had crossed over the rim. They'd worked their way half way up the canyon when she noticed multiple cattle tracks with horses trailing.

"Len!"

The ranch hand reined his horse around and trotted over. "Yeah?"

"Take a look at those tracks." She pointed to the ground.

Len dismounted and crouched, studying the hoof prints. "Looks like someone took off with about ten head, I'd say."

"Go get Skip and Abe. I'll follow the tracks." Mariella pressed her heels against Dash's ribs.

Len caught hold of her reins, halting the horse. "Mr. Weston wouldn't want you trailing after cattle rustlers by yourself. You get Abe and Skip. I'll follow the tracks."

Mariella glared down at the man. "I don't care what Mr. Weston would want. I'm the one here dealing with rustlers and I am your boss."

Len shook his head. "Yes, you're my boss, but I'm not allowing you to chase after rustlers by yourself." He nodded to the other canyon wall. "Let's both go get Abe and Skip. Then when we find the critters we can round them up and bring them back."

Mariella's anger wasn't really at Len. He made sense. It was at the boldness of rustlers to come on their land and take their cattle. But she didn't like wasting so much time going after Skip and Abe.

"Shoot your rifle in the air and see how long it takes Skip and Abe to get here."

Len grinned. "That would save time." He pulled his rifle from the scabbard and pointed it at an angle in the air. Two booms, one after the other, echoed through the canyon.

"That should bring them." Len replaced his rifle and walked over to a rock and sat. "You might as well get off and wait, too."

Mariella dismounted, but she couldn't sit still. Knowing her cattle were being driven farther away with each passing minute had her pacing the ridgeline.

Heaves, snorts, and the creak of leather announced the arrival of Skip and Abe thirty minutes later.

"What's wrong?" Abe asked as they pulled their horses to a stop beside Dash.

"Someone herded our cattle out of the canyon," Mariella mounted.

"R-rustlers?" Skip asked.

"Looks like. Come on." Mariella wasn't waiting any longer. There was no telling how much of a start they had. One thing was certain, they were most likely taking the cattle to the Diamond Ranch to change the brand.

***

Davis ignored the way Jedidiah's lips quirked into a smile as they trotted down the road toward Blitzen

Valley. The old ranch hand had ribbed him more than once about hurrying back to Mariella. He wouldn't admit it to the old man, but he did miss her. If anyone had told him a year ago, he'd miss a woman more than he missed Sarah, he would have punched them in the face. But he and Mariella had formed a connection he still didn't fathom but wanted to explore. It wasn't just his body missing her. He craved her smile, her laughter, and the way her colorful eyes could scorch him one minute and turn soft with desire the next.

Two miles beyond the road leading to the Diamond Ranch, he spotted a horse and rider running hell-bent toward them.

"W-weston! M-mr. Weston!"

"That's Skip." Jedidiah said, racing toward the rider.

Davis urged Poker into a lope to catch up with the two.

"Mrs….Len…Abe…trying…cattle…from…D-diamond Ranch." His young face was red and his eyes wide. "….hands…guns."

Davis didn't wait to hear any more. He dug his heels into Poker's sides and headed toward the ranch. The thundering hooves of two horses behind him said the others were following. He hadn't suspected the Diamond Ranch foreman to be so brazen. He had dozens of questions swirling in his head but all that mattered was keeping Mariella and the hands safe.

As he approached the ranch, he spotted cattle in the corral and Mariella, Len and Abe on horses with men holding them at gun point.

Without thought to his own safety, Davis charged

through the circle of men holding rifles and stopped beside Mariella. Her red face and narrowed eyes told him she wasn't backing down and would take a bullet rather than let the men have her cattle.

"What is this?" he asked, staring straight at the Diamond Ranch foreman.

"Your wife and hands are accusing us of stealing cattle." Tucker had his arms crossed and his feet spread wide.

Davis twisted in his saddle. He didn't even have to ask.

"Len and I found tracks of cattle herded over the canyon rim by horses. We called Abe and Skip over and followed the tracks. They stop here. At the corral." Mariella pointed to the cattle in the corral bawling and mulling around.

Davis dismounted. "Jedidiah, come with me. We'll inspect the cattle in the corral."

Tucker stepped forward. "You'll do no such thing. This is property of Mr. French. You can't go where you want."

"Fine. Skip, take my horse and ride to Canyon City and bring back the sheriff. We'll wait here to make sure these cattle don't disappear." Davis glanced up at Mariella. She smiled and dismounted.

"Abe ride to our ranch and bring back food and bedding for us. Let's see, Two days to Canyon City, two back. Better make it enough food for four days." Davis glanced around. "Len, we'll make camp over there." He pointed to a spot right beside the corral gate.

"Now see here, you can't squat on this land." Tucker put his hand on his revolver.

"We aren't squatting. We're waiting for the officials to get here and inspect the cattle in this corral." Davis looked up at Skip. "What are you doing still here? Go!"

Skip dismounted from his horse and started loosening the cinch on his horse. Jedidiah stepped up to Poker and started loosening his cinch.

"There's no need to bring in the law." Tucker waved a man forward. "Tell the Westons what you told me about the cattle in this corral."

Davis stared at the man. He was the same one with Tucker the day Davis and Zach spotted them on Bar S land.

"I was riding the rim during the storm and saw a herd of our cattle race up the canyon wall. I went after them even when they went into your land."

Mariella stepped forward. "Liar! There were three horses herding our cattle over the rim. There were no tracks coming from this side other than horses."

Len stepped beside Mariella. "I saw the same thing as Mrs. Weston. The cattle didn't come from this side."

"Mr. Tucker, if you don't allow us to take our cattle, Skip is ready to bring in the officials." Davis motioned for Skip to take off.

The young man leaped into the saddle and had Poker at a dead run in four strides.

"Get your cattle out of my corral," Tucker said.

Jedidiah shot his rifle in the air.

Skip sat Poker on his haunches and looked back.

Davis motioned for the rider to come back.

Jedidiah, Len, and Abe all mounted and headed to the corral.

Davis motioned for Mariella to help. He walked up to Tucker. "If you do something this stupid again, I won't hesitate to take matters into my own hands."

Since his saddle was on Skip's horse, Davis mounted and followed along behind the twelve head of cattle his wife and ranch hands were pushing out to the road.

He was glad Skip had found he and Jedidiah before things had taken a turn for the worse. Davis angled the horse up alongside Dash.

"Are you all right?" he asked, Mariella.

She nodded. "We shouldn't have let him get off so easy. We know he stole other cattle from us."

"No one was hurt and we have the cattle back. That's the main thing." Davis put a hand on her arm. He'd had a hard time refraining from touching her the minute his feet hit the ground. But he'd known she'd have hated him pulling her into his arms like she was fragile.

"But he shouldn't get away with it." Mariella glanced at him. Her eyes held a steely glint.

"He won't. I'll write up a complaint and send it to Mr. French. While the man is land hungry, I don't think he would condone his foreman stealing. Who knows, Tucker could be stealing cattle from French."

Mariella's eyes lit up. "Oh, that would put him down the road or possibly shot, knowing Mr. French's temper." She giggled. "I could live with that."

Davis grinned and shook his head. "No, you couldn't. You wouldn't wish a man dead."

"I know, but sitting there with all his ranch hands pointing rifles at us, I wished one of them would miss us and get him."

"I'm glad no one was hurt." Davis wasn't going to tell Mariella he'd threatened the man. It was out of his character, but he would not allow anyone to bring harm to his family. And if he had to go through with the threat to save them, so be it.

**

It was after dark when they drove the cattle through the two gates and up to the ranch buildings.

Davis rode next to Jedidiah. Mariella had ridden ahead of the herd to tell her mother what had happened and tell her they'd be late for supper.

"Push them past the buildings and then come in for supper," Davis told the foreman.

"Will do. Hep!" Jedidiah rode over to Len and he relayed the message to the others.

Davis rode to the barn, dismounted, and led Skip's horse in. He lit the lantern, hanging it from the hook on a beam. Loosening the cinch, he heard scurrying in the loose hay. The sounds continued as he rubbed down the horse and gave him a portion of grain.

His curiosity couldn't take it any longer. Davis walked over to the pile of loose hay and discovered a tri-colored puppy. The animal was playing with a knotted sock. A soup bone lay beside a folded up blanket. Clearly someone knew the puppy was here.

He grinned. Who was hiding this? Tomorrow was Mariella's birthday. It could be a gift from someone. Jedidiah? Her mother? He'd keep the person's secret. Davis patted his pocket. He'd picked up something for Mariella while in Canyon City in case the buggy he'd ordered didn't arrive tomorrow.

277

Davis put the horse out into the corral and headed to the back door to wash up and see his family. It had been a long five days. He'd missed each of them. Even Mariella's quiet mother. She allowed Mariella to be outside and do what she loved.

He stepped in the door and little arms circled his legs.

"Daddy!" Lizzie squealed.

"Did you miss me as much as I missed you?" he asked, pulling her up into his arms for a hug.

"Yes!" She kissed his cheeks and snuggled her head to his chest.

Davis peered at Mariella's smiling face. She'd not only come home and caught her mother up on what was happening, she'd cleaned up and put on a dress. The one he liked because it showed off her womanly curves.

Zach burst through the door from the main room. "You're back!" He hugged Davis around the waist.

Davis put an arm around the boy and felt his heart burst with pride and love. How different his life would be right now if Ernestine hadn't encouraged him to come west and help out a friend.

"This is indeed a warm welcome." Davis placed Lizzie in her high chair and patted Zach on the back. "Mrs. Simon, this meal smells delicious as always."

The older woman blushed and put another bowl on the table.

Mariella floated across the floor and wrapped her arms around his neck. "Welcome home."

One look in her eyes and he knew this night would be memorable. "Thank you. It's good to be back." He settled his lips on hers and kissed her as if he were a man lost in the desert without water. Her lips were his sustenance.

Stomping outside the door registered and he slowly drew out of the kiss. It was one thing to have the family watching them and another to have the hired help. He moved to Mariella's side and escorted her to her chair.

Jedidiah and the men entered, hanging their hats by the door and taking their seats on the chairs opposite the children and Mrs. Simon.

"Thank you for looking out for the herd today, and my wife," Davis said, leveling his gaze on each man and smiling.

The brothers mumbled something, and Len stared him square in the eye. "Mr. Weston, I don't envy you keeping her safe."

Jedidiah chuckled.

Davis shot his attention to Mariella. Her cheeks were as red as apples, and her gaze was narrowed on Len. It was obvious something happened today. But rather than bring it up at the table, Davis let it pass and started handing platters of food around.

When the men finished and excused themselves, Davis whisked Mariella out the kitchen door. He looped her hand through his arm and strolled toward the stream that trickled through the canyon.

Stopping at the rock that had become their evening spot, Davis sat and patted the hard surface next to him.

Mariella continued to stand, facing the stream.

"What happened today?" he asked.

"When Len and I found the tracks, I told him to go get Abe and Skip. I'd follow the tracks. He refused to let me go."

Davis stood and drew Mariella into his arms. "I'm glad you didn't charge off after the rustlers. There's no telling what could have happened to you. I'm giving Len a raise."

"He disobeyed my order." Mariella pushed against him but he kept his arms wrapped around her.

"For your safety." Davis kissed her temple. "Len is a good hand. He was right to keep you from harm, that's part of his job."

Mariella peered into his eyes. "Have you told the ranch hands they are to take care of me?"

Davis wasn't going to lie, but he also didn't want her to think someone was always watching out for her.

"When they signed on, I told them you were the cattle savvy owner of this ranch. That to keep their jobs, your safety was necessary."

She narrowed her eyes. "Len said you wouldn't like me following the rustlers."

"That's true. I would be worried for your safety." Davis touched his lips to hers in a brief kiss. "Mari, I couldn't live with myself if something happened to you or the children. I lived through that once, but if it happened again, to you, Zach or Lizzie, I wouldn't be able to start over again."

Mariella's eyes softened. Her arms wound around his neck. "I feel the same about you and the children."

Their lips met. He'd never had a woman admit this devotion to him. Deepening the kiss, tangling her tongue with his, he savored her taste, her lips, and her heart.

The scream of a mountain lion echoed in the valley.

Davis drew out of the kiss and whispered, "Let's continue our talk in our room."

"It's been empty without you," Mariella said, linking her hand with his.

He didn't think he'd ever been as happy as he was at this very minute. In all his years, nothing had prepared him for this complete bliss.

Chapter Twenty-nine

July fourth Davis found himself driving their new buggy to the P Ranch. Everyone in the two valleys had been invited to a Fourth of July celebration at the ranch. Mrs. Simon had packed two baskets of food to feed not only the family, but their ranch hands. The family rode in the two-seat buggy and the hands trailed along behind on their horses.

Pulling onto the main road, they fell in with the ranch hands from the Catlow Ranch headed to the P Ranch.

Davis grasped Mariella's hand and leaned close to her ear. "I don't want you going out of my sight. There's going to be a lot of lonely cowboys at this thing."

She faced him and grimaced. "I can't have you following me around." Her fingers played with the locket he'd given her for her birthday. They'd cut up photographs of the children placing each one's face in the locket halves.

He smiled thinking of Mariella's thank you. It was a short night of sleep and a long night of pleasuring one another.

"I won't follow you around. Just stay where I can see you. If you need to use the privy come get me. I'll escort you." He kissed her cheek. "I'm sure the other husbands will be just as vigilant."

Whining from the back seat was followed by Zach piping up, "Ma's puppy needs to get down."

Davis stopped the buggy and watched as Zach jumped out and then lifted his present to his mother out of the wagon. The two wandered around the sagebrush. Soon the boy was relieving himself on a bush and the puppy squat beside him.

Mariella laughed. "Zach went to a lot of trouble to get that puppy for me, but I have a sneaking suspicion it will be his dog."

Davis laughed. "I agree. He gave himself a gift. But every boy needs a dog. I can't believe the little imp planned it with Mr. Farley's son."

Mariella laughed. "True. He was scheming with another boy while all the adults were worrying about Mr. French."

She glanced over her shoulder. "Lizzie has the kitten and now Zach has a dog." Mariella hugged his arm. "And a wife needs a husband."

He flicked the reins and the horses continued down the road. The ranch hands from Catlow had long since passed them and were a small cloud of dust in the road ahead.

An hour later they pulled into P Ranch, the headquarters for all of Mr. French's holdings. Twenty buggies and wagons sat in the open area in front of the house. Horses were tied up all around the outside of the corral. Jedidiah and the other ranch hands rode their horses to the corral.

Davis stopped the horses and buggy at the end of the line and set the park brake.

By the time he had Mariella, the children and Mrs. Simon out of the buggy, Skip had the horses unharnessed and was leading them to water. The young man had a soft spot for animals and preferred them over people. Mostly because he had a hard time communicating. Abe told them his brother was called Skip because he tended to stutter or skip words when he talked.

Jedidiah and Len grabbed the baskets of food, and they all headed to the barn that was a flurry of activity. Zach spotted Sammy Mulligan and took off at a run with the puppy at his heels.

"It will be good to see Ernestine and the other women," Mariella said.

Glancing at his wife, he noticed her hand resting on her belly. He'd caught her this way several times the last few days. He remembered Sarah doing the same thing when she'd been with child. Davis's heart raced thinking of him and Mariella making a child. He wasn't going to ask. He'd wait for her to say something.

"I'm sure your mother is good company but not the same as other women your own age." Davis tightened his grip on Lizzie who had started squirming. "Where do you think you're going?" he asked.

"Follow, Zach."

"No, young lady. You will stay with me, your mother, or your gran. You are too young to be running about." Davis kissed her cheek.

"Let me take her. You have people to speak with." Mariella held out her hands for her daughter.

Davis spotted J.P. and Mr. Emmet talking in the shade of a tree. He strode over to them.

"Davis, we were just wondering if you've heard anything," J.P. said when he was close enough no one else would hear their conversation.

Scanning the area, Davis said, "Mr. French should have received a letter from the lawyer by now. If he tries to detain you, just tell him to talk to me. I know more about it than you do."

J.P. studied him. "You think that's wise to have all his anger on you?"

Davis shrugged. "I am the only one who knows everything. I'd like to talk to all of you, but if we gather together French might think we are here to confront him."

"I agree," said Mr. Emmet. "My Ruthie wants to have a good time. I don't want to ruin it for her."

Davis sent a glance the direction he'd last seen Mariella talking with Ernestine. She wasn't there. He scanned the area he could see and came up empty.

"I agree," he said quickly and started off in the direction of his sister.

"Where's Mariella?" he asked, as soon as he was within earshot of Ernestine.

"She took Lizzie to the privy." Ernestine stared at him. "What's wrong?"

"I asked her to stay where I could see her and to ask me to escort to her to the privy." Davis scanned the area between him and the privy. No groups of cowboys hung out between him and the small building.

"Why would you need to keep such a close eye on her?" Ernestine sucked in air and put a hand to her mouth. "Is she having difficulties with her condition?"

His sister just verified his assumptions. He wasn't about to let her know Mariella hadn't told him yet. "No. She had altercations with some ranch hands the last social we attended. I don't want a repeat."

He strode toward the privy, knocked on the door and found it empty. Stepping behind the building, he scanned the area and found his wife and daughter petting the noses of several horses in the corral. Gathering his emotions so as not to make a spectacle, he walked up to the corral and stood with Lizzie between them.

"I asked you to remain where I could see you," he said calmly while stretching his hand out to one of the horses.

"You found me. You must have seen me."

He heard the challenge in Mariella's voice.

Davis faced her. He couldn't read her face. But the tears gleaming in her eyes stalled his heart.

He reached out, cupping her chin. "What's wrong?"

She glanced down at Lizzie and shook her head.

286

Understanding was easy. She didn't want to talk about it with Lizzie present.

He released her chin and put an arm around her waist. "Let's find Gran. I bet she has something tasty for Lizzie."

The child clapped her hands. Mariella grasped one of the child's small hands and Davis took the other. They walked back to the barn and found Mrs. Simon visiting with Mrs. Ridley.

"Ma would you get Lizzie a snack. Davis and I have something to talk about." Mariella placed her daughter's tiny hand into her mother's and then linked hands with Davis.

After speaking with Ernestine, she had a heavy heart. While the woman had been happy for she and Davis, her stories of miscarriages had spiraled fear into Mariella's heart.

Davis led her over to a secluded spot in the shade of a tree. He helped her settle onto the ground and sat next to her. "What's wrong?"

A lump clogged her throat and she couldn't speak. She reached over, clutching his hand between her two.

"Nothing is this bad." He plucked a tear from her cheek.

She swallowed. Davis's love for her glistened in his eyes. The concern showed in his wrinkled forehead.

"I'm with child," she finally blurted.

His lips tipped into a smile. "I know."

Her thoughts scattered. "How?"

He placed a hand on her belly. "I've noticed how lately you place a hand on your belly. Sarah did that when she was with child."

287

His hand warmed her body. How would he feel if she couldn't carry this child to life?

"Did you have a hard birth with Lizzie?" His eyes darkened with worry. "Do you fear giving birth to our child?"

How did she answer?

"Lizzie came early. After Hugh was killed. She wasn't breathing at first, but then she started. She's been weak ever since."

"You won't have the stress of losing a husband this time." Davis put a finger under her chin, making him look into her eyes. "I promise."

She did see that promise in his eyes. But he didn't know what could happen between now and seven months from now. "I don't want to lose this baby." Tears trickled down her cheeks. Her heart cracked with sorrow. "And I don't want to lose you."

Davis pulled her into his arms. "Mari, you'll never lose me. I'm here to stay no matter what. If the child lives, we will love it just as we do Zach and Lizzie. If the baby doesn't make it, we'll grieve and give the two we have the best life we can. I won't leave you if our baby dies."

She'd known this man was special from their first conversation. Over the last month and a half, she'd discovered just how special.

"Come on wipe those tears. We have a day of socializing and having fun ahead of us." He kissed her lips and wiped her tears away with his fingers. "When we need to worry about the baby we will. Right now, let's think of the two that are with us."

She drew in a steadying breath and peered into his

eyes. "Mr. Weston, I have never known a man like you." She hiccupped, unsure whether now was the time to tell him her heart.

"Mrs. Weston, you are a remarkable woman and one I am proud to call my wife." He stood and reached down for her hand. "I'd like to show off my lovely wife."

Mariella sniffed, drew a handkerchief from the pocket of her skirt and blew her nose. She raised her hand, and Davis pulled her to her feet and straight into his arms.

"Never doubt my affection for you." His lips descended on hers.

The kiss took away her doubts and filled her heart. Unlike the long, devouring kisses when they came together, this kiss talked to her heart.

Davis drew away and kissed her forehead. "We'll get through this and all challenges together."

"Thank you."

He grasped her hand and led her back to the people visiting and children playing games. It appeared two of Mr. French's ranch hands were in charge of games for the children. Zach was participating with the puppy nipping at his heels.

A roar from the corrals stole her attention. "Look! They're having ranch competitions."

Davis steered her to the corral. "I hope Abe and Skip enter a roping competition."

They leaned against the corral fence alongside Jedidiah. He nodded to the far side of the corral.

There sat Abe and Skip waiting for the P Ranch hands to shove a steer into the corral. The gate opened.

The steer ran into the corral. Abe dug his heels into his horse with a rope loop flying over his head. He caught the animal around the neck and before Mariella moved her attention to Skip the calf was strung out and ready for someone to throw and brand.

The spectators roared their approval.

They watched half a dozen more roping pairs, but none had a calf caught as quickly as Abe and Skip. When that event was finished, Mr. French himself walked into the corral with an envelope.

"Would Abe and Skip from the Bar S please join me," he bellowed.

Mariella watched as her two young cowhands walked into the corral. Mr. French handed them the envelope, shook hands, and then talked to them. She saw both men shake their heads and turn their backs on Mr. French.

"I wonder what that was about?" she said to Davis and Jedidiah.

"I can guess," Jedidiah said. "I bet Mr. French tried to talk those two into working for him."

Mariella fisted her hands and jammed them into her hips. "The nerve of that man!"

Davis rubbed her shoulders. "Calm down. Those two aren't going anywhere. They're loyal."

"I agree." Jedidiah nodded toward Len who was about ten feet down the corral from them. "He's not going anywhere either. Those three are your hands for life."

Mariella leaned against Davis. That was the second best information she'd heard all day.

***

It was about dark when Davis had a chance to speak to Ernestine without Mariella nearby. He couldn't believe his sister of all people had sparked fear for the unborn child in Mariella.

Ernestine was sitting on the blanket she'd spread for her family next to their blanket. He had Mariella, Mrs. Simon, and Lizzie in his sight as the three made a trip to the privy. Davis sat down, watching the women of his family.

"It's good to get a chance to visit with you," Ernestine said.

"I've wanted to talk with you ever since I caught Mariella crying." He slashed a pointed glance at his sister then shifted his gaze to the privy.

"Crying? Why?" Air whooshed out of his sister. "I should have kept my mouth shut about a woman her age and having had complications before."

"Yes. She doesn't need to fear losing a child for eight months. It will only make it more likely." He put a hand on his sister's shoulder. "I know you were only repeating what you knew, but please, don't tell her anything negative. She already was worried before you added more."

Ernestine's eyes glistened. "I'm truly sorry. Seeing the two of you together makes me happy. I worried you would never know happiness again and here you are talking about Mariella as if you love her."

Davis glanced at the women walking toward them. His gaze latched onto Mariella's. "I do love her."

Davis rose, taking Lizzie from Mariella's arms and leading her away from Ernestine. "I heard Mr. French bought fireworks. Let's sit in the buggy and watch."

291

The sky had barely darkened when booming, whirring noises assaulted their ears and colors shattered in the sky. Lizzie stayed awake for the first two then slept in his lap as he sat on the seat with one arm around Mariella, watching the fireworks.

"This has been a nice day," Mariella said.

Davis squeezed her shoulders and kissed her temple. "I agree."

She laid her head on his shoulder and sighed.

It had been several years since he'd been this content. In fact, he was pretty sure it had been closer to his childhood than his adulthood.

As an adult he seemed to always be trying to prove himself. Right now, he didn't need to prove anything to anyone. He had Mariella, two children, and a ranch.

"I've been looking for you."

Davis knew that voice. Their host, Mr. Peter French.

Mariella straightened.

Davis settled Lizzie in Mariella's lap and slipped out of the buggy.

"Mr. French, you've found me."

"I received a letter from a lawyer in Canyon City stating he was working for you and several others."

"That's true," Davis said, trying to decide if he should lead the man away from Mariella. He knew she'd be upset if he did.

"I've already contacted my lawyer. I'll fight all of you." He spread his arms. "And as you can see, I have more money and power than you do."

"That may be true, but we have the law on our side. You are illegally keeping people from land you don't own." Davis crossed his arms. This man was not going to intimidate him.

"I also received your allegations against my foreman Tucker."

"And?"

"He's been asked to leave my property, and I've told my ranch hands to shoot him if they find him on my land."

Davis nodded. "That's a good decision. If he was stealing from us, he was no doubt stealing from you."

Mr. French turned to walk away then pivoted back toward them. "You may want to watch out. He was talking about getting revenge on the person who had him dismissed."

Davis wasn't scared for himself, but for Mariella. It had been her tenacity that had followed the cattle tracks.

"Thanks for the warning."

Jedidiah appeared with Zach and Mrs. Simon. "I figured it was time to head home."

"It is." Davis helped Mrs. Simon and Zach into the back seat of the buggy.

Davis climbed up. Skip had hitched the horses to the buggy before dark. They were ready to head home.

He clucked and flicked the reins, starting the horses on the way. Out on the road he looked back and found all their ranch hands following. Davis smiled. He'd figured the young hands would stick around, but with so few women in the area, and he hadn't taken the three for drinkers, there wasn't anything left at the celebration to keep them there.

"What are we going to do about Tucker?" Mariella

whispered.

"Nothing. We can only hope he moves on without a chance of finding a job here." Davis wasn't going to tell her, he'd tell the men to keep a watch out for the man. And he wasn't going to let her or Zach ride off alone.

"I don't think he's the type that will move on without taking his revenge."

Davis put an arm around Mariella. "If he does, we've been warned and will be ready for him."

Chapter Thirty

A week after the Fourth of July celebration Mariella wanted to take one of the geldings she'd been working with for a ride. Zach had mentioned fishing, and she didn't see any reason why they couldn't ride up the stream and spend the morning catching trout.

Davis had gone down to the meadow with Len to check on the grass. She'd told him it was too soon to cut, but he wanted to make sure it was all getting water.

Abe and Skip were checking the cattle at the far end of the canyon and Jedidiah had been sent to the settlement of Harney to post letters. The establishments that were left after the military pulled out of Fort Harney the previous month still conducted business.

She led the gelding out of the corral and caught Zach's pony, Thunder. Tying the two to the hitching post in front of the barn, she entered the house by the front door. Zach was sitting at the desk, writing a lesson. The puppy, she'd yet to name but Zach called Shorty, lay at his feet, sleeping.

"Zach, want to go fishing?" she asked.

"Yes!" He dropped his pencil on the page he was writing and jumped up.

"Grab some worms and your pole. I have the horses ready." She smiled at his enthusiasm. For a boy who was always on the move, he enjoyed sitting still and fishing.

Mariella walked into the kitchen. Ma and Lizzie were making cookies.

"I'm taking the new gelding up the stream. Zach's going with me to do some fishing. We'll be back by noon." Mariella picked up a cookie and took a bite.

"Davis said you should stay close," Ma said, raising an eyebrow.

"I'll only be a short distance up the stream. I promise." She hugged Ma and kissed Lizzie's floured cheek.

Mariella picked up three more cookies and exited the back door. Zach was sitting on Thunder, his pole in one hand and the reins in the other.

She handed him two of the cookies. He gripped them between his fingers on the hand holding the reins. Shorty lay across Zach's lap sniffing the air.

Poking the last cookie in her mouth, Mariella mounted the gelding and reined him up the canyon. Zach rode alongside, telling her where he wanted to stop to fish. The spot he requested was a bit farther up the canyon than she'd planned to ride, but the squaw currants near that area would be ready to pick. Ma could make preserves or pies from the berries.

They continued up the stream about a mile until she spotted the currant bushes. Zach dismounted, tossing his fishing line in the stream.

Mariella dismounted and placed a rock on the ends of the reins. She had just started to teach the horse to ground tie. He needed to learn dropped reins meant to stay. The only problem with her idea to pick currants as an afterthought, she didn't have a container to put them in. Pulling off her hat, she decided it was the closest thing to a bucket she had. If that became full, she'd borrow Zach's hat.

Tossing a glance toward the stream, she smiled. Zach was already stretched out on the ground with Shorty lying next to his crossed legs which held the pole, waiting for a trout.

She walked over to the bushes, shooed a couple bees away, and started plucking the round, red berries the size of the tip of her little finger from the stickery bushes. Her hat was half full when the horses nickered and the puppy yelped.

Mariella spun around. Her heart jumped into her throat, and her legs propelled her toward the stream. The puppy lie on the ground whimpering.

Zach was crying and slugging, Tucker. The man held her son by one arm, dangling the boy from up on his horse.

"Put Zach down!" She would kill the man with her bare hands if he harmed her son.

He laughed. "I figure if I have your boy, you'll follow me and do what I want." He spun his horse and took off into the trees.

Mariella's heart thudded in her chest. She had to follow the man. But first she had to send word that they were in trouble. She pulled her neckerchief from around her neck and made a sling. She put the puppy in the sling and tied it to Thunder's horn. Tying the reins up so the horse wouldn't step on them, she slapped him on the rump. "Go! Go home!"

Watching Thunder run down the canyon, she mounted the gelding and headed into the trees where she'd last seen Tucker and Zach. Reaching down to the scabbard, she realized the man had taken her rifle.

***

Davis stopped his horse as Zach's pony came running down the canyon and into the barn yard. He leaped off of Poker and grabbed the pony's bridle. That's when he saw the limp puppy in the sling made from Mariella's neckerchief.

"Mariella! Zach!" He shouted, staring up the canyon.

Mrs. Simon came running out of the house. She spotted the pony. "No!"

"Where are they?" It took every ounce of Davis's will to stop the dread and fear pounding in his head. You won't get to them in time. You didn't last time and you won't this time.

"Mariella said she was taking Zach fishing. That they'd be back by noon."

Davis swung up on Poker. "We'll find them." He dug his heels into Poker and loped up the canyon alongside the stream. He heard Len following.

I won't lose another wife and son. He repeated over and over as he scanned the ground along the way. He spotted Mariella's hat moments before he saw Zach's pole and can of worms.

Len dropped to the ground and studied the tracks. "Two horses went that way." He pointed to the trees across the stream, headed to the north ridge.

If it was Tucker, Davis had an idea where the man was heading.

"I think he's headed to that draw that comes down the north ridge with the cluster of aspens."

Len nodded he knew the place.

"I'll go straight there, you circle down and come to it from the west. If I have him paying attention to me, you can sneak up on him."

"You think Tucker has Mrs. Weston and Zach?"

Davis nodded and set out for the trees, hoping he reached the two before Tucker did something stupid. He hadn't thought the man vile enough to kill, but he wouldn't put it past the man to hurt Mariella. That thought pressed him forward, ducking and dodging trees as he loped Poker toward the draw.

***

Mariella pulled the gelding up short at the sight of Zach tied to a tree.

"Where are you, you coward!" she yelled.

Tucker stepped out from behind the tree buttoning the fly on his pants. "Right here. The only coward I see is that man you call a husband hiding behind your skirts, then writing to Mr. French that I stole your cattle and possibly his."

"Davis isn't a coward. He's more man than you'll ever be." She scanned the area for the man's horse and her rifle.

He grabbed a rifle leaning against the tree he'd tied Zach to. "Get off your horse and come over here."

She glared at him.

He put the barrel end of the rifle against Zach's head.

Mariella scrambled off the horse and charged the man, slamming him in the gut with her head like she'd seen Davis do at the Diamond Ranch social.

"Don't you ever put a gun to my child's head." She bent to untie Zach. Before she could get him lose something hard struck her in the shoulder knocking her sideways. Pain shot through her shoulder and down her arm. She couldn't make her arm move.

"No woman will get the better of me. Not even one your size." Tucker stood over her the barrel of the rifle pointed at her belly.

Our baby! She wouldn't let this man hurt Zach or the unborn child. "Let Zach go. He's just a child."

Tucker grabbed the front of her shirt, pulling her to a sitting position. "You can take him with you when I'm done with you. Right now, he's the only thing that makes you behave."

The man tore her shirt open.

She didn't want Zach to see what she feared this man was about to do. "No!" She glanced at her son.

Zach's eyes narrowed and he kicked at the man. "Leave my Ma alone!"

Tucker shoved the rifle backward, catching Zach in the belly with the butt end.

"Don't hurt him. I'll give you what you want, but not here, where he can't see." She hoped to get the man out of sight of her son, and then find a way to get the upper hand. Until someone found them, she was the only person who could keep Zach alive and safe.

***

Davis heard Zach's shouts and dismounted. He dropped Poker's reins, pulled his rifle out of the scabbard and worked his way closer to the draw. He spotted Zach tied to the tree. The boy's body jerked back and forth as he tried to see around the tree. Tucker must have Mariella back there.

His heart pounded in his constricted chest. He had to save them both. His heart couldn't take losing two more people he loved. But how did he know someone wasn't waiting for him to walk up to the boy?

He scrounged the ground and found a round rock about the size of a marble. Placing it on his curled fingers, he flicked it with his thumb. The small rock thunked Zach in the chest. He stopped squirming and stared into the trees. Davis moved catching the boy's attention.

"P—!"

He waved his hand to keep the boy quiet.

The boy mouthed Ma and nodded behind the tree.

Davis sprinted across to the tree, grateful his wife made him wear a knife sheath in his boot. He cut Zach free.

The boy clung to him. "Pa help ma."

Having Zach call him pa buoyed his heart, but the sounds of a struggle behind the tree clenched his gut. Mariella and the baby had to live. He leaned down and

301

whispered to Zach. "Go to Poker and stay there until I come." The boy started to protest. "Go." Davis shoved the boy back the way he'd come and peeked around the tree.

The sight started his head pounding with rage. The man sat on Mariella's belly facing the tree. He tore at Mariella's clothing as she struggled against him. Tucker raised a fisted hand. Davis didn't even think twice, he leveled the rifle to his shoulder, took aim, and pressed the trigger.

Tucker flopped backward, pinning Mariella's legs.

Davis dropped his rifle and sprinted to his wife. "Mari. Mari, did he hurt you?" He shoved the man off her legs, dropped to his knees beside her, and pulled Mariella into his arms.

"Ow!" she cried out.

He loosened his grip. "Where did he hurt you?"

Mariella wrapped one arm around his neck. Wetness heated his cheek where she pressed her face against his. Her body shook.

"Zach?" she asked.

"I untied him and sent him to Poker." Davis leaned back, wiping at the tears on her face. "What did he do to you?"

Crashing through the trees brought a panting Len bursting into the draw. He glanced at Tucker, then stared at them.

"Is she—"

"I sent Zach to my horse. Find him and take him home. We'll be along shortly." Davis returned his attention to Mariella.

"What about Tucker?" Len asked.

"We'll take care of him after my family is taken care of."

He didn't spare a glance at Len but heard his footsteps retreating.

Davis focused all his attention on Mariella. "Mari, honey. Look at me."

She lifted her face to him. He noted a bruise on her cheek and one on her forehead. If he hadn't already killed the man, he would do it all over again. Her right arm hung loose at her side.

Rage thundered through his mind like a violent storm. He had to control the rage. Being angry wouldn't help Mariella. The target of his anger was dead. He didn't need to check the man to know he was dead. His aim had blown a hole in the man's chest.

"Where all are you hurt?" He had to help Mariella. She was alive and he could help her.

"He slammed the butt end of the rifle into my shoulder. I can't move my arm." Tears streamed down her face.

"Is this the worst of your injuries? Did he?" Davis glanced down at her torn clothes, the buttons ripped from her trousers.

"No. I told him I would do what he wanted to get him away from Zach." Her face darkened and anger sparked in her eyes. "Tucker hit Zach with the rifle."

He knew she'd do anything to protect her children. He also knew she wouldn't have given her body to him easily.

His other fear surfaced and he asked. "Did he hit you in the stomach?"

"No. I wouldn't let him hurt that child either."

303

Davis grasped her head and kissed her. He needed the contact. Lips to lips, heart to heart.

Mariella returned the kiss with the same relief and love.

Drawing out of the kiss, Davis released her head. "We need to get you home where your mother can doctor that arm."

"Yes. I want to go home."

Davis helped Mariella to her feet. Her shirt hung open. He hunted for buttons to fasten it closed and found none. Her corset had the top hooks pulled straight. She grasped her trousers as they started to fall. Davis took off his vest and gently slid it up her injured arm. Her other arm slipped through the arm hole and he buttoned it.

"Hold your pants on with your good arm until we get to the horse." He held her elbow, escorting her to Poker. "What horse were you riding?" he asked, pulling the knife out of his boot and cutting a length off of the rope tied on the pommel.

"The gelding I've been working with." She nodded to the right. "He should be over there with Tucker's horse."

Davis wrapped the rope around Mariella and tied it to keep her pants up.

He didn't want any riding mishaps. Mariella was injured enough. "You ride Poker. I'll get the other two." He helped Mariella mount Poker and walked the direction she'd indicated for the other two horses. He found both and mounted the gelding, leading Tucker's horse.

Chapter Thirty-one

Mariella lay in bed, thinking about how lucky she was to have such an attentive husband. When Davis brought her home, he'd helped her off the horse and escorted her straight into their bedroom, only stopping long enough for her to hug Zach and kiss Lizzie's soft curls. He'd undressed her and put her in a night dress, all but her hurt arm and shoulder. Then Davis stood by as Ma pronounced her upper arm broke and helped Ma set it.

The children had been in this morning. Zach read to her and showed her his numbers. Lizzie had brought her a half a glass of water and two cookies, before snuggling beside her along with the puppy for a nap.

She missed Davis even though he'd only been gone half the day. She shuddered thinking about what he and the ranch hands were doing.

Davis told her they would load Tucker's body onto his horse and Len would take it to the sheriff in Canyon City along with Mariella and Davis's accounts of what happened. They didn't expect any problems with the law, but as usual Davis wanted to make sure they had everything covered.

Lizzie woke, yawned, and stretched. "Mama," she said and hugged Mariella's injured arm.

Mariella grimaced and accepted her daughter's love. While the child didn't know what had happened, she knew her ma was hurt and wanted to give comfort.

"Thank you, baby." She patted Lizzie's blonde curls. "Could you scoot on out to Gran and see when she's bringing me something to eat?" Mariella wasn't hungry, but she wanted the pain to go away. She also wanted out of the bed, but Davis had made her promise to stay in bed today.

Her heart frolicked, remembering how he'd gently placed his hand on her belly and stared into her eyes. "You say you're fine and all that's hurt is your arm, but for me and the baby inside you, please stay in bed today. Just to be safe."

She'd started to protest and he'd said the words she'd hoped he'd one day say.

"Mari, I love you and I love the child inside of you. Please remain in bed. I couldn't bear if anything happened to either one of you when I can prevent it."

Tears had slid down her cheek.

He'd plucked one from her cheek. "What did I say

to make you cry?"

"They aren't tears of sorrow. They're tears of happiness." She'd leaned forward kissing him. "I've wanted to tell you I love you. But I feared you'd think me a ninny for having these feeling so soon."

Davis had smiled, crinkling the corners of his eyes and glinting mischief in his eyes. "I know."

"You knew I loved you?"

"Yes. You aren't a woman to give your loyalty or heart away. I knew you loved me after the social when you took me to your bed." He glanced down at the bed they sat on. "Our bed."

Stomping at the back door sent her heart racing. Davis was back. Voices and chairs scraping told her the men were back from gathering Tucker's body. She shuddered thinking of what could have happened to her and Zach if she hadn't had the good sense to send his pony back to the house.

Davis filled the doorway and her heart raced. He carried a tray laden with food. "Mind if I share dinner with you?" he asked.

"No."

He kicked the door shut and placed the tray on the table by the bed. Leaning over the bed, bracing a hand on either side of her, his lips met hers. The kiss was soft and lingering. Her lips tingled when Davis pulled back and looked into her eyes.

Davis stared into Mariella's eyes. He saw his future in them. A future of love, family, and good times. He needed to get the letter J.P. delivered discussed then tell her his thoughts about her and their family.

"J.P. dropped off a letter from the courts. There has

been a court date set for our claims against Mr. French. The lawyer believes he has all he needs but requests we show. It's in a month."

"Do you think this will settle things?" Mariella asked.

He shook his head. "Even if we win, it won't keep him from continuing and keeping out others." Davis pushed that away. He wanted to concentrate on the woman that had entered his heart.

"Mariella, I never expected to find love when I followed my sister's wishes and came out here to marry you." He kissed her lips again. He couldn't resist being this close and having nearly lost her yesterday. He'd never miss a chance to kiss her. This time he opened his mouth, tasting the sweetness of his Mari with his tongue. She responded, darting her tongue to touch his. Before his desire flamed uncontrollably, he drew away, staring at her half-closed lids and wet, swollen lips. "But I have." He nipped her chin and her eyelids rose. Her hazel eyes were dark with desire. The golden brown color sent his heart pumping.

"You have what?" she whispered in her husky voice that stole his heart the day he married her.

"Found love." He dipped down to kiss her chastely.

Mariella wrapped her good arm around his neck, pulling him down on top of her.

"I have too," she whispered and nibbled on his ear.

For the first time in over a year, he was looking forward to a long life. With this ardent woman by his side and in his bed, he knew it would be filled with love and adventure.

About the Author

Award-winning author Paty Jager and her husband raise alfalfa hay in rural eastern Oregon. On her road to publication she wrote freelance articles for two local newspapers and enjoyed her job with the County Extension service as a 4-H Program Assistant. Raising hay and cattle, riding horses, and battling rattlesnakes, she not only writes the western lifestyle, she lives it.

http://www.patyjager.net

Letters of Fate Series
Davis
Isaac

Halsey Brother Series
Marshal in Petticoats – Gil's story
Outlaw in Petticoats – Zeke's story
Miner in Petticoats – Ethan's story
Doctor in Petticoats – Clay's story
Logger in Petticoats – Hank's story
Halsey Brothers Series – Box Set
Halsey Homecoming trilogy
Laying Claim – Jeremy's story
Staking Claim – Colin's story
Claiming a Heart – Donny's story
A Husband for Christmas - Shayla's story

Historical Western Anthologies
Sweetwater Springs Christmas: A Montana Sky Short Story Anthology
Rawhide "N Romance: A Western Romance Anthology
Silver Belles and Stetsons: A Western Christmas Anthology

Historical Paranormal Romance
(Native American)
Spirit of the Mountain
Spirit of the Lake
Spirit of the Sky

Thank you for purchasing this Windtree Press publication. For other books of the heart, please visit our website at www.windtreepress.com.

For questions or more information contact us at info@windtreepress.com.

Windtree Press
www.windtreepress.com
4660 NE Belknap Court
Suite 101-O
Hillsboro, OR 97124